# TREASURE TRAIL

## MORGAN BRICE

eBook ISBN: 978-1-939704-93-1
Print ISBN: 978-1-939704-94-8


Cover art by Lou Harper
Darkwind Press is an imprint of DreamSpinner Communications, LLC

# TREASURE TRAIL

By Morgan Brice

# ONE

# ERIK

"If the show proposal goes through, it will really put *Treasure Trail and Trinkets* on the map!" Corinne Scott had the bouncy enthusiasm required of an agent, and it came across as clear over the phone as it did in person.

"It's exciting, but let's wait before we break out the champagne," Erik Mitchell protested. He had been dealing with the chaos of unpacking boxes and living out of a suitcase for two weeks, since his move to Cape May, New Jersey, and the complete uprooting of his life. "If they're counting on using my supposed notoriety to sell the show, they might be disappointed. There's a lot I can't talk about—and it's mostly the exciting parts."

"You traveled the world stopping art and antiquities fraud," Corinne continued, undeterred. "It's like something out of Indiana Jones."

Erik winced. Much as he loved those movies, Indy was more like the kind of guy he helped bust for swiping relics. "Um…not really. I spent a lot of time in the back rooms of museums going over old stuff with a magnifying glass. And I only got shot at a few times."

That was enough. A collector with a very rare Fabergé egg music box wanted Erik to authenticate the egg for the buyer. Unfortunately, there were other interested parties, and they all brought more muscle than brains. The deal went sideways when they decided to negotiate with guns; all hell broke loose, and Erik nearly died. He ended up with a concussion, a bullet wound in his shoulder, and nightmares verging on PTSD.

"This wouldn't be anything so dangerous!" Corinne was in full sales mode now. "It's only six episodes, and it's the local PBS station. All the crimes have already been solved. You're just on camera for the expert cameos, and to toss out some advice on how to avoid buying fake art or accidentally stealing priceless relics."

The longer Corinne talked, the more Erik became convinced the whole TV show was a colossal mistake. He had relocated to Cape May from Atlanta to get away from the sensational—and dangerous— aspects of his old life. Sure, chasing down art fraud had been his dream job, like something out of a thriller novel. His younger self had relished the constant travel and intermittent danger, and the work paid well—in headlines and in a very healthy salary.

Then there was the clusterfuck bust and Erik's injury. He realized that he was ready to move on, settle down, and step out of the spotlight. He'd thought his boyfriend, Josh, would be happy about the change. Then he got home a few days earlier than expected and found Josh banging Erik's personal assistant on the dining room table.

After all the shouting and tears were over, Erik found himself single and lacking an assistant. He'd decided right then to leave his old world behind. That meant getting out of Atlanta, out of the apartment he'd shared with Josh, and going somewhere he could get a fresh start.

He surfed real estate sites and found a beautiful Victorian in Cape May at a great price. Even better, it was part of a package deal and included an established antique store on the main floor, inventory included. Suddenly, the daydream Erik had indulged about starting a blog on trendy antiques and running a boutique service for designers all came together. The next thing Erik knew, he was standing in front of his new home and business with the keys in his hand, wondering whether he'd lost his mind.

Now, he was certain that the answer was "yes."

"Let's see if the proposal even gets interest," Erik protested. "And if it does, it's going to depend on what they actually want, and we'll take it from there."

"Party pooper," Corinne joked. "Fine. I'll let you know when I hear from the producers. But I'm telling you, Erik, this would be a great way to start your new business off with a bang!"

*That's what I'm afraid of.*

Corinne conveniently seemed to forget that some of the thefts, forgeries, and smuggling rings he'd helped bust had ties to the Mob and the cartels, or left a trail of pissed off billionaires who were used to getting what they wanted. Death threats had been common, and for a while he'd had a bodyguard. While Erik wanted his new venture to succeed, he didn't want to attract the wrong kind of attention.

"Look, I need to finish what I'm doing," Erik said. "Call me when you hear something. And...thanks." Corinne might be exasperatingly upbeat, but she had stuck by Erik through all the changes in his life, and she had been a good friend—especially when there was a commission in it for her.

Erik ended the call and slipped the phone into his pocket, turning to look around the downstairs of the grand old house. It had been updated by the prior owner to create a shop on the first floor and an expansive living area on the second and third floors. Boxes and packing peanuts littered the floor, along with crinkled paper shred. He sighed, completely overwhelmed.

"It can't be that bad." Susan Hendricks, Erik's new next-door neighbor, looked up with a grin from where she sat on the floor, helping to unpack some of the items Erik had shipped from Atlanta. His condo and office had been full of antiques he had bought in his travels, but he'd decided to sell them all and start over, using his personal collection as part of the inventory for Trinkets. "You've got some real pretty pieces here."

"I'm just feeling a little out of my depth," Erik admitted. Susan was probably the same age as his mother, but far more energetic and approachable. Her short salt-and-pepper hair framed a youthful face, and he suspected her wardrobe of T-shirts and yoga pants saw real gym time. She'd been the first person other than his real estate agent to welcome him to Cape May, and won him over with her genuine friendliness and no-bullshit attitude.

"I couldn't help overhearing," Susan said. "There's nothing wrong with spreading things out instead of doing everything all at once. You don't have to say no or yes…you can say 'later.'"

That sounded like the best thing Erik had heard all day. "Thank you. You're a genius."

Susan laughed. "No, I've just felt overwhelmed a time or two myself, and I'm happy to pass along the tricks that worked for me, for what it's worth."

*If I just take one room at a time, it might be all right*, Erik thought. The front parlor was the main showroom, and the furniture was already in place, providing plenty of places to display the additional inventory he had brought with him. He bent down to pick up a vase, trying not to wince at the thought of the pricy piece sitting on the floor.

"You might change your mind about only being open by appointment," Susan said as she carefully unwrapped a vintage tea set. "The folks who visit Cape May have refined tastes—and money."

Erik figured he would get everything safely off the floor and out of boxes and rearrange them for maximum impact later.

"I know. Just trying not to bite off more than I can chew. I want to get the blog up and running because that will not only bring people into the store, but it should attract decorators and curators looking for the perfect piece. If I can attract those folks, they'll be steady business even in the off-season." Given his knowledge and reputation, Erik's collection was likely to attract attention from museums looking to round out their collections, and designers searching for eye-catching and unusual items for their clients' homes. He could make more money with less overhead.

"Sounds like you've thought everything out," Susan said, wiping some stray paper fibers from an inlaid music box.

"Not really, but it's nice of you to say so." Erik felt like he'd been careening from one major life decision to another since he'd woken up in a hospital in Antwerp with a concussion and a gunshot wound, and decided the paycheck and fame weren't worth dying for. Now here he was, relocated, single, a new homeowner, taking over a business and finding his way in a vacation town he vaguely remembered from a few trips when he was a kid. He'd been outrunning his dumpster fire of a life, and Erik was ready to slow down and try to find some kind of new normal.

"Have you done anything except unpack, move furniture, and work on your website since you got to town?" Susan raised an eyebrow to tell him that she already knew the answer.

"Guilty as charged. But there's so much to do, and…"

"And you know what they say about all work and no play," Susan said with a grin. "You need to go out, meet some people, let the town get to know you. Maybe meet a cute girl—or guy," she added with a wink.

"Definitely guy," Erik replied.

"Well then, you've come to the right place. Cape May is very welcoming. My son is probably a few years younger than you, and he and his friends never seem to have any trouble finding dates."

Erik's escape plan hadn't been quite as headlong as it sometimes felt. He'd done his research on Cape May, a town he visited several times vacationing with his aunt, uncle, and cousins when he was in middle school. He remembered the beach and all the classic Victorian houses—and the ice cream. When he went looking for a place to relocate, he checked out the town on a whim and discovered it was gay-friendly and eclectic. While that was definitely true of his former home in Atlanta, the same couldn't be said about everywhere else in Georgia, or in his native South Carolina.

At thirty-five, Erik was ready to put down roots, settle in, and settle down. He never really liked hookups, even before his relationship with Josh, and while Josh's betrayal had rocked Erik's confidence, he still hoped that there was someone out there for him.

"Don't worry. All in good time," Susan reassured him. She got to her feet with a gracefulness that only came from hours of asanas and dusted herself off. "Let me help get everything up on shelves, and by then the meatloaf in the slow cooker will be done. I don't know about you, but I'm starving!"

"It does smell good." Erik knew he'd lucked out with a neighbor like Susan. She had refused any pay for helping him unpack and insisted on bringing over dinner. He'd been wary about her friendly overtures at first, but she quickly won him over.

"It was one of Keith's favorite recipes," Susan said, and her smile grew wistful. "Nothing fancy, just good comfort food." She had mentioned her husband's death to Erik not long after they met, and they had commiserated about how scary it was to get back into the dating game.

"I just bought ice cream, so I can at least contribute dessert," Erik said.

"Sounds like a plan," she answered. Together, they made quick work of moving the antiques out of harm's way and cleaning up the packing materials. Then Erik led the way into the next room, where the slow cooker sat on the table, along with the paper plates and plastic utensils Susan had brought. A two-liter bottle of soda and red cups made for a picnic-style supper.

Susan filled plates while Erik brought chairs. He had to admit that the smell of a home-cooked meal made the place feel more welcoming. He'd been surviving on takeout subs and pizza delivery.

"Tell me about Cape May's ghosts," Erik asked as they sat down to eat. "I've read that local ghost whisperer's books, and I've got to admit, I'm very curious."

Susan wiped away a bit of tomato sauce. "Oh, there are plenty of them, enough to go around, if all the tales are true. It's almost a point of pride to claim you've got a resident ghost."

Erik ate and listened as Susan recounted what she knew. Most of the stories told of victims of swimming or boating accidents who never left, or jilted lovers who died of grief or by their own hand. The fierce storms that had pummeled the beach town added a few more spirits to the tally, as did old local scandals.

"But you know, I think the biggest ghost story in Cape May isn't a 'who.' It's a 'what,'" Susan said with a conspiratorial smile. "A big old hotel that took up two city blocks—the largest hotel in the United States when it was built back around the turn of the last century."

"A hotel?"

"The Commodore Wilson Hotel was quite the showplace back in the day, and everyone who was anyone stayed there. But the hotel was snake-bit from the start. Or cursed, maybe. Ruined everyone who owned it and seemed to be a magnet for tragedy."

Erik vaguely remembered seeing the hotel mentioned when he had researched Cape May, but hadn't seen anything that resembled what Susan was describing. "Where is it? I can't believe I missed it!"

She paused to take a few bites of meatloaf. "Oh, they finally tore it down years ago. It was a grand place in its prime, and it was a shame to see it fall into disrepair. In the end, no one could afford to fix it, so they brought the hotel down with dynamite, and the whole town held a wake."

Erik made a mental note to do some online digging. The Commodore Wilson sounded like the sort of hotel he always sought out when he traveled, a place with a rich history and the kind of architecture no one could afford to build anymore. "You said the place was cursed?"

Susan shrugged. "Maybe that's not literally true, but it sure seemed like it. Five owners went bankrupt. A mobster got gunned down in the lobby. Several celebrities committed suicide there. Its real heyday was probably during Prohibition and the Second World War, but it was still *the* place to be seen into the seventies. Then a shady televangelist bought it and brought all his followers in for big events. It was all fun and games until he up and vanished, leaving a pile of debt and a bunch of pissed off followers—and a lot of unpaid taxes."

"Did they ever find him?" This story was better than anything on the History Channel.

"Nope. Hard to imagine someone who'd had his face all over TV like that could just disappear, but everyone figured he probably went to Brazil or somewhere else without extradition," Susan said. "If so, I guess he was smarter than that TV preacher from South Carolina. He went to jail."

Erik remembered. He'd grown up in Columbia, South Carolina, and the infamous preacher's scandal had unfolded when he was a child, but it had been impossible to live in the state and not know. For a while, it seemed like all anybody talked about.

"Wow. That's a lot of excitement packed into one building," Erik said. "But I hate to see landmarks like that destroyed. They're a part of history."

Susan grinned. "Oh, the Commodore was so much a part of this town's history I swear it's like a ghost itself. Everyone who grew up here had a story about the hotel—working there, wedding reception, going to prom, drinking too much in the bar, spotting someone famous. And after it closed there were paranormal investigators and urban explorers—and local kids who dared each other to go inside and bring out a souvenir."

She sighed. "You should have seen the crowd when they finally sold off all the Commodore's stuff. People who used to live here or stay at the hotel came from all over the world to buy a memento. Monogrammed china sets, silverware, knick-knacks, even the metal fobs for the room keys. It was quite the media circus."

Erik grabbed another slice of meatloaf and gestured for her to continue. "Sounds like my kind of event."

Susan raised an eyebrow. "Actually, you'd have been right at home. Even at the end, there were rumors that some of the artwork and antiques were fake. So many of the hotel's owners were strapped for cash, I wouldn't be surprised if they'd sold the originals and put good forgeries in their place."

"It happens more often than you'd imagine," Erik replied. "I've had to break the news to European nobility that their 'priceless' Monet or Rembrandt was just a very good copy."

Susan sat back and took a sip of her soda. "So, you're interested in ghosts? See any yourself?"

Erik hesitated, but figured that in a place like Cape May, where the local spirits were practically celebrities themselves, it wouldn't hurt to tell the truth. "I've seen a few," he admitted, although the real number was more than he could count. "Guess it goes with knocking around museums and historic old mansions. I can't talk to them or hear them say anything, but I've seen some things I can't really explain."

He didn't mention his odd hunches, the ones that always seemed to know the forgeries from the real deal. They were never wrong. Erik also didn't mention his second sight, the way some objects gave him flashes of their history, showing the world as the object had seen it, a window in time.

Thank God that didn't happen with everything. But it occurred often enough that he usually wore gloves to handle new acquisitions, until he could check them privately to avoid an embarrassing incident. He'd only told one person about that ability, Simon Kincaide, a grad school friend who was a psychic medium. Simon had understood. Erik knew others wouldn't.

"I believe. In ghosts, I mean," Susan said. "There are plenty of things about the world we don't understand. Seems a little arrogant to think we've got it all figured out, don't you think? I don't understand why some people can see ghosts and others can't, but I know enough people who have that I can't dismiss it."

Erik relaxed a little. Susan set him at ease. Most of his friends in Atlanta and on the cases he had worked were situational, so when they weren't forced together by circumstances, the connection withered. He could count the friends who didn't fit that pattern—Simon included—on one hand. It felt good to make a new friend who liked him just for being him.

"So every now and then, I pick up a hint of a drawl from you," Susan said, going back for another small slice of meatloaf. "I get the impression you're not a Jersey boy."

Erik usually didn't say much about his family, but he appreciated that Susan hadn't just Googled him. "I'm from Columbia, South Carolina. State capital and all that. But I've been gone for a long while, and I've lived in New York, London, Rome, and Atlanta. I think the accent comes out most when I'm tired." Or stressed or hurt, he didn't bother to add. Josh had always chided him when his drawl slipped out, calling him a "redneck" and spewing bigoted stereotypes.

*And yet, I sat there and took it. So what does that say about me?*

"Your parents must be so proud. I imagine they'll be the first to tune in if your TV show comes through."

Susan meant well, but she didn't know his family. "My sister was an Olympic athlete—brought home two silvers and a bronze in gymnastics—and now she coaches. If the TV is on at home, it's usually because Macy has a televised meet."

"That sounds exciting." Susan didn't press for more, and Erik got the impression that she read between the lines.

When Erik was growing up, Macy was being groomed for gold medals. All of his parents' time and money went toward coaches, lessons, and going to competitions all over the country and later, the world. That usually meant no one was around to go to his high school plays or other events. Erik had worked part-time jobs and gotten scholarships to put himself through college and graduate school. He loved his sister, and he did his best not to hold his parents' favoritism against her, but they weren't really a close family.

"How about ice cream?" Erik asked. It wasn't the smoothest segue, but it worked to get past an awkward moment. It wasn't Susan's fault that a question normal people could answer without blinking was such a minefield for him. Even now, with all his accomplishments, Erik had to remind himself that he wasn't as invisible and replaceable as his parents' indifference always made him feel.

"Count me in!" Susan replied with a grin. "And I know it's still off-season, but once everything opens up for the summer, there are some fantastic local ice cream shops that make everything from scratch. I'll have to take you!"

"You're on." He ran upstairs to get the ice cream out of the freezer and returned a few minutes later with a scoop and bowls.

"I'm really looking forward to seeing the town wake up from its winter nap," he said as he set out generous portions of vanilla bean for both of them, finishing off what was in the carton. Once he got settled, he'd have to see about adding toppings to his grocery list. "I know a lot of shops and restaurants close in the off-season. I'm looking forward to getting the whole Cape May experience!"

He had fond memories of the seaside town with its stately Victorian homes and yellow-striped beach tents. Aunt Karen and Uncle Jim included Erik whenever they could in their vacations, saying it was because he was the same age as their boys. Now that he looked back on it, Erik guessed that they were doing their best to make up for his parents' indifference. Their visits to Cape May had left a lasting impression.

"Oh, you'll love it," Susan gushed. She was definitely the town's biggest booster. "I mean yes, there's more traffic. But there's also a lot more energy. Plus even more theater and music, live bands in the bars, fireworks—I wouldn't want to live anywhere else!"

They chatted about favorite kinds of ice cream and desserts, fun topics without any stress. Once Susan scraped her bowl clean and licked every drop from her spoon, she sat back with a satisfied sigh.

"This has been fun. Thank you."

Erik gave her a perplexed look. "You volunteered to spend an afternoon helping me unpack and brought dinner. I owe you a big thank you!"

Susan shrugged. "I enjoyed the company and got to see some lovely antiques up close. I stay pretty busy, but it's nice to get out. Tank and Ziggy are good company, but the conversation gets a little one-sided." Erik had already met Tank, the bulldog, and Ziggy, the black cat.

"Anytime," Erik said. "This was fun." Once he unpacked his kitchen boxes, he'd have to find the few recipes he could make well enough to serve to company and repay the favor.

Susan helped clean up the garbage and went to grab the slow cooker. She divided the leftover meatloaf and put half into a plastic container for Erik. "Here. It makes great sandwiches."

"I never turn down good food," he assured her. "Thank you—for everything."

She grinned. "You're very welcome. Don't forget it's Friday night—why don't you wander into town and see if there's anyone worth meeting? You never know if you don't try!"

With that, she was out the door and across the yard. Erik watched out the window to make sure she got in safely, still thinking about her words. Before he could second-guess himself, he pulled out his phone and downloaded a dating app. As soon as the app registered his location, he uploaded a photo and sketched out a quick bio.

He hesitated, staring at the photo, worried it might not attract interest. He considered his looks fairly average, and he hadn't devoted enough time to the bar or club scenes to gauge his effect on other men. He hadn't had difficulty finding casual boyfriends in college and graduate school, but then he'd connected with Josh and taken himself off the market.

His light blond hair had a bit of a wave no matter how he styled it. Erik had always considered his blue eyes to be his best feature. They were dark like sapphires, and he thought they made up for other unremarkable features. At five foot ten, Erik wasn't short, but he wasn't terribly tall, either. Running and lifting weights kept him in good shape, although he doubted anyone would mistake him for an underwear model. His build remained on the slender side, even now that he was in his mid-thirties. He'd discovered long ago that he preferred men who were taller and more muscular, and had found that interest was often returned.

Erik paused. He really wasn't looking for a quick fuck. The appeal of hookups had gone cold in grad school. Trying not to overthink this, he dismissed the profiles that made it clear they were "one and done." Whether they were telling the truth, a few of the profiles indicated they wanted friends with benefits or were willing to start slow and see where it went.

For once, his intuition wasn't telling him a damn thing as he looked through the remaining profiles. He picked one for "David," a good-looking man with dark hair, a muscular build, and the promise of intriguing tattoos peeking from beneath the sleeves of his T-shirt. Then Erik gathered his courage and hit "send."

TWO

BEN

"What the hell did you pack in these boxes? Rocks?" Sean Meirlach shifted the heavy moving box on his shoulder. Sean looked and sounded like the Jersey Shore guy he was, brawny and blunt.

"Books," Ben replied. "You know, those rectangular paper things? Ever read one?" The teasing was good-natured. Ben Nolan had spent most of his summers working for his cousin's mom, and they were thick as thieves. Which, Ben reflected, was a poor analogy for an ex-cop-turned-former-private-investigator. And now, at least for this summer, a vacation rental manager in beautiful Cape May, New Jersey.

"Yes, dumbass. I've read lots of books. And not just the ones with pictures in them," Sean said with a smirk. Sean played up his bad boy persona, but Ben knew his cousin had plenty of brains, hustle, and street smarts.

"Good to know. I'd hate to have to break it to Aunt Meg that her favorite son was illiterate."

Sean snorted. "Favorite son? I'm her *only* son, asshole. And she's already pissed at me because I just want to run my food truck in Wildwood. Which is why you're doing me a huge solid, taking over the family business."

"Whoa, there! Hold up. I'm here for the summer. *Just* the summer. I said I'd see how it went. No promises."

"Just the summer? You sure brought a lot of shit with you if it's just for the summer." Sean set the box down a little harder than necessary on a table in the upstairs apartment over the rental office, which would be Ben's home for the next few months. Ben dumped the tangle of odds and ends he had carried up from the rented van and flopped onto the couch. He had put most of his things in storage when he left Newark and brought what he didn't want to do without, or what the apartment didn't have. Sean had driven the truck up to Cape May, while Ben drove his black Mustang, packed to the roof.

He owed Sean a lot for helping him move—and, if truth be told, for pushing him as the perfect candidate for the job to Aunt Meg.

"Don't screw up the master plan, dude!" Sean chided. "You're sick of the big city and getting shot. And I need a little of that good life, somewhere not quite as buttoned-down." He reached for a bottle of water and took a swig. "I love this town, but I need to stretch my wings. And the vibe in Wildwood is different. People come for the Pier and the Boardwalk and the rides. More singles, not just families. And they all have to eat!"

Sean's truck, *Put A Ring On It*, specialized in kickass onion rings, which went on everything—burgers, hot dogs, chicken wings, even chili. The combination of great food, a catchy name, and Sean's outgoing personality had made for a very successful launch.

Ben knew that his cousin had dreamed of owning a restaurant for years, almost as long as Ben had wanted to be a cop. While Ben had earned his badge with the Newark Police Department, Sean had been the good son, helping his mother with the rental business after his father was sidelined with emphysema.

"I am really happy that you're finally living the dream," Ben said, and meant every word.

"We had a great first summer, and even though we're in the off-season, there are enough events every weekend that we're doing better than just okay." Sean's love for the truck and his new-found freedom were clear in his tone and in his radiant smile. "So I think we're gonna crush it this summer. And if we do, maybe it won't be too long before I can buy a second truck. It's really happening, Benny, just like I always said."

Ben took one look at how happy Sean was and felt like a jerk. Yeah, becoming a cop hadn't worked out quite like Ben had expected, but he'd had a shot at his dream. Sean deserved his turn, and Ben could do worse than taking over an established business with a decent salary and an absentee boss who also happened to be his aunt and his biggest supporter.

"I'm sure I'll love it here," Ben said, trying to make amends. "My head's spinning and I haven't even unpacked my suitcase. I just need time to settle in."

"Then let's get to it so we can have a little fun later!" Sean and he were the same age—thirty-three—but Sean still acted like he was twenty-three and holding. Ben felt every moment of those years.

Maybe taking a few bullets had something to do with that.

The nightmares and PTSD were easing up, but his department-ordered therapist warned him that they might never completely go away. Three years later, Ben hadn't seen as much of a difference as he'd hoped.

He'd been undercover on a racketeering bust that had been in the works for more than a year. His boyfriend hadn't been able to take Ben's absence and the secrets being undercover meant Ben had to keep. Caleb had bailed on him, moving out and leaving a note while Ben was on the job. Then someone in the department had tipped off the racketeers, the bust turned into a shitstorm, and Ben ended up shot twice and nearly died.

When he finally recovered, he had no desire to go back to the department, especially since the traitor was never caught. He took his settlement from the department and got his private investigator license. But after more than two years as a PI, seeing the worst of human nature, Ben was depressed and drinking too much, with night-mares worse than before. That was when Aunt Meg threw him a lifeline, offering him the chance to step into the family vacation rental business. They'd agreed he would work the season, and if he liked the job, Meg wanted to arrange a gradual buyout, since Sean had no interest in taking over. And so, here he was.

"What kind of fun?" Ben asked. God, when had he become such a wet blanket? He remembered their teens and early twenties, partying all night. Even his early years on the force had been all about "work hard, play harder." Blowing off steam on the weekends diffused the terror of the worst moments on the job. Now he sounded like he planned to watch *Jeopardy* and fall asleep on the couch by ten.

"Chill, Badge-Boy. Nothing illegal. There's a great bar—The Spike —with a fire pit, live music, and drink specials. We can walk, so no ride-share required. Some of my boys are coming down from Wild-wood. You'll like them."

"Okay. That sounds good."

"Do you remember Sherri, from when you worked summers up here?"

Ben searched his memories and came up with an image of a blond girl with short hair and a wide smile. "Yeah, kinda."

"She and Jo own The Spike. Best bar in Cape May."

"So did Sherri and Joe get married? We always thought they would."

Sean chuckled. "That's right, you've missed a few years. Yes, they're married. And Joe is now Jo without the 'e.' Or, as *she* puts it, 'same person, new and improved packaging.'"

"I guess I was away longer than I thought." The town itself hadn't changed much, but Ben figured he shouldn't be surprised people he knew had moved on. He certainly wasn't the same. Bullet wounds and a broken heart had made him wary of trusting, afraid to risk another betrayal. Maybe that was more proof that coming back to a familiar place was the right move.

Ben and Sean got the sound system set up first, and jokingly argued over whose playlist to blast while they finished unboxing and got Ben's stuff squared away. Aunt Meg had paid her housekeeper to stock the fridge and freezer like she did for rental clients, so Ben could put off grocery shopping for a while and not starve. The apartment came furnished, but Ben had brought towels, and a stash of kitchen appliances, pans, and gadgets that went beyond the basics.

"Do you like the couch where it is?" Sean asked as Ben got his printer and computer station arranged and connected.

"Can I see the TV from the couch? If so, then yeah."

"Just asking. I think we're pretty much done with the heavy lifting." Sean stood with his hands on his hips and turned in a circle, surveying the apartment. "Let's get your art up, and then we can hit the town."

Ben could have hung the pictures by himself, but it was so much easier with someone else to tell him when the height was right. Removable sticky hooks made short work of the task, and when he stepped back to admire their handiwork, he had to admit that his collection of framed Marvel movie posters went a long way toward making the apartment feel like his space.

"Not too shabby," Ben said, pleased with the way things looked. He had been afraid that his decorations would be as bland and lifeless as he felt inside. The movie posters had been packed away for a while because Caleb hadn't been a fan. Other pieces were souvenirs that brought a smile when he looked at them. A painted vase from a long-ago trip to Cancun. A conch shell was a reminder of a vacation to the islands. German beer steins he had bought when he and Sean had done an Oktoberfest tour through New Jersey and Pennsylvania.

His awards and commendations stayed in storage. But over in the corner, he had the big Spider-Man statue Aunt Meg had bought him as a graduation present, next to a large—and transformable—Optimus Prime. Caleb had shamed him about his "geeky" favorites, and Ben had gradually hidden them away. Giving them prominent display in his new apartment felt like coming out all over again, a statement that he was never again going to hide who he really was.

Then again, he wasn't expecting that he'd have many visitors other than Sean. Caleb walked out two years ago, and Ben still wasn't sure he was ready for another relationship. His cop wariness made him leery of picking up guys at bars, and he wasn't much for the club scene. At thirty-three, the idea of an anonymous fuck in a back room held no appeal. So far, he'd kept himself busy to stay distracted, and rubbed one out in the shower when he needed to scratch that itch. It wasn't where he thought he'd be at this point in his life, but he hadn't expected to end up managing rental real estate property, either.

*I've still got my New Jersey PI license if I decide I want to go swimming in the sewer again.*

"Tomorrow I'll give you the tour of all the rental properties that aren't occupied," Sean promised. "But we've worked hard enough today. Let's get cleaned up and go down to The Spike. I'm hungry, and I could use a couple of cold ones."

Ben let Sean get the first shower, while he put his clothes in the dresser and chest of drawers in the bedroom. He snorted when he found a bottle of lube and a string of condoms, and tossed them into the nightstand drawer, figuring they'd probably pass their expiration date, unopened.

The bedroom had a king-sized bed, which Ben appreciated. At six foot one and a solidly muscled two hundred pounds, he liked room to stretch out. He'd brought his own comforter and sheets, which automatically made the place feel more like home and less like a hotel. While he waited for Sean to get out of the bathroom, Ben unboxed the books and put them on shelves, along with a few small knick-knacks from trips to Vegas, New Orleans, and New York.

A faded photograph in a frame lay in the bottom of the box. Ben stared at it, an image of him and his mom, on a trip to the planetarium at the Newark Museum for his eighth birthday. It hurt him to see the smiles on their faces, knowing how soon everything would go so wrong.

Erin O'Connor had been a good Catholic girl from a strict home when she'd gotten pregnant in high school. Her family forced her to marry her boyfriend, who hadn't planned on a wife and a baby on the way at eighteen. Patrick Nolan took out his frustration with alcohol and his fists. Ben remembered Patrick as a mean-tempered drunk who smacked them both around until he walked out and didn't return. Ben had been ten at the time, and he was surprised his dad had stuck around as long as he did.

Erin felt the shame of being a single mother, and the judgment of a priest who told her Patrick's abuse was her fault. A divorce meant she couldn't receive Eucharist. She'd seen Ben as her redemption, pushing him to go into the priesthood. When he had finally rebelled at seventeen, on the grounds that he had no calling and was gay, Erin considered it the final indignity and threw him out. He'd moved in with Aunt Meg and Uncle Stewart while he saved up enough money to go to Newark to join the police department.

So yeah, he owed Aunt Meg. Big time.

He took the photo out of the box and placed it face down on the shelf in the back of his closet.

"All yours," Sean called as he headed down the hall to the guest bedroom.

Ben grabbed a towel and rummaged through his clothes to find something to wear. Newark was solidly a jeans and T-shirt city. Wildwood was board shorts and knock-off Hawaiian shirts. Cape May had a prep school vibe, a reminder of the Northeast money that had built the huge Victorian homes and flocked to the seaside at the turn of the last century.

He finally picked a black polo that played up his green eyes and short dark hair, and a nicer pair of jeans he saved for going out. He liked the way they fit, even if he didn't expect anyone else to notice. The shirt sleeves were short enough to reveal some of his tats, mostly Celtic designs and protective symbols that seemed like a good idea in a dangerous job. *You can take the gay boy out of the Catholic Church, but you can't take the Church out of the gay boy.*

The shower felt good, easing sore muscles from carrying boxes, and cleaning away the sweat. Ben was just glad to do the move in mid-May before it warmed up. He got out, toweled off, and paused when he caught sight of his scars in the mirror.

Two pink, round scars that would likely never fade. He'd refused to wear a protective vest because he didn't want to give himself away as an undercover cop. The traitor had done a good enough job doing that. Ben didn't remember the worst of it, but Aunt Meg did. She was his designated next of kin, the ICE contact on his phone.

Ben pulled on his clothes and gave himself the once-over. He was resigned to the faint lines starting at the corner of his eyes. He'd earned them, and felt lucky to have lived long enough to show his age a little.

Ben ran a hand through his hair. *Now that I'm not a cop or a PI, I could grow it out again.* He'd kept his hair long when he was under-cover, but he didn't really want to be reminded of those days every time he looked in the mirror. The fade he sported worked with his thick dark hair, and it was simple to manage without a lot of fuss.

"Are you ready? Since when do you take time to primp?" Sean teased when Ben walked out to the living room. One look at Sean, and he wondered why he bothered to stress about his clothing choices. Sean wore a T-shirt that strained across his sizable pecs and a pair of skinny jeans.

"And you look like an extra from Real Housewives," Ben shot back.

Sean shrugged. "I may have been raised in Cape May, but I've always been more Wildwood at heart." His phone buzzed, and he glanced down. "The guys are here. Let's go!"

Three men waited for them at the curb, next to a sleek red Camaro. "All right! You made it!" Sean greeted them. "Guys, this is my cousin Ben, the one I told you about."

The redhead looked Ben over. "The cop?"

"Ex-cop," Ben clarified.

"Ben, this is Darius, Taylor, and Mateo. We have an apartment together up in Wildwood."

Taylor, the redhead, wore his curly hair long over skin so pale Ben wondered how he didn't fry to a crisp working a beach job. Mateo was stocky with two full sleeves of impressively inked tats. Darius, tall, slender and dark-skinned, looked like the quiet one of the bunch.

"Nice to meet you," Ben said. "Do you all have food trucks?"

They broke out laughing. "If I wanted to slave over a hot stove, I'd have stayed home and worked at my *abuela's* restaurant," Mateo said. "Are you kidding? I live for ink." He showed off his sleeves. "I've got a good spot in the hottest tattoo shop on the boardwalk, but one of these days I'm going to open my own place. I figure if this loser can buy a truck, anything's possible!" He shoulder-checked Sean, who pushed back playfully, and the whole group laughed.

"I'm a bartender at Tahiti Tiki," Taylor said. "The cocktail prices are high enough that we don't attract the puking college kids. Better tips, too." From the look on his face, Ben figured Taylor had worked his way up from places that drew a different crowd.

"I'm a lifeguard," Darius said with a shrug. "It's boring until there's an emergency, and then it's boring again."

"Pretty much sums up being a cop, too," Ben said. "But more doughnuts."

The Spike was about a mile away, but a pleasant ocean breeze and a clear night made for a nice walk. In a couple of weeks, more cars and pedestrians would crowd the streets and sidewalks. Cape May wasn't a town for cruising. Nobody circled the block unless they couldn't find the perfect spot to park their BMW or Tesla.

Sean and his friends laughed and joked, with the kind of comfortable familiarity that came from long experience—and probably shared adversity, Ben thought. He hung back, feeling more like a world-weary older brother than part of the group, although they were all close to the same age. The four weren't being overly loud, but they still drew a few disapproving looks from older couples dining on hotel patios, and Ben wondered if the diners were the kind to call the cops on anyone they thought didn't look like they belonged. If so, it would be a mistake. Sean was born and raised in Cape May, and his parents had run the rental business for more than twenty years. He belonged, far more than any tourist.

*Will I ever actually belong here?* Ben had grown up in Newark. For as much as the city was often the butt of jokes—not as much as Trenton, but often enough—he'd met a lot of good people and felt at home. Cape May was a tourist town, a little buttoned-up, but still welcoming to the LGBT community. Maybe with time, he'd find his place. Ben hoped so, because he had no intention of going back to Newark.

"So Sean said you're going to run the rental business, and spring him so he can keep his truck going full-time," Mateo said.

Ben realized he'd trailed the others, staying quiet, and appreciated the effort Mateo was making to include him. "Yeah. I'm trying it out for the season, and if it all goes well…we'll see what happens."

Mateo nodded. "You're smart to keep your options open. See how it feels. Me, I like the energy at the boardwalk. Always something going on." He grinned. "And I don't think there's as much call for tattoos here."

"You're probably right," Ben agreed with a laugh.

"I noticed your ink," Mateo said. "You get that done in Newark?"

"Yeah. I had a guy who did nice work. I gave him a lot of business."

"That's good, when you find someone you trust. The tattoo business, it's all about trust. My customers, they have to trust me to keep things clean, so nobody gets sick. And they trust me not to fuck up their designs. Nobody wants a crappy tattoo."

"I've been thinking about maybe getting some more work done. If I do, I'll look you up." Ben didn't think he'd be adding anything right away, but Rod, his regular artist, warned him ink was addictive. Ben hadn't believed him then, but one look in the mirror when he was shirtless proved Rod had been right.

"Do it. I'll give you my friends and family discount," Mateo promised.

Ben couldn't help sizing up his new companions, a side effect from all those years as a cop. Sean and Taylor were the extroverts, egging each other on, joking and laughing. Darius and Mateo chimed in now and then, clearly part of the group, but they weren't quite as boisterous, or maybe they just were okay with playing wingmen and letting Sean and Taylor do their thing.

Ben wondered how it would go when they got to The Spike. Sean had been bi—or maybe pan—since high school. He had no idea about Taylor, Mateo, and Darius, although if they were used to going out on the town with Sean, they clearly didn't have a problem with Sean's choice in partners. Ben had no intention of cruising the bar for a hookup, and he doubted the other men had that in mind tonight. That took the pressure off and made Ben relax, just a little.

*Maybe it wouldn't kill me to lighten up. It's been a long time.*

Ben shook off his thoughts, reminded himself that he was lucky to have family, a job, and a place to live, and decided that he would have a great time with Sean and his friends at The Spike tonight if it killed him.

# THREE

# ERIK

After Susan went home, Erik got in the shower and washed away the stress of the day. He reminded himself that he had no intention of bringing his date home with him, let alone making out in a dark corner at the bar. *He said he was open to friendship and seeing where it goes. So...that's all I'm offering. If we hit it off, we'll take it from there.*

Still, it had been a long time since he'd been on a date. He and Josh had been together for three years, and Erik had been seriously considering popping the question—before he found Josh popping Lee's cherry. In the months since then, he'd kept to himself. But Susan was right. New town, new beginnings. And it wouldn't hurt to make some friends.

So he took a bit more care than usual with his blond hair. After he walked away from the fraud and forgery unit—an interagency collaboration between U.S. and European law enforcement entities—he let his hair grow longer on top. He'd kept it shorter to fit in with the agents, most of whom were ex-military. Erik hadn't worn it longer since graduate school, so the style felt rebellious and a bit like reliving happier days. That, and Josh hadn't cared for this style, but Erik thought it looked good.

*Screw what Josh thought. I'm over him.*

*Yeah, keep telling yourself that.*

Erik sighed. Both were a little true. He was long past wanting Josh back. But the hurt still felt fresh and sharp at the damnedest moments, usually when he thought he was finally getting his shit together. Maybe the best way to forget an old lover was by taking a new one. Erik had kept himself so busy tying up the loose ends of his old life and getting ready to move that he hadn't had time to think. *Nice coping strategy,* an inner voice mocked.

He refused to let his nerves—or the past—get the best of him. Erik went into his closet and found a navy button-down that brought out the blue in his eyes, and a faded pair of skinny jeans that showed off his ass. He didn't intend to sleep with David, but it certainly didn't hurt to showcase the goods.

Erik had been to the restaurant part of The Spike on his first visit to Cape May, but that was during the winter, and the fire pit and outdoor bar hadn't been open. So he knew where to head, and was glad that the bar was in walking distance, which meant he didn't need to call for a ride. He tried to imagine what the town would look like once tourist season was in full swing. He'd gone to Myrtle Beach a few times on Spring Break, but Cape May had a totally different vibe. Erik looked forward to seeing the beach resort come alive.

*Maybe it'll resuscitate me, too.*

He'd kept himself busy with a whirlwind of activity because he hadn't wanted to face how empty Josh's betrayal had made him feel. Sometimes, Erik was afraid he'd never feel anything again. Then a hint of excitement about Cape May and starting up the *Treasure Trail* blog gave him hope that, in time, he might find his way back to feeling passionate about something—and maybe, someone.

The Spike opened onto the sidewalk with the enclosed restaurant on one end, the outdoor bar in the middle with its back to pedestrians, and a large sandy area on the other side. Fire pits, Adirondack chairs, a small stage for performers, and wooden corn hole games gave the bar the feel of a well-attended beach party.

Erik resisted the urge to check his hair in the reflection of a darkened window as he approached the bar. His hands were sweating. *Shit. I haven't been this nervous since the first time I asked a guy out.*

"It's just a drink," he muttered to himself. "That's all. No big deal."

Erik walked up to the outdoor bar and found a seat with an empty stool next to it. He checked the time on his phone and saw that he was five minutes early. *That's okay. Good to be on time, but not so early it looks desperate if he's watching.*

He'd glanced out over the crowd and hadn't seen anyone who matched the picture on the app. Maybe David liked to saunter in right on time. Erik forced himself to relax.

"Whatcha drinkin'?" the bartender asked.

"Give me the Cape May IPA," Erik replied, having at least looked up the local brew. He preferred wine—and the area had some nice local wineries—but he didn't want to look pretentious. And since he wanted to keep a clear head, cocktails and shots were out. Beer was neutral. *I'm overthinking this.*

"You starting a tab?" the bartender asked when he brought the drink.

"Yeah. I'm meeting a friend. Sure."

The bartender nodded and walked off. Just as Erik lifted the can, a man slid onto the stool next to him.

"Can't believe the traffic around here, huh?" the stranger said with a grin. He flagged the bartender like a regular and ordered a Dogfish Ale.

"It's practically bumper to bumper," Erik replied, although only a handful of cars had passed on his walk to the bar.

"Can't wait to see what it's like when the season starts. Hope it picks up."

Erik shifted on his seat to get a look at his new companion. Short dark hair, a bit of scruff, and bright green eyes made him catch his breath. Broad, muscled shoulders filled out the black polo, tapering to a trim waist. The edge of a pattern in dark ink showed just below the shirt's short sleeves. Erik caught a whiff of burnt orange and cedar that went right to his groin *Hot damn.*

"You're not from here?" Erik had gotten the idea from David's profile that he had lived in Cape May for a while.

"Nah. Barely had time to unpack. I'm from Newark. Just here temporarily, helping out my aunt. You?" the guy said.

The bartender brought the man his Dogfish, and he paid cash with a good tip. *Maybe I shouldn't have opened a tab. He doesn't look like he's planning to stay long. Shit. Did I manage to disappoint him already?*

"Here and there lately, but South Carolina originally," Erik replied.

The man snorted. "Oh, you're gonna love the winters. Hope you packed your long johns. That sea wind'll cut you to the bone."

"Well, at least the food is good," Erik answered. He'd forgotten how bad he was at small talk. Still, David hadn't run yet, so maybe he was doing all right. "I've eaten here a couple of times. Their breakfast is amazing."

The man leaned back and seemed to just now notice his new companion. Erik felt the stranger's gaze rake over him like he could see every sin and desire. He fought a shiver at the appraisal that laid him bare. "Yeah? Good to know. I never turn down bacon." His smile eased the tension.

"Me, neither. So David, how does Cape May compare to Newark?"

The handsome stranger startled. "I'm not David. I think you have the wrong guy."

*Fuck.* "I'm sorry," Erik apologized. "I'm supposed to meet someone here, and you look a lot like his picture."

The stranger didn't say anything, but Erik could practically see the pieces of the puzzle assembling in the man's mind. Picture = dating app = hookup.

"Ah, no. Sorry to disappoint." He licked his lips as if the mix-up made him uncomfortable. "So, I guess I'd better free up the chair for your date. I need to go anyhow." His discomfort vanished behind a smirk. "Hope your evening has a very happy ending."

With that, the man slid off the stool, grabbed his beer, and walked over to where four men waited near the corn hole game. One of the men slung an arm over the stranger's shoulder and pulled him in against his side. Since all of the men were holding drinks, Erik guessed they'd been here for a while.

He turned back to the bar, not wanting the stranger to catch him watching. Still, Erik thought the man didn't quite seem to fit with his companions or the Jersey Shore tough guy who stood too close to be just a friend. *Damn. He was hot—and just my type. Fuck. It's like they say —all the good ones are taken.*

"Are you Erik?" The voice at his elbow nearly made Erik spill his beer.

"Yeah. Are you David?" This time, Erik intended to be certain.

"Yep. Sorry I'm late." David scooted onto the stool and leaned forward to catch the bartender's attention. "You got Nattie Light?" he called to the bartender, who was cashing out a tab.

While David focused on getting a drink, Erik gave him the once-over. The picture didn't exactly lie, but it was probably a couple of years old. A couple of *hard* years. David's wrinkled shirt and mussed hair suggested that he hadn't bothered to make an effort to look his best. In person, there was an edge that didn't come across in the photo.

*I liked the first guy better.* A burst of laughter came, right on cue, from where the stranger had gone to catch up with his boyfriend and their buddies. *Fuck. No use crying over spilled milk. He's already taken. And if that's the sort he goes for, I'm not even in the running.*

Back when he had helped infiltrate art theft rings, Erik had never bothered to try to pretend to be a tough guy. He'd taken martial arts classes because the work was dangerous and he wasn't an idiot. He'd gotten good with a gun, but hated to carry. But never once did he need to try to come off as tough. It had been to his advantage to play to the nerdy professor stereotype that people expected, overeducated and high-strung. "Poncy" one of his Brit colleagues had called him, managing to insult his orientation and his masculinity, all at once.

Erik tuned back in as David sparred with the bartender over what beer was available, settling on one that even Erik knew tasted like piss. He paid in cash, with no tip. "So, you been in town long?" David asked, finally turning his attention to Erik after he'd taken a long pull from his beer. He smelled like Axe and stale cigarettes.

"Couple of weeks. Getting settled." Erik tried not to sound short with the man, but everything so far had been a turnoff for a friend, let alone anything else.

David looked him up and down. Unlike the stranger's gaze, which had sent a jolt right to Erik's cock, David's appraisal held an air of disapproval. "You'll get the hang of this place. I've lived here all my life. You find out real quick there are the tourists and the townies. Tourists come here to drop a bundle. Townies can squeeze a buck tighter than a nun's knees."

He laughed at his own joke. "So whaddya do for a living? Me, I have a boat, and I take people out to fish. I usually catch some dinner, too."

Before Erik had a chance to answer, David barged on. "Let me guess. Professor? Teacher? You kinda got that look."

Erik felt his eye twitch. He'd met guys from the Russian Mob with better manners. "I handle antiques."

David shot him a sidelong glance. "What do you mean, 'handle'? Like, fence?"

Erik closed his eyes and counted to five. The bartender seemed to pick up on the tension, because he brought Erik's bill without being asked. "No. Nothing like that. Nothing at all."

David raised his hands like Erik had pulled a gun on him. "Geez. Don't get your panties in a twist. Can't a guy make a joke?"

Erik paid in cash, not wanting David to see the name on his credit card. He made sure to add a high enough tip to cover what his boorish "date" didn't.

"I don't think this was a good idea," Erik said, standing. "I'm sorry to have wasted your time." His voice automatically took on the chilly note he had once reserved for thieves and forgers.

"No kidding," David muttered. He turned his back to Erik. "Hey, bartender! Gimme another."

Erik squared his shoulders and held his head high, although inside, he felt utterly embarrassed. He dared to shoot a glance to where the stranger and his friends had been, but they were, mercifully, nowhere to be seen.

He could have walked home, but David's whole manner squicked him out, so Erik called a ride-share, and took the driver the long way, although David had been far more interested in his second beer than in following Erik for nefarious purposes.

"Well, that was a disaster," Erik murmured as he let himself into his apartment. The charm and personality of the big Victorian house that had originally entranced him eluded him, and the old house now seemed dark and empty. He locked the door, turned on all the lights, and went to change clothes. Erik came back out in a worn sweatshirt and track pants, and then stood in the kitchen, debating whether he wanted ice cream or scotch to soothe his wounded pride.

In the end, he decided on both. He carried his consolation prizes to the couch and flipped on an action movie marathon.

Erik's phone buzzed. He thought about ignoring the call, then noticed the caller's name. "Simon?"

"Got the feeling you were having a rough time, and I thought I'd check in with you."

"How—?"

"Hello? Psychic here." Simon's fond exasperation suggested an eye roll. "I got a vision of scotch and ice cream. And since you're the only person on the planet who considers that pairing to be comfort food, I knew something was up. Spill."

Despite his mood, Erik had to smile. Simon knew him so well. "I had a shitty date, and I'm home licking my wounds...instead of anything else."

"You had a date?"

"You don't need to sound so surprised," Erik muttered. "I've been on dates before."

"Uh-huh, but not since the *incident*. Unless you've been holding out on me."

Erik sighed. "No, I haven't been withholding juicy stories. This was the first time I stuck my toe back in the dating pool, and it was a clusterfuck."

He and Simon met during graduate school at the University of South Carolina, when Simon had been working on his Ph.D. in Folklore and Mythology, and Erik had been pursuing the same degree in Art History and Preservation. Some of their required classes overlapped, and they had ended up best friends. Over the years since then, while other college and grad school friends drifted away, he and Simon stayed in touch. Despite how well they got along, there had never been anything between them except friendship, which made it easier to talk about bad dates.

"Fill me in. Vic's working a case, so we won't be disturbed." Simon's partner, Vic D'Amato, was a homicide detective.

Erik told the whole tale, complete with the mistaken identity of the sexy stranger. "And then I walked out," he concluded. "God, that's so pathetic." He was tempted to knock back the scotch all at once, but a good bottle of Glenmorangie didn't deserve to be treated like that.

"It's not pathetic, and neither are you," Simon replied, after having listened in silence. "It took a lot of courage to set up a date, even if you weren't really expecting it to go anywhere."

"That's the problem," Erik said. "That first guy—I wouldn't have minded things going somewhere with him. I haven't had a reaction like that to anyone since…in a long time."

"Have you actually looked at anyone closely enough to have a reaction to them?" Simon asked.

"Not really. But this guy pressed all my buttons—and he's taken." *And just here temporarily.*

"You don't know *how* taken," Simon pointed out.

"Aargh. That's almost worse. I'm not looking for a player. If I do this again, get serious about someone, I want there to be a good chance from the start that it can last. I did my jet-setting. I'm ready to settle down." Erik really wanted the kind of relationship Simon and Vic had: honest, committed, and strong.

"If that's what you want, then keep looking," Simon urged. "He's out there."

"Well, he wasn't in London, New York, Rome, or Antwerp—or Atlanta," Erik said, a hint of bitterness coloring his tone. "What are the odds he'll be in Cape May?"

Simon laughed. "Maybe the same as they were that I'd find my forever guy in Myrtle Beach. You know what I wreck I was when I moved down here."

Erik remembered. Back at the university, they had mourned bad grades and broken hearts at the bars catering to broke grad students. In the years since then, email, phone, and texts had kept them in touch. Simon had lost his teaching position when the zealot father of a student falsely accused him of teaching "witchcraft." His tenure-track fiancé had broken up with him, afraid of damaging his own prospects. Simon had gone to the beach to get his head together and never left. Now he owned Grand Strand Ghost Tours, had a home, and a great partner.

"Do you see anything? I mean, about me?" Erik didn't ask his friend questions like that often. Simon was a psychic medium, and his talent was strong enough that he now worked as an official consultant with the Myrtle Beach Police Department after having helped solve several high-profile cases.

"Other than the whiskey and ice cream?" Simon was silent for a moment. "I see an antique clock, and an impressive brick and stone building. It looks old. Everything else is blurry. That usually means there's too much in flux to get a solid read. Sorry."

"That's okay," Erik said. "Thanks. Did I tell you about the TV thing? Or do you already know?"

Simon took the change of subject for what it was, and let Erik fill him in, commenting enthusiastically at all the right spots.

"It sounds like a fantastic opportunity. You've got a lot on your plate right now, getting the blog and the shop up and running, planning the TV show. Why not put dating on the back burner and see what happens?"

Erik had already come to that decision, but it helped to have his old friend provide confirmation. "Yeah. You're right. There's a lot of good stuff coming together." He paused. "And despite tonight's disaster, I like the town so far. More than I thought I might."

"Isn't Cape May really haunted? Run into any ghosts?" Simon asked.

Erik's abilities differed from Simon's, although their shared "weirdness" had been part of what had bonded their friendship. Simon was a true medium: he could summon and dispel ghosts, speak to them and hear their replies. His psychic visions revealed glimpses of things in the present and future. Erik could see ghosts, but he'd never been able to actually communicate with them. And while his touch magic let him see through the "eyes" of an object, it certainly didn't provide any predictions of things to come.

"There's an old woman who shows up on the third floor of my house. I call her Millie. Nobody seems to know who she was. I hear her walking around, and I saw her near the window a few times. So maybe she's watching for her husband's ship to come back," Erik replied. "And I spotted a man on the beach who looked like he might have been from Victorian times. But honestly, I haven't been many other places in town yet to see any other ghosts."

"I never knew how haunted Myrtle Beach was until I moved here," Simon replied. "But I guess it's good for business." Simon did psychic readings and séances, as well as leading ghost tours. "Speaking of business, if you ever need any help with your touch magic, don't forget that my cousin Cassidy down in Charleston can do that stuff."

"Thanks. I might take you up on that once I get settled in." The visions he received from antiques with an "interesting" history had grown stronger and more detailed over the years. Erik chalked it up to improving with practice like any other talent, but he'd never really had anyone but Simon to talk to about it. Certainly no one in his old life.

Erik already put the ice cream back in the freezer and sipped at the scotch. He yawned, and Simon chuckled.

"Sounds like you're done for tonight. Go get some sleep. Things'll look better in the morning," Simon told him and said good night.

Erik ended the call, tipped his head back, and swallowed the last of the whiskey. Simon's call had helped him get his priorities straight. *Sort out the business, and then worry about everything else.*

He went to bed, resolutely refusing to think about the dark-haired stranger at the bar. But the dreams that woke him, sweaty and hard, desperate for release, made it clear his subconscious had a different agenda.

FOUR

# BEN

"I had forgotten about the ghosts." Ben followed Sean into the fourth rental house that morning.

Sean clucked his tongue and shook his head. "Benny, what are we gonna do with you? This is Cape May. Ghosts cost extra."

Personally, Ben wasn't a fan, but he knew many other people—including well-heeled tourists—felt differently.

"Do you remember the time mom had us doing the move-out clean-up on the big gray Victorian, and that man with the top hat popped through the floor, right in front of you?" Sean started laughing at the thought. "You shrieked so loud. I didn't think a guy could hit those notes after puberty."

Ben remembered a heart-stopping moment of terror. Nice to know that, even now, it was on Sean's mental gag reel.

"Yeah. I remember. And I also remember that you just about wet yourself when that pervy old lady ghost slapped your ass." Ben had plenty of cringe-worthy memories of Sean if they were going to play that game. All in good fun, of course.

"Oh. My. God. I thought you were messing with me until—"

"—She smacked your butt, and I wasn't even on the same floor," Ben finished for him, laughing.

"We cribbed some of Dad's beer that night," Sean recalled. "I think we absolutely deserved it. Hazard pay and all, you know."

They had been sixteen, and Ben had been up for the summer, happy to make some extra cash and get out of his mother's hair for a few months. Looking back, it seemed like a cheesy coming-of-age movie. Pilfering beer from the fridge, sneaking a smoke, staying out late on the beach with Sean and his friends, setting off illegal fireworks and outrunning the cops who tried to catch them.

"We were almost juvenile delinquents," Ben replied, but he couldn't keep the fondness out of his tone.

Sean made a dismissive noise. "Fuck, no. Come to Wildwood—I'll introduce you to some real juvenile delinquents. We were just making the most of a slightly misspent youth," he replied with a grin.

They hadn't actually done anything too bad, nothing malicious or dangerous. At the time, he and Sean thought they were putting one over on Aunt Meg. Now, he was pretty sure his aunt knew and figured it was safer to let them blow off a little steam than crack down and send them looking for real trouble.

"I always wished we'd gotten up the nerve to explore that big old abandoned hotel," Ben said wistfully.

"The Commodore Wilson? No thanks. The place was cursed, I shit you not," Sean replied. "I knew some older kids who broke in there one summer. Bad stuff happened to all of them."

Sean gave him the grand tour of the rental house, noting selling points and things that were likely to break. "This house usually stays rented all summer," Sean told him. "But watch out—there's something about the garbage disposal that seems to break at least once a month. I used to think it was the renters, dropping in bottle caps or some shit like that. Now I just think it's a crap unit. But expect a call."

"Great." Ben added it to his notes. He had to admit that it impressed him how Sean could rattle off the selling points and candid problems of each property. "You're really good at this. Are you sure you don't want to keep your options open?"

Sean had been walking across the large upstairs game room. He stopped with his back to Ben. "You don't think I can make it, with the truck?"

*Shit.* "No. That's not what I meant at all. It's just, seeing the business here with fresh eyes, as an adult instead of a teenager, I see what your mom and dad built. Assuming I decide to stay…what if you and I worked out some kind of partnership? You've already put in a lot of sweat equity. I need a job and a place to live. Maybe we could figure something out where you wouldn't have to be here full time—so you could run the truck—but you could cover for me sometimes, help with some of the maintenance stuff you'd always done. You'd have a backup income, to get you through dry spells and invest in your business." *And I wouldn't be in this all by myself.*

Sean turned, a questioning look on his face. "You mean it? You'd do that?"

Ben shrugged. "Sure. Why not? It only seems fair. We can draw it all up, legal and official. *If* I decide to stay."

Sean's eyes narrowed. "Would that cute blond with the nice ass at the bar last night have anything to do with getting you to stay?"

Ben sighed. "I wish. We were having a great chat, and then it turned out he'd mistaken me for his hookup…from an app."

"Ouch," Sean commiserated loyally. "You mean that loser who sat down after you left?" He shook his head. "If that's the kind of guy he'd pick over you, you're better off without him. On the other hand, if it really just was a hookup, he's probably still available."

"Not really what I'm looking for," Ben replied, not planning to admit the same thought had crossed his mind, and he'd squashed it. "If that's all he wants, it's not going to work out."

"Or, he could help you get over Butthead, and then you could move on to someone who might be a keeper," Sean suggested, then went into an exaggerated—and off-key—rendition of Marvin Gaye's *Sexual Healing.*

"My ears! My ears are bleeding!" Ben protested although he couldn't stop laughing. Sean had gotten him through the aftermath when Caleb had packed his stuff and moved out, and they'd taken to calling his ex "Butthead." It was completely immature—and satisfying, nonetheless.

"I mean it, Ben. Sometimes a fuck buddy is all you need. Or if it makes you feel better, friends with benefits."

"Ugh. I hate that phrase," Ben said, knowing he should be paying more attention to hardwood floors, crown moldings, and kitchen appliances as they walked through the house. "I'm pretty sure that one person in that arrangement really wants more and just goes along with it."

"Who knew that beneath that tough Newark cop exterior lurked a true romantic?" Sean's tone was snarky but not mocking.

"It's not like I watch the Hallmark Channel," Ben protested. "I just don't want to play games anymore. Look at it this way—if I'm not playing, there's less competition for you." His smile said he knew he was poking the bear.

"Oh my dear, slightly confused cousin," Sean said, shaking his head with mock pity. "There's no competition. Not everyone can be…me. Just accept it and move on." He grinned, falling right back into the banter they perfected in high school.

Sean went into his practiced patter about the house, and Ben resigned himself to making notes. Still, he couldn't help that his thoughts strayed to the handsome blond at the bar. Ben bet the man would be a few inches shorter than his own height, nice to tuck against him standing up—or in bed. He'd rocked the academic look, but Ben wondered if he could also rock a bit of "hot for teacher" roleplay. Something told him that in the right setting, for the right person, that nerdy professor might be fun between the sheets.

More to the point, he'd been smart as well as flirty. And from the way that blue shirt fit his shoulders and the jeans outlined his ass, Ben guessed the body underneath would be prime real estate of a different kind.

*Shit.* Just thinking about the man was making Ben hard, and he really didn't need that right now. He tried to adjust himself surreptitiously as he and Sean locked up to go to the next property, but he should have known Sean wouldn't miss a chance to razz him.

"Thinking about Bar-Guy again? Seriously, you need to get laid."

"Can we not call him Bar-Guy?"

"Did you get his name?"

"No. But the loser's name was David."

"Not helpful. He told you he had just moved here? So, ask around. Keep your eyes open. Cape May isn't that big of a place, especially off-season. You'll see him again. And when you do, just slide right in like the smooth devil you are," Sean teased.

Yeah, no. "Smooth" was Sean's gig, not Ben's. "Anyhow, what can you tell me about the next house?" Ben hoped Sean would take a hint and change the subject.

The properties Nolan Resort Real Estate handled ranged from tidy bungalows to seaside mansions, with some stately Victorian "painted ladies" and a few modern condos thrown into the mix. Aunt Meg and Uncle Stewart had quietly put together a real estate empire, with their own properties and the ones they managed for absentee owners. Ben was suitably impressed.

"This one's a real charmer," Sean said as they walked a few blocks to the next property on the list. "Modern appliances, gourmet kitchen, with Victorian charm. The place was built in 1900, it's been fully refurbished, with original pine flooring and some nice stained-glass accent windows."

Ben followed him onto the porch, taking in the white filigree trim that set off the blue paint. *His eyes were blue. Very blue. Was that his real eye color, or contacts?* Ben shoved the thought aside, determined to stick to business.

"So is it already booked?" he asked as they walked in. The furnishings maintained the Victorian feel, but Ben knew most were reproductions sturdy enough to survive real use. The decorations adorning the mantle and bookshelves were antique, but nothing terribly expensive or irreplaceable. Given how much it cost to rent the houses—and the required renter's insurance—their properties didn't generally draw a crowd likely to cause problems.

"It's not a problem of getting it booked," Sean said as he closed the door behind them. "It's keeping it booked. This one has a ghost problem—and Casper *isn't* friendly."

"I don't remember this house," Ben said, taking a look around. The place was beautiful, and it probably looked like a showplace in the online photos. But now that they were inside, Ben felt unsettled, like they were being watched.

"You wouldn't. Mom bought it a couple of years ago, right before Dad got sick. It had stayed in the same family until then, but the owners weren't here that often. Now we have a clue about why."

The room seemed cold, despite a pleasant temperature outdoors. Ben didn't see a ghost, but he sensed that something just wasn't right.

"Did you ever see a ghost in here?" he asked.

Sean shook his head. "See one? No. But weird stuff happens. We can rarely get the same cleaning people in here twice between rentals. They don't want to come back. And some renters up and leave halfway through their week."

"What kind of weird stuff?"

"Cold spots. Their car keys go missing and end up somewhere they never would have left them. Milk sours overnight. They hear footsteps on the stairs, and people who sleep in the third bedroom sometimes wake up to find a man in a forties-style suit and hat sitting on the edge of the bed."

"Okay, that's creepy," Ben said. "Any idea who he might be?"

Sean shrugged. "We even had this guy in who's a local historian and ghost-whisperer, to see if he could figure it out. The best anyone can guess, the ghost is someone who might have rented a room here when this was a boarding house."

"There used to be some Mob stuff going on, back when that big old hotel was in its heyday, wasn't there?" Ben tried to remember details that his teenage self had noted only in passing. "Maybe he got whacked and didn't want to leave."

"The Commodore Wilson? Yeah, everyone says it was all mobbed up from Prohibition through the War. But the ghost guy wouldn't have to be Mafia. He might have just had a heart attack or something."

"Not nearly as dramatic," Ben said. "And if the ghost is causing problems, I think that supports the violent death theory."

Right on cue, heavy footsteps sounded overhead, and Ben caught a whiff of cigar smoke where none had been present minutes before.

Sean raised an eyebrow. "Then again, maybe you're on to something. You up for seeing the rest of the house?"

"Yeah. Now I'm curious." The same instincts that made him a good cop and a decent private investigator told him there was more to the story.

Sean gave him the full tour, pointing out architectural details and modern upgrades. *It's a shame the haunting drove off renters*, Ben thought, because the house really was a gem. Maybe they could get to the bottom of the problem and put its cranky ghost to rest.

"And this is the room where the ghost puts on the biggest show," Sean said as they walked into the back bedroom. It had a lovely view of the ocean and a deep-set window seat.

Ben felt the hair on the back of his neck stand up an instant before something shoved him hard enough to send him flying. He crashed down onto the window seat and felt the wood splinter beneath his back.

"Great. First day on the job and I'm breaking things." His heart pounded, and it didn't escape his notice that if he hadn't hit the way he did, he could have gone right out the window—and onto the concrete sidewalk below.

Sean had gone pale. "Fuck. Are you okay? My God, you could have—"

"Yeah, but I didn't," Ben said, trying to extricate himself from the broken boards without having the splinters turn him into a pincushion. All those years as a cop and PI had taught him to avoid thinking about the "what ifs."

He stood up, knowing he'd be bruised and sore tomorrow, and frowned. "Hey, wait. Did you know this window seat opened? Look," he added, pointing. "There are hinges."

Sean shook his head, still looking spooked. "Never noticed. It's probably been painted shut for years."

"Not anymore," Ben replied ruefully. He reached down to pull away a few of the broken boards and grabbed the remains of the ruined seat and yanked upward, exposing a dark compartment.

"Find anything? Pirate booty? A stash of old Mob money?" Sean edged closer to get a look.

Ben reached in and pulled out the "treasure" hidden inside. The rectangular clock looked old, with four gilt-covered columns—two on each side of the face—against a black lacquered background. He looked up at Sean, totally confounded.

"It looks old, but if it was valuable, why nail the lid shut and leave it behind? And why haunt the place over it?"

Sean shrugged. "Dunno. But Mom always worked with an antique shop in town when she needed pieces to decorate a new property or fix something that got damaged. I'll look for the information when we get back to the office. And I'll let Mom know. She'll probably want to put in a good word for you with the owner."

Ben nodded absently, still trying to wrap his mind around what just happened. "Yeah. Okay. And we'll need to get someone in to fix the seat, but let's take the property off the website for now. I don't want anyone to get hurt."

"Speaking of which, you're bleeding."

*Son of a bitch.* Now that the adrenaline rush had faded, Ben could feel where the shattered wood had raked skin through the fabric of his shirt.

"I hope you didn't have more places to show me today," Ben said. "I think I'm done for now."

Sean watched the window seat as if it would bite, which was a little too close to the truth for Ben's comfort. "There are more, but we can do them another day. I wasn't going to be able to show you a few of them until the weekend anyhow because they've got renters in them."

As soon as Ben lifted the clock from its hiding place, he stopped noticing the weird vibes and the odd chill, and the sense of being watched. Had the ghost used up all his energy hurling Ben across the room? Or had Ben found what the ghost had been trying to reveal? And if so, why wait until now? Ben had no answers, but plenty of questions, and they all made him wonder if he was really cut out for the rental business.

Fortunately, they didn't have a long walk back to the office. Ben planned on taking some ibuprofen, because he knew sore muscles would tighten up as soon as he sat for too long. He tried not to limp but knew he didn't fool Sean.

"Be glad you're not a racehorse," Sean teased. "I'd have to put you out of your misery."

"Bite me," Ben muttered. "And I didn't break my leg."

"You don't have to be embarrassed, you know," Sean replied. "Just tell that hot blond that those scratches are your souvenirs from a night of rough, sweaty sex."

"You're impossible."

"No imagination," Sean chided.

When they reached the office, Sean went in search of the first aid kit while Ben gingerly removed his ruined shirt. The wood had gashed through the fabric, and it was stiff with blood. He took stock of the rest of his body. His thighs, lower back, and ass had taken the worst of the impact. No doubt he'd have some spectacular bruises to show for it, and sore muscles, but he couldn't find any other open wounds. It didn't bear thinking about what would have happened if he'd gone out that window.

"So I found it, but I don't know whether we've got enough bandages—holy fuck!" Sean stopped in his tracks. "Damn. Your back looks like it's been mauled by a bear." Then he waggled his eyebrows. "You can take that any way you want."

Ben turned to glare at him. "Seriously?"

"I remember you being a lot more fun."

"I am fun—when I'm not being thrown at windows."

Sean ripped open an antiseptic wipe and daubed at the deep scratches on Ben's back. Ben swore through gritted teeth. "Good news —no need for stitches. Probably won't scar, either." He smoothed ointment over the wounds and taped large gauze patches over top.

"The bandages aren't pretty, but it should all be healed by the time it's swimming weather."

"I've had worse." He stood and turned before thinking.

"Ben—those scars, is that from when you got *shot*?" Sean's eyes had gone wide, and his mood sobered.

Ben sighed. "Um. Yeah. A bust went wrong. It happens."

"I remember when Mom went up to Newark. She said you'd gotten shot. But she obviously didn't give me the whole story."

Ben's memories of the first part of his recovery were hazy from the painkillers. "I woke up after surgery, and Aunt Meg was there. I had her down as next of kin. She stayed until I was out of danger, and my captain told her the department would take care of me."

"You could have come down here to recuperate."

"I didn't know how long I'd be in the hospital, and the department needed me in reach so Internal Affairs could sort through all the shit. And honestly, there's a lot I don't remember."

"Wow. I...don't know what to say."

"Well, now I know what it takes to make my mouthy cousin speechless," Ben joked to lighten the moment. He crumpled up his ruined shirt and tossed it in the trash.

Sean rooted through a drawer and pulled out a "Nolan Resort Real Estate" polo shirt. He tossed it to Ben, managing to hit him in the face. "Have a free shirt."

Ben winced as he lifted his arms and flexed the muscles on his back. "Thanks. I think I'm going to go upstairs while I can still walk."

"I'll get Mom to call you with the name of that antique shop," Sean promised. "And seriously—I think you should find that hottie from The Spike and play the sympathy card. He'd probably be willing to kiss all your boo-boos and make them feel *much* better."

"Hold that thought until I'm not walking like an eighty-year-old man," Ben replied.

Sean left, and Ben hobbled up the steps to his apartment. He figured he'd have a frozen dinner for supper, since he didn't want to cook, and he sure as hell wasn't going to go up and down the stairs again soon, even for pizza delivery.

Ben eased out of his jeans and took a look at the damage in the full-length bathroom mirror. It was a good thing he didn't plan on getting naked with anyone soon. Several large bruises were already forming, and he knew they'd be Technicolor by morning. He found a pair of sweats and a soft T-shirt to replace the scratchy polo and changed, before shuffling into the kitchen.

Tomorrow he'd take the clock over to the antique shop to see what was so special about it. He and Sean could probably finish up the walk-throughs for the available houses and spend the rest of the day going over the computer system. Maybe he'd have things pretty well in hand by the time Sean went back to Wildwood. Or well enough to manage, at least.

Ben thought back to the conversation with Sean about finding a way to share the business. He'd been surprised that Sean was willing to consider it, almost as much as he'd surprised himself by suggesting it. Was he seriously considering staying?

*Too soon to make any promises.*

He was certain he didn't want to go back to Newark, but he was less sure he wanted to stay here. Still, he wouldn't mind running into the cute blond again. Maybe Sean was right about that, at least. Perhaps Ben needed to take things less seriously, have a fling, and get "Bar-Guy" out of his system. He wouldn't have to get permanently involved—with the blond, or with Cape May.

With a little bit of luck, he could have a good summer and still keep his options open.

FIVE

ERIK

"The PBS station wants to know if you're open to calling the show something less...suggestive," Corinne said.

Erik rolled his eyes. "*Treasure Trail* is the name of the blog. The name of the store is Trinkets. But remember—if I'm going to do the show, I want visibility that promotes the blog and the store, and if we can't use the real names, then I'm out."

Corinne hesitated. "I'll try. But you know how they are."

"They want all the salacious details about old scandals, but we can't say 'Treasure Trail'? Make up a story. Say it's about pirates. Or a mysterious gold mine. Bluebeard. Lost Dutchman. You spin stories for a living. I believe in you."

"Uh-huh," Corinne replied, unconvinced. "I'll see what they say." She ended the call, leaving Erik to go back to the task of matching up the items in the store against his inventory list.

Robert Pettis, the prior owner, had run the store for fifty years and said in the sale listing that he wanted to go live out his golden years somewhere warm. Erik had seen the listing pop up almost as soon as it came into the system, and when he'd read down through the description, he couldn't help feeling that it seemed like it was written just for him.

*Ideal buyer shares a love of antiques and an appreciation for art history. Strongly prefer a background in appraisal and authentication, preference given for hands-on experience. Must be good at researching provenance. A healthy respect for the unexplained is required. Serious inquiries only.*

Erik had called right away and hit it off with the old man from the start. He'd asked Simon for help doing due diligence, and Simon had pulled in his cousin, Cassidy, who ran a family-owned antique shop in Charleston, for advice. Simon's research and Cassidy's enthusiasm had won over Erik, and he'd closed the deal quickly. He doubted there'd been time for anyone else to even make a bid.

Now, Erik wondered if he'd been rash. The previous owner had a good eye, and so far Erik hadn't found any counterfeits or questionable items. But some of the pieces were definitely haunted. Erik could see spirits hovering near them as if waiting to be noticed. A few gave Erik the willies, and he had absolutely no desire to pick them up and have his touch magic trigger. The vibe they gave off told Erik that whatever he saw from the objects' perspective would be the stuff of nightmares.

Interestingly, all those questionable objects had been grouped together in what had probably once been a pantry. Had the former owner had a touch of the Sight, too? Or maybe he'd just sensed that something was "wrong" about the pieces and they needed special handling.

Erik had no idea what he was going to do about the problem antiques. *Maybe a blessing? I wonder if I can get a priest to come in, say a prayer, sprinkle some holy water? Might be worth a try.*

Before he worried more about the spooky pieces, Erik had plenty of other work to do. He hadn't met the prior owner in person; the man had already been on his way to Florida when Erik picked up the keys. All the paperwork was in a file on the front counter, and everything about the apartment was on the kitchen table. As usual, the devil was in the details. Erik really couldn't open for business until he could confirm the inventory he'd purchased, on top of what he'd brought with him. Susan helped when she could, but Erik didn't want to take advantage of her goodwill.

Which made for long days and longer nights, checking off one item at a time, out of hundreds.

It didn't help that his thoughts kept straying to the sexy guy from The Spike. He'd seen those green eyes in his dreams, imagined the brush of those pink lips, and come harder than he had in a long time imagining those inked arms around him, with that fine ass bucking between his legs. Erik had woken just as he climaxed, unsure whether he was more chagrined at having jizzed his sheets like a teenager, or at just how much that dark-haired stranger had turned him on.

After what happened with Josh, Erik had wondered if he'd ever be interested in anyone again.

Just his luck, the guy was taken.

Erik's phone buzzed in his pocket, reminding him he had an appointment. He looked around at all the work yet to be done and had a moment's regret about taking time out. Then again, a walk in the sunshine would clear his head, he told himself. Maybe he could be twice as productive once he got back.

The sunny spring day lifted Erik's mood as soon as he locked the shop door behind him. He'd been surprised to get an email through the store's old account from Jaxon Davies, chairman of the Cape May Center for the Arts, asking Robert—the former owner—to come take a look at an item brought in for a new exhibit. Jaxon had been surprised when Erik answered, but seemed happy to get a professional opinion, regardless of whose.

The Center for the Arts was a new brick building at the edge of Cape May's vibrant shopping district. The designer had done a good job making the modern structure fit its surroundings, and Erik's curiosity to see inside caught him by surprise.

"I'm looking for Jaxon Davies," Erik told the man at the information desk. "Erik Mitchell. He's expecting me."

While the man placed the call, Erik glanced around. One wall of the lobby was all glass, while an interior brick wall curved around toward the mood lighting of the exhibit areas. Erik had been behind the scenes in every major art museum on three continents, working with some of the best curators and preservationists in the business.

But the tingle of anticipation he felt went back to his memories of the first field trip to the Columbia Museum of Art that sparked his interest in the field. Every museum was like an adventure, a treasure to be discovered. Erik felt grateful that he hadn't lost that feeling.

"Erik Mitchell. I have to say, I never expected that you of all people would practically be a next-door neighbor!"

Erik didn't recognize the tall, slender man striding toward him, but his brain—for just a moment—conjured up an image of David Bowie in his Thin White Duke period. The man was handsome—or maybe beautiful—with high cheekbones, piercing eyes, and a sense of presence Erik associated with the celebrities he occasionally crossed paths with in New York or London. From his Armani jacket to his Prada shoes, Jaxon Davies looked ready to walk the red carpet at Cannes or a gala at the Met.

"I'm sorry—have we met?" Erik hated to admit it, but his work had left him siloed from most things outside his area of focus.

Fortunately, Jaxon accepted his admission with a genuine laugh. "Not to my knowledge, though we have run in some of the same circles. Plenty of time to rehash old times later. Thank you for coming on short notice. Let's do this properly." He extended his hand. "I'm Jaxon Davies. Pleased to meet you."

"Erik Mitchell," Erik replied, still surprised at the star wattage his host projected. The man's name triggered a memory deep in the back of Erik's brain, but it eluded him for the moment. "I take it you didn't know Robert had sold the store."

Jaxon shook his head. "No idea. Then again, as dear as that man was to all of us, he was also very private about his personal plans."

"I don't think the store was on the market long," Erik confessed. "I seem to have been in the right place at the right time and scooped it up."

Jaxon gave him a look that made Erik suspect the man guessed there was more to the story, but he didn't press for details.

Erik fell into step beside Jaxon as they headed into the exhibit area. "Robert was an important part of the arts community here in town," he said with a tone that made his affection for the old man clear. "We host traveling exhibits relevant to the area and put on installations and retrospectives of our own. Robert served as a consultant when we needed to validate the provenance of a piece on display or get an appraisal for insurance purposes. I wished I would have known he was moving. I would have thrown him a going-away party."

Erik nodded, making a mental note to see if Robert's records showed whether he'd been paid for those consultations or if they had been done in the spirit of goodwill and volunteerism. He was beginning to get the feeling that the former owner's shoes would be big ones to fill if Robert and Trinkets had been fixtures in the community.

"How can I help?" Erik cast a practiced eye toward the displays they passed as Jaxon led him deeper into the exhibits. Everything was top notch, as professionally presented and curated as he'd expect at a much larger institution.

"We aren't going to be able to give you the kind of excitement you might be used to," Jaxon went on. "No purloined Picassos or rustled antiquities."

Erik's heart sped up. He might not be able to place Jaxon, but clearly the other man knew exactly who Erik was. Not that Erik meant to make a secret of his past; it certainly wouldn't be under wraps if the PBS show actually went through. He hadn't moved to Cape May to hide, not exactly. But knowing he'd been made left Erik feeling oddly vulnerable.

Jaxon must have guessed his thoughts. "I go back a long way with Jacinda Hamilton at the Met, and Lawrence Taylor at the Tate Modern, and there was always an incestuous amount of interplay between the Broadway crowd and the MOMA."

Erik's forgotten memories stuttered to life. Jaxon Davies had been the toast of Broadway in the mid-nineties, starring in a number of celebrated and socially relevant plays that came in the wake of the success of works like *Angels in America* and *Rent*. He'd spent a good twenty years in the spotlight, gracing magazine covers and being chased by paparazzi, then suddenly stopped performing and stepped into the role of doyen and patron without missing a beat.

And if the names Jaxon had just dropped were any indication, he and Erik had a lot of the same high-profile people on speed dial.

"I'm sorry I didn't make the connection right away," Erik said, feeling a blush rise. "I've been focused on inventory."

Jaxon's laugh sounded natural and with no hint of wounded ego. "No harm done," he assured Erik. "I'm glad you're Robert's successor. I trusted his judgment, and I can't say that I would have felt confident about just anyone stepping into his shoes. But you…are definitely a worthy successor."

In another setting, Erik might have wondered if Jaxon was flirting. But the diamond band on the man's left hand suggested otherwise, and Erik seemed to remember hearing about a wedding that managed to elude the press. "Thank you. What can I do for you?"

Jaxon's smile was warm and genuine. "We're putting together our big summer installation, which always celebrates part of the area's history. This year, the theme is "By the Sea: Where New York Went to Play," and it's looking at the Jersey coast's emergence as the place New Yorkers—of all classes—came to spend the summer."

They turned a corner and stepped around a pipe-and-drape barrier and a sign that promised an exciting new attraction. Half-assembled displays and partially-emptied crates littered the large area, but even so, Erik could see the bones of the exhibit and knew it would be a blockbuster.

"We couldn't do a retrospective without including the Commodore Wilson Hotel," Jaxon added, in full impresario mode. "It was the jewel in the crown in its day—although perhaps more like the Hope Diamond, given its bad luck."

"So I've heard."

"We have some wonderful photographs from its heyday, as well as some exceptional decorative items from the hotel that came into collectors' hands after everything was auctioned off. And there's one in particular I'd appreciate your opinion on."

Erik followed Jaxon into a side room which held a variety of small items that would no doubt go into display cases. "What do you make of that clock?" Jaxon asked, pointing to a dark rectangular box in the middle of the table.

Erik stepped closer and bent over to examine the piece without touching it. He didn't have cotton gloves to keep oil from his fingers from marring the finish, and he also didn't know what kind of images the clock might trigger. He'd already embarrassed himself once by not recognizing Jaxon; he didn't want to make a fool out of himself again. "I'd need to examine it more closely to be sure, but I'd say it's an Ingraham. Nice faux marbling on the pillars on either side of the clock face, gold leaf around the face is in good condition, and it's got both lions' heads," he added, noting the decorations that graced both sides of the clock.

"Authentic?"

Erik frowned. "An authentic Ingraham? Yes. But I think you're looking for more than that."

Jaxon nodded and picked up a photograph from the table, which he handed to Erik. The black and white picture probably dated to the 1940s, given the clothing styles. A smug man in a tailored suit stood next to a taller, heavy-set man with a cigar chomped between his teeth. They were in front of a fireplace, and two identical clocks graced each end of the mantle.

"Could it be one of those clocks?" Jaxon asked.

Erik drew in a breath. "The age on it looks right. You say the clock was sold to a collector?"

"He bought it when the hotel's assets were liquidated. But it's the other clock that's famous."

Erik glanced around but saw no matching piece. "I don't have it," Jaxon said. "It's been missing for almost seventy years. It vanished the same night that Vincente Cafaro was murdered."

"Who?"

Jaxon raised an eyebrow. "The Commodore Wilson financially ruined its first owner, who was shot in the lobby by his wife's lover back in 1918. The Mob took it over, and all through Prohibition, the Commodore was the best-known secret speakeasy and a big player in the rum-running business. Several high-profile mobsters died there over the years. Vincente Cafaro bought the place at a fire-sale price in the 1950s and owned it until he died in a car bombing."

He paused dramatically. "A car bombing that was never solved."

Erik frowned. "Great story, but what does it have to do with the clock?"

Jaxon tapped the photo. "The pudgy guy in the photo is Cafaro. This was taken the night he died. Both clocks are there. But within a week of his death, one of the clocks went missing, reported stolen, never recovered."

"You think it's somehow linked to the murder?"

"Maybe. It's certainly suspicious. Might be just coincidence, but who knows?" Jaxon smiled. "But what I do know is that scandal sells. So if I can say that we've got one of the two 'Cafaro murder clocks' on display, it'll sell tickets."

"And the town fathers are all right with airing the dirty linen?"

"This is New Jersey. We have cheap linen and expensive linen, but it's all dirty," he replied with a sly grin.

Erik couldn't deny being intrigued. He also figured that Jaxon Davies was a good ally to have, and he could do a little bridge-building by agreeing to check into the clock.

"All right," he said. "How about if I come back tomorrow and I'll bring some of my appraisal equipment. That way, the clock remains in museum custody, but I can also look it over the right way."

"Wonderful!" Jaxon said, with a clap of his hands. "I'm thrilled to have you onboard." He dropped his voice conspiratorially. "I've followed your career for years. This wouldn't be your first brush with the Mob and artifacts."

"They certainly seem to have fingers in everything," Erik said noncommittally. *The less said about the Russians, the better. Although the Sicilian and Corsican Mob were a terror, back in the day.* "And I'd like to take a picture of that photo if you don't mind."

"Snap away."

Erik used his phone to get a couple of pictures, figuring they might help him research the clock's provenance. So many pieces had an interesting oral history attached to them, which couldn't be substantiated. He found himself hoping that this would work out differently. He took a few pictures of the clock, too.

"When you're all moved in and ready to do a grand reopening for Trinkets…and that new *Treasure Trail* blog I've heard you're doing… we'll have to make sure to hold the proper coming-out party!" The amused glint in Jaxon's eyes told Erik the double entendre was not accidental.

"That would be great," Erik replied. He could certainly do worse than having a mover-and-shaker like Jaxon rooting for him. "What do you want to do about tomorrow?"

Jaxon inclined his head, inviting Erik to walk with him back toward the foyer. "Brian at the desk handles all my appointments. Work out a time with him. Whenever is best for you—you're the one doing me a favor. I'm in your debt."

Erik understood the conversation for what it was, navigating a complex social web of mutual obligation. "Happy to help," he replied. Jaxon shook his hand and left him at the front desk, and Erik worked out a time to come back the next day.

On the walk back to the shop, Erik couldn't help thinking about the clock, and Jaxon's tantalizing information. If the TV show came through, the Cafaro clock mystery could be an intriguing possible episode.

He roused from his thoughts, startled, when he realized a man was waiting in front of Trinkets with a large box in his arms.

"Are you the owner?" the man asked. He looked to be in his late twenties, with a mop of curly brown hair and a husky build.

"I'm the *new* owner," Erik said. "Can I help you?"

"Can we go inside please? This box is heavy."

Erik unlocked the door and led the way. The man plunked the box down on the counter.

"I'm Justin Kramer. My grandfather just died, and I'm the lucky guy who gets to clean out his attic." He sighed. "I'm pretty sure he bought this box of stuff when the old Commodore Wilson Hotel had its bankruptcy sale. He worked there as a bellboy when he was a teenager, and that's where he met my grandmother. Anyhow, I don't think anyone else even looked in the box since the day he carted it home and stuck it in the rafters—until now. I took a quick glance—there's nothing that interests me, but it's all old. I was hoping you'd want to buy it."

Justin looked exhausted, and Erik wondered how much of cleaning out the old man's house had fallen to him. Before his conversation with Jaxon and the clock incident, Erik might not have been inclined to buy the memorabilia. It probably had little value aside from nostalgia. Now, he couldn't help indulging his inner Hardy Boys inclination to do a little harmless sleuthing.

"So you can't tell me anything more about what's in there?"

Justin shook his head. "I had to move half a dumpster's worth of old magazines just to get to the box. The newest magazine in the pile was from 1996, so I guarantee you no one has been close to that box since then."

"What would you consider a fair price?"

"I'd be fine with a hundred bucks," Justin replied. "I need to pay the dumpster bill."

"Mind if I take a look?" Erik asked. Justin shrugged. Erik picked up a pencil and opened the box, using the pencil to move items around so he didn't run the risk of getting a touch-magic surprise. "I hate spiders," Erik said when he saw Justin looking at him. The mystery box intrigued him, and he closed the flaps, then pulled out the shop's checkbook.

"Here you go," he said, upping the amount to one-fifty because Justin's ask was too low to be fair, and Erik figured he'd still gotten a bargain or at least a few evenings' entertainment. *Who knows? I might even find something Jaxon would want for his exhibit.*

He carried the box into the back and set it on the desk in the store's office. A ringing noise startled Erik, and it took him a moment to realize the sound came from a landline telephone near the register in the front of the shop. He sprinted for the call, hoping he could grab the receiver before the caller hung up.

"Hello? Uh…Trinkets and *Treasure Trail.*" Shit. He still wasn't used to owning the store, and the blog was barely more than a few hasty articles. Erik knew he had a long way to go.

"Robert?" The woman's voice was unfamiliar.

"I'm sorry—Robert sold the store and moved south. I'm Erik Mitchell, the new owner."

"Oh, my. I hadn't realized. That must have been sudden."

"I got the feeling it all came together quickly," Erik replied. "Is there something I can help you with?"

She chuckled, getting past the initial surprise. "I hope so. I'm Meg Nolan, of Nolan Resort Real Estate. Robert was my go-to guy for more than twenty years, any time I needed just the right antique or curio for one of our properties, or help with a hard-to-fix piece. Which is why I'm calling."

Erik's thoughts spun, trying to remember if the owner had said anything about long-time clients. Was the shop on retainer? Did they have a contract? He was going to have to dig deeper into that pile of papers Robert had left behind. "Are you looking for something specific?"

"Actually, we found an antique that had been forgotten about, and I'd like you to look it over, see if it's valuable, and see if there's a reason someone might have wanted to hide it."

Erik's training from his old job put him on alert. "Is there any chance it might have been stolen?" There was no good way to ask that question, but best to get it over with up front.

"If so, it was a long, long time ago. Doesn't look like it's been touched in ages. No way to tell, because the house was in the same family for a hundred years, and the owners died shortly after they sold it to us. So there's no one left to ask."

Maybe not, Erik thought, but there were possibly other resources he could tap into, assuming the piece was actually worth the effort. Curiosity zinged through him, and even though he had come here intending to leave his old life behind, it couldn't hurt to poke around a bit. *After all, it's Cape May. I doubt I'm going to stumble onto an international art theft ring.*

"If you'd like to bring it over, I'm happy to check it out," Erik replied. "Um, this is awkward, but I haven't gotten through all of Robert's notes. Am I on retainer?"

Meg laughed. "No, although for as much business as I did with Robert, he probably should have been. I'm actually on an extended vacation, but my nephew who's taking over the business will bring it by. I had expected to just give Robert a heads-up. I do hope you can help us."

"Happy to give it my best shot," Erik said.

"Good. I'll let him know. I hope you two get along as well as Robert and I always did. Thank you—and welcome to Cape May!"

SIX

# BEN

Ben told himself that he didn't have time to take the clock to an antique shop. He thought about sending Sean, but his cousin seemed like an unlikely messenger. There were so many details Ben still needed to handle before Sean went back to Wildwood and left him on his own. And while his cousin would only be a phone call away, Ben wanted to show he could handle the job. He didn't want to let Aunt Meg down.

Even if it was only for the summer.

He paused at the door. Trinkets had been a fixture in Cape May for decades. It sat on a tree-shaded street in an old Victorian house, not in the relatively new shopping district. Ben had a half-forgotten memory of riding bikes with Sean during one of his summers here and catching a glimpse of an old man opening up the store. But if the owner only just retired, then either he was immortal, or Ben's teenage self had badly misjudged his age.

Ben glanced at the clock in the box he held. He had no idea how to explain how he found it since the truth sounded ridiculous. Only the knowledge that Aunt Meg had already called the new owner and told him to expect Ben kept him from turning around and going back.

*What the hell? Won't be the first time I looked like a fool. Probably not the last time, either.*

Ben hesitated at the door. Should he knock? Ring the bell? Then he remembered that the house was really a shop, and he pushed the door open and walked in. His cop instincts worried when no one was in sight. Were people really trusting enough to walk away from the register and leave the door unlocked?

"Hello? Anyone here?"

"Sorry, I just stepped away—"

*Oh, shit.* The harried blond man who came around the corner from the back room stopped in his tracks, with a deer in the headlights expression that probably mirrored Ben's.

Ben suddenly found himself tongue-tied, like he was fifteen again and trying to muster the nerve to talk to his first crush. "Oh. Hi. I'm Ben Nolan. We met—"

"Yeah," the blond cut him off. "I remember. I'm Erik Mitchell, the new owner."

The comments Erik had made at The Spike that night fell into place. "So—you took over for the old man?" Ben didn't mean the comment to come out quite the way it did. Erik's expression of disapproval was there and gone, but watching people closely had kept Ben alive for years as a cop, and old habits died hard.

"Robert. Never met him, actually," Erik said, his tone all business. "Did everything long-distance. Still getting things sorted out."

Jesus, Erik was even more attractive here in his element than he'd been at the bar. He wore a faded T-shirt and a ripped pair of jeans more suited to cleaning out the storage room than greeting customers, but then again, that's probably what Ben had interrupted. Erik's blond hair was mussed, he had a day's reddish scruff, and whatever he'd been doing must have been physical enough to raise a sweat, because a slight sheen glistened on his forehead. He was exactly the height Ben had guessed at the bar, and while Erik had a slighter build, the damp T-shirt and short sleeves revealed defined pecs and strong arms.

*Say something.* Ben realized he was staring. More to the point, Erik was staring back. "Um…I understand. I'm new here myself." He wanted to kick himself immediately, realizing he'd already said that at the bar. "I mean—"

"Your aunt said she worked with Robert quite a bit. I got the impression you're taking over for her?"

"Maybe. I mean, I'm here for at least the summer. We'll see how it goes."

Another fleeting expression crossed Erik's face, and Ben had the feeling he'd once again said the wrong thing.

"What can I do for you?" Erik's tone sounded a little stilted. Almost…hurt. That didn't make any sense. Erik had been at The Spike waiting for a hookup. He had no reason to care if Ben stuck around town. Did he?

Ben realized that Erik was watching him, and the gaze made Ben feel exposed. Or rather, made him wish he was exposed, because the intensity of that stare made his cock twitch and gave him all kinds of ideas that were definitely not suitable for work.

"Oh yeah. The clock." *Smooth*, Ben's inner voice chided.

"What clock?" Erik's whole manner changed. His gaze was suddenly wary, and his body tensed.

Ben set the box on the counter. "I was doing a walk-through of one of our properties and had an accident—broke through the top of an old window seat that had been nailed shut years ago. And found…this."

Ben lifted the clock out of the box. Erik caught his breath. When Ben looked up, Erik seemed a little spooked.

"You found this in a window seat?" Erik looked suspicious and intrigued.

"Aunt Meg just bought the house recently. Before that it had been owned by the same family, although it was used as a boarding house long ago."

Ben had the feeling he'd become invisible, and that Erik hadn't heard a word he said. The blond man took the clock out of Ben's hands, then seemed to repress a shudder. For just an instant, Ben thought he saw fear in the man's blue eyes.

"Was there anything else with the clock?" Erik asked, turning it one way and another and peering closely at the workmanship.

"No," Ben replied. He had an unreasonable stab of jealousy at the intensity in Erik's gaze as he stared at the clock. Especially since he seemed to have been almost forgotten.

On the other hand, he was at the perfect vantage point to appreciate how the slim fit of the man's jeans clung to slender, muscular thighs and a tight, rounded ass. *Did he top or bottom? Would he switch it up?* Too late, Ben realized his cock had been paying full attention, and he needed to shift to relieve the pressure.

"No," Ben repeated, fighting to keep his mind on the topic instead of on Erik's perfect ass. "There was a lot of dust. I can't imagine why someone would hide a clock like that. Is it valuable?"

Erik looked up. "Actually, it's a fake. Old enough to be considered an antique, but not an original Ingraham. But it might have been part of something bigger. Maybe insurance fraud. Maybe…murder."

"Murder?" Ben cursed himself. He might not be as smooth as Sean, but he usually wasn't completely inarticulate.

"Do you know anything about the Commodore Wilson Hotel?" Erik's blue eyes were focused on Ben now, taking his measure. Ben made himself meet that gaze and felt the tension of their showdown. Erik looked away first, but somehow Ben felt like he'd lost instead of won.

"The big old place they tore down like twenty years ago? Do you think the clock came from there?" Ben had to remind himself that he wasn't a cop anymore. Fraud and murder weren't his problem—especially if they happened before he was born.

On the other hand, he was still a licensed investigator. And he couldn't resist the pull of a good mystery.

"Yeah. I was just over at the Arts Center. They're doing a retrospective, and I saw the clock that should have been the twin of this one." Erik dug out his phone and pulled up a photo. He handed it to Ben, who saw two identical clocks on a mantle, with a guy who looked like an extra out of *The Godfather* standing in front.

"They have another clock just like this one?"

Erik shook his head. "They have an authentic Ingraham. This is a fake. The gold leaf isn't as thick, the numbering on the face of the clock is sloppy, the lion heads on the side are all wrong, and the box itself isn't the same kind of wood."

"Go back to what you said about fraud and murder."

Erik shrugged. "Just a hunch on the fraud. The second clock went missing. It's not uncommon for collectors who get strapped for cash to sell a valuable item, try to report it stolen, and then double-dip with the insurance payout."

Ben tried and failed to keep from going into cop mode. "And you know this, how?"

Erik must have picked up on the shift in tone, giving Ben a weird glance in return. "Because my job, for fifteen years, was dealing with fraud, theft, and forgeries. There's more of that stuff than you'd think."

Ben snorted in reply but didn't say anything. *Actually, you'd be surprised at what I think.*

"If the switcheroo happened, it was before we were born. I don't imagine there's anyone around to arrest. Where does murder come in?"

"The guy in the photo I showed you. Cafaro. He bought the Commodore Wilson when it went through one of its many bankruptcies. Then a car bomb killed him. Probably the Mob. It was the fifties."

"How is the clock involved? It's just background for the picture."

A strange look crossed Erik's face as if he had a brief, silent debate with himself. He froze, staring over Ben's shoulder, then roused himself from his daydream. Ben couldn't help glancing in that direction but saw nothing. *He's holding back,* Ben thought.

"Call it a hunch," Erik replied. "An educated guess." His eyes and his tone confirmed Ben's suspicion that Erik wasn't saying everything he knew.

"So what happens now?" Ben asked, because despite the conflicting signals Erik threw off, Ben found himself still very attracted to the man. And from the way Erik stood just a little too close, held his gaze a few seconds longer than necessary, and let his fingers lightly brush against Ben's hand, Ben was willing to bet that the blond felt that pull, too.

"Probably nothing official," Erik admitted. "As you say, too much time has passed, and most of the people involved would be dead by now. But I've got some resources from my old job I can use to see if a claim was ever filed and if so, what came of it. Maybe there'll be a connection to Cafaro to back up my hunch," he added as if he could read Ben's skepticism.

This could be the excuse to get to know Erik better, Ben thought. He rubbed the back of his neck, then dove in. "I might be able to help." At Erik's raised eyebrow, Ben found himself defensive. "I used to be a cop. Still have my private investigator's license. So if there's anything out there on Cafaro—cold case file, that sort of thing, I might be able to get to it."

"Why?"

Ben flashed what he hoped was a disarming smile. "Sounds exciting. The rental business is a little slower pace than what I'm used to."

If Erik was curious about what led Ben to make the change, he didn't press. "Sure. Can't hurt to play a little Jessica Fletcher."

"Speak for yourself. I'm much more the Magnum type."

That won Ben a genuine smile, which softened Erik's features and seemed to make him relax.

"So, did your friend show up the other night at The Spike?" Ben thought he knew the answer, but if Erik's date actually had turned into something, it would be good to know that now.

Erik's smile faded. "Ah...yes. But not really a friend—more of an unpleasant acquaintance." He shrugged like it didn't matter. "But it looked like you and your boyfriend were having a good time."

Ben's eyes widened. *Boyfriend?* Then he remembered walking back to Sean and his Wildwood friends, and how Sean had slung an arm around his shoulders. Ben hadn't thought anything of the gesture—it was just the way Sean was, especially after a few beers.

"Um, *not* my boyfriend," Ben managed. "Sean's my cousin. Came down from Wildwood to help me move. Give him some alcohol, and he's everyone's best friend. Hell, you're just lucky he didn't start singing along with the band."

The look in Erik's eyes told Ben the other man had registered that intel loud and clear. Ben decided to plunge ahead before he could second guess himself. "So, you have plans for dinner? My aunt says there's a good Greek place a few blocks down. Diner style—good food, great price. We could talk about the case. I mean, the clock."

Erik hesitated, and Ben found he was holding his breath. He didn't know why Erik's reaction mattered so much to him—he barely knew the man—but there was definitely a spark between them, and Ben wanted to see where it would take them. At least until the summer ended.

"Sure," Erik said, with a friendly smile that didn't completely reach his eyes. "Sounds great. We're not really open to the public yet, so I can go whenever."

"How about if I pick you up here at seven?" Ben asked.

Erik nodded. "I'll see you then. And maybe I'll have more info about the clock by that time."

"Sounds like a plan."

SEVEN

## ERIK

E rik wasn't sure what surprised him more—having the missing clock show up just hours after his meeting with Jaxon or having the hot guy from the bar be the one to bring it to him.

Just his luck to get both a flash of insight from the clock and a sighting of its dead owner right in front of the man who'd been starring in his dreams for the past few nights and in his shower-time fantasies by day. He could still kick himself for picking the clock up without gloves. Something he would never have done if he wasn't so distracted by the guy.

Still, his weirdness hadn't stopped Ben from asking him out to dinner. Was it a date? Erik felt certain Ben sensed the attraction between them. But he'd said something about only being in town for the summer. So maybe he was just looking for a fling.

Still, Erik could do worse to get back into the dating game. If anything happened between the two of them, the relationship came with an expiration date. No pressure, no expectations. That should have made Erik feel relieved, but oddly, it stung. *Lighten up*, he warned himself. *Sometimes dinner is just a meal. He might really be more interested in the clock.*

Though from the surreptitious glances Ben had been sneaking, Erik figured the other man was interested in more than the antique. After all, Ben had brought up the situation at the bar, which had to have been a way to see if Erik was available. And Erik had to admit he was relieved to find out Ben didn't have a boyfriend. Still, he refused to read too much into their dinner tonight. But his imagination suggested plenty of ways they could finish off the night other than dessert.

Erik locked the front door and made sure the sign read *"Closed."* Then he grabbed a pair of cotton gloves to avoid handling the clock here in the main shop and carried it gingerly into the back room. The box of memorabilia took up his whole desk, so Erik took the clock to the small kitchenette.

The little room held a mini fridge, hot plate, coffee maker, and sink, as well as having room for a small table and a couple of chairs. Erik set the clock down and went to retrieve a set of jewelers' tools from behind the counter.

Before he tried taking the clock apart, he wanted to get another read on it with his Second Sight, in private. He tugged the gloves off, steeled himself, and laid both hands palm-down on the rectangular box.

He saw an ornate foyer, with marble columns, a parquet floor, and domed skylights. The images came from the clock's point of view, not any person or owner, so Erik couldn't pick up emotions or conversation. He had the impression it was nighttime since the huge room was empty. Hands lifted the clock, and then everything went dark.

Erik gasped for breath as if he were coming up for air after a deep dive. The temperature in the break room had plummeted, and Erik shivered. The antique in his hands was no longer a window into a long-ago time and place. But standing between the table and the small counter was the ghost of the man from the photo, Vincente Cafaro.

Cafaro resembled his photograph. Average height, balding, and the kind of paunch that came with too much fine living. The deadness in his deep-set eyes had been there before a bomb blew him sky high, and Erik felt sure Cafaro had been a man with no compunctions about breaking the law or getting rid of anyone in his way. Except that, someone had gotten rid of him, first.

Erik figured out years ago that he saw ghosts in more detail than many of the others who were sensitive to spirits. He couldn't summon them or dispel them—at least, he'd never tried—and he couldn't hear them speak, although Erik thought the ghosts might be able to hear him talk to them. He knew he didn't have the same level of talent that his friend Simon did.

Some of the spirits were just repeaters, a faded memory strong enough to make itself seen, but lacking awareness. But others, like the dead mobster standing in front of him, seemed to cross the Veil with their sense of self intact. And right now, Vincente Cafaro fixed Erik with a gaze that chilled him to his core. He didn't have to hear the ghost to get the message. Cafaro wanted Erik to find his killer—or else.

The fact that sixty years had passed probably wouldn't work for an excuse.

"I'll give it my best shot," Erik said. "But you've been dead for a long time. The trail is cold." Cafaro's expression spoke eloquently, letting him know that failure wasn't acceptable. Then the image shifted, from showing Cafaro as he appeared in the photo to the charred and shattered corpse he'd become. The ghost blurred, then winked out, leaving Erik alone with the clock.

"That was fun," Erik muttered under his breath. He eyed the clock warily. It probably wouldn't run anymore, but he couldn't check since the key apparently hadn't been hidden with it. That would make sense if someone had stolen it, since the key was probably entrusted to a hotel worker who minded all the clocks.

Up close, the forgery wasn't hard to spot. In good light and under a magnifying glass, the problems were glaring. Erik frowned, thinking. Maybe the clock had never been meant to pass muster under expert scrutiny. Maybe it just needed to be seen in the background long enough after the original was sold to increase the chances of getting away with the switch.

The clock would show up in press and tourist photographs, since the Commodore Wilson played host to celebrities from around the world. Those photos established that both clocks were in their rightful place and established an alibi as good as a timestamp.

Erik lifted the clock again and thought the weight felt odd. He laid it on its face and carefully opened up the back with a tiny screwdriver from the kit. Erik wasn't sure what he was expecting, but it wasn't two faded, folded ledger pages and a yellowed photograph of Cafaro standing over a man's dead body, holding a gun.

He sat back and stared at the clock, wondering what Ben would make of this new development. Somehow, it hadn't surprised him that Ben had been a cop—or an investigator. He had a hardness to him that suggested law enforcement, or at least ex-military, even though Ben was trying to start over.

Which meant that it probably hadn't escaped Ben's notice when Erik had zoned out as he touched the clock and got a flash of insight, or there at the end, when he had been staring at Cafaro's ghost over Ben's shoulder. Erik wondered how Ben would take it if he told him the truth, and decided it wouldn't go over well. Cops stuck to what they could see and prove.

Since Cape May had more than its share of documented hauntings, claiming to have seen Cafaro's ghost wouldn't be too strange. Ben might not believe, but perhaps he wouldn't think Erik was lying or crazy—or making a dramatic bid for attention. The mental images from the past, though, that would be asking too much.

Erik had seen TV shows featuring psychics and mediums. His buddy Simon was both and made his living from what Simon called his Gifts. Simon seemed comfortable in his own skin, so if he'd ever had a problem with his abilities, he'd made peace with it, owned it just like he was open about being gay. Erik had come out as gay a long time ago. But he was still in the back of a haunted closet when it came to his visions. He'd always thought of his abilities as a burden. Ben was likely to see them as a liability.

Maybe it wasn't a bad thing that Ben might not stay in Cape May. Despite their attraction, even if Ben was really interested, he wouldn't stick around. Not when he found out what a freak Erik was, and not even the sexy kind.

EIGHT

BEN

Ben rushed upstairs as soon as he finished going over the books with Sean, glad to close the rental office for the night. He hadn't told his cousin about meeting Erik for dinner, but Sean guessed something was going on and had surprised Ben by not ribbing him about it.

In fact, in his own affectionately obnoxious way, Sean had urged Ben to have a good time, then asked if he needed to pick up any "supplies" before the big night out.

Ben let his imagination supply the images that would require those "supplies." Erik's lean chest against his own, his strong, slender body naked and his cock hard and leaking. Would that happy trail of his be blond or ginger? Ben wondered. Was he cut or uncut? Ben's mind supplied the details, and his cock stiffened eagerly.

*It's just dinner. Doesn't mean anything's going to happen.*

Maybe not, but that didn't keep Ben from wishing. He rubbed one out in the shower, but that only took the edge off. Nothing compared to the real thing.

Ben took more time to get ready than usual, even though he wasn't sure their dinner counted as a date. Or, more to the point, Ben wasn't sure Erik considered the night out to be a date. But with luck, maybe the evening would end that way.

He'd finally decided on a blue shirt over black jeans. Nice, but not too fussy. Despite the disastrous first attempt at The Spike, Ben knew he was seriously out of practice. He'd liked Erik after just one meeting. The run-in this afternoon just confirmed that attraction.

He still wondered what Erik was holding back. Then again, it was hardly like Ben had spilled his entire life story, either. By the time anyone was over thirty, there were likely to be ghosts and scars, topics that would take years of trust to discuss, and some that might stay buried forever. Absent a fresh corpse and a smoking gun, Ben resolved to give Erik that space and see what happened.

The walk to Trinkets wasn't far, and Ben arrived a few minutes early. He had checked out the store's website and found a little about Erik's background. The bio on the site listed Erik's Ph.D. in Art History and Preservation from USC and mentioned having worked with museums around the world, although the nature of those jobs was vague. Part of him felt guilty for having checked up on Erik, while his cop self wanted to dive deeper.

Once again, he had the feeling that Erik was hiding something. Ben pushed it from his mind. Tonight, he hoped to get to know Erik better. If that worked out, perhaps he'd eventually get the answers he needed to put that annoying inner voice to rest.

This time, the *"Closed"* sign hung in the window, so Ben knocked. He heard footsteps on the other side, and then Erik opened the door. His hair still looked damp from the shower, and he smelled of citrus and coffee. The pale green shirt played up the blue of Erik's eyes, and his distressed jeans showed off his lower body to good advantage.

"Hi," Erik said. Ben thought he looked pleased and a little awkward, which just added to the charm.

"Hi," Ben replied. "It's a nice night—are you all right with walking?"

"Sure." Erik locked up, then fell in stride beside Ben. The rhythm felt natural, happening without thought. Ben hoped that was a sign.

A sea breeze stirred the night air, cool enough to remind Ben that it wasn't summer yet. Only a few weeks until the season kicked into high gear, and already many of the shops and restaurants that shuttered for the colder months were opening up, cleaning away the remnants of the winter, getting ready for business.

"I spent summers here when I was a teenager. Helping out my aunt and uncle. Sean and I got up to shenanigans," Ben recalled fondly. "Nothing too bad. Just burning off some energy."

"Funny. I came here with my aunt and uncle, too. My sister was always training for one gymnastic meet or another, so my parents were usually too busy to vacation. We only came a couple of times, but something about the place stuck in my mind." Erik looked toward the dark horizon where they could hear the ocean waves.

"That's what brought you back?" Ben tried to be careful not to use his cop voice. He didn't want Erik to shut him out.

"I was ready for a change," Erik replied. "You know what they say about life in the fast lane. Makes you lose your mind," he added with a chuckle.

"So you just bought the shop and moved in?" Ben had thought his move from Newark was gutsy, but he had a known situation and supportive family. Showing up to a brand-new town, taking over an unfamiliar shop—that took brass balls in Ben's book.

"Pretty much. I just—when I saw the listing for the shop, it felt like it was supposed to be mine." Erik smiled self-consciously. "Probably sounds crazy, right?"

Ben shrugged. "Sometimes when it's right, you just know."

When they reached Peter's Place, Erik looked up at the sign, puzzled. "I thought you said this was Greek?"

"It is." Ben pointed to the lettering on the door, which proclaimed *"Damian Petrakis, Owner."* "It's good stuff. Better than anything I had in Newark."

"Then what are we waiting for? I'm hungry."

The restaurant didn't usually take reservations, but Ben had leveraged a favor and snagged them the table all the way in the back, where they could talk undisturbed. He waited while Erik examined the menu, which covered both sides of a large sheet.

"It's all good," Ben assured him.

A dark-haired young man came to take their order, and Ben felt certain he was the owner's grandson. "We want some stuffed grape leaves and spanakopita to share," Ben ordered. He glanced to Erik and raised an eyebrow.

"Souvlaki for me, please," Erik asked. "And water."

"Moussaka, please. And a Coke." The server nodded and headed off, only to return with their drinks, warm pita bread, and a bowl of olives while they waited for the rest of their food.

"Have you been here a lot?" Erik asked.

Ben shook his head. "A few times with my aunt, but she knows everyone. I know they don't serve alcohol, but it's also quiet enough we can actually talk."

"That's fine," Erik replied, starting to look more comfortable. "And the food smells amazing."

They chatted about the weather as they waited for the appetizers, and Ben felt his stomach rumble. Beneath the table, his longer legs brushed against Erik's, and when the other man didn't move away, neither did Ben.

"So, you were a cop?" Erik asked, in a tone that suggested he was doing his best to make the question sound off-handed.

"Twelve years. Took my exam a month after I turned eighteen, started out as a dispatcher, worked a lot of different beats, and ended up getting moved to undercover." Ben felt his smile dim. This wasn't something he enjoyed talking about, but if he and Erik were going to get more than a one-night stand off the ground, he knew he needed to open up, at least a little. To his surprise, that wasn't difficult with Erik. "Believe me—it's nothing like you see on TV."

"What made you quit?" Erik's gaze felt supportive, not judgmental.

"Two bullets. A bust went bad and—*wham*! Almost lights out." Ben tried to keep his tone conversational, but he didn't quite manage it.

"And you thought being a private investigator was safer?"

"Nothing's really safe in Newark. Have you been there? Being a PI meant I could set my own hours and stay out of department politics." The answer sounded good. Ben had rehearsed it well. He just left out the part about being betrayed by a dirty cop and having the "thin blue line" close ranks around the traitor instead of him.

"How about you?" Ben asked, eager to step out of the spotlight. "You said something about tracking art theft?"

Erik hesitated long enough that Ben thought the other man wouldn't answer. "I worked with law enforcement agencies in various countries to authenticate stolen and recovered items, relics with a shady provenance, forgeries. Saved a lot of art, returned some important pieces to their rightful owners, and pissed off a bunch of folks who didn't get what they wanted."

Ben saw the change come over Erik's green eyes, a haunted look he'd seen on the faces of plenty of career cops. Erik had obviously been playing at a much higher level than Ben had originally supposed. He didn't have to guess what kind of enemies might be made cutting power brokers out of deals for items they coveted.

"Sounds exciting. Why give it up to come here?"

Erik shifted and cut his gaze to the window, a classic tell that the subject made him uncomfortable. Ben resigned himself to the futility of completely turning off his cop brain.

"A sting went wrong. The people involved weren't happy about it. I got shot and got a concussion out of the deal. A couple of my team members didn't make it back."

"I'm sorry."

Erik shrugged, but it looked more like a flinch. "It's over. I had time to think in the hospital, and I figured I'd used up my luck, tapped out my guardian angel. And then I saw the listing for Trinkets, and it was like the daydream I'd always had was right there for the taking."

The similarities in their backgrounds didn't escape Ben's notice, despite their different professions. Shared experiences—especially traumatic ones—sometimes also meant similar old wounds to overcome. He tried not to look surprised when Erik disclosed that his work had taken him around the world.

*Even if the sex is fantastic—assuming we ever get to that point—a guy like him won't be interested in a damaged Newark ex-cop for long. But maybe I can keep him for the summer.*

They polished off the appetizers just in time for their entrées. Ben regaled Erik with some of the funnier moments from his police years, and Erik matched him tale for tale with stories of travel screw-ups and cultural snafus. Through it all, their knees remained touching beneath the table, and occasionally their fingers brushed as they reached for bread or dolmas. Ben did his best to flirt, and Erik flirted right back, reassuring Ben he hadn't read the signals wrong.

When the plates were cleared away, and they had ordered home-made baklava for dessert and strong Greek coffee, Erik pulled out his phone. "I had another look at that clock you brought in," he said, pitching his voice low so that the bustle of the restaurant and the canned music covered his words. "And it turned out to be loaded."

He slid the phone with its photos of the old picture and the ledger sheets across the table. "Whether or not the clock was stolen or part of an insurance scam, someone thought they had the goods on Cafaro."

Ben let out a low whistle. "Can I get a copy of the ledgers? I'd like to have a look at them."

Erik nodded. "Sure. The clock and what's in it belongs to you. I can give you the originals, when we're done with it. From a quick glance, I'd guess someone was keeping two sets of books, but we'd need to spend some time on them to be sure."

"The photo is pretty damning. It's long before Photoshop."

"So here's a question for you—who hid the clock, and why? And… why there?"

"I don't know, but I did put in a request at the recorder of deeds to double check the history of who owned the house. Maybe there's more to it than what we know," Ben replied.

Ben had been turning the same question about who and why over in his mind since he'd been thrown through the window seat. He wondered how Erik would react if he told him the full story.

"And…I guess if we're going to take this thing further," Erik said, leaving it unclear whether he meant the mystery or their mutual attraction, "I should probably tell you something else." He cleared his throat. "I see ghosts sometimes. Just see them—I don't hear them, can't make them do anything. And today, when you were in the shop, and then when I opened up the clock, I swear I saw Vincente Cafaro's ghost."

The rush of relief Ben felt at Erik's confession surprised him. "Welcome to Cape May, the haunted gem of the Jersey Shore," he replied with a wry grin. "Just about everyone here has seen a ghost or two, I wager. And so have I."

Erik's smile lit up his eyes, and Ben felt a warmth that started in his chest and then moved south, right to his groin. Damn, Erik was beautiful.

"I'm glad. I mean, that's good to know." Erik licked his lips, giving Ben all kinds of ideas. "I wasn't sure how you'd react."

Ben slid his hand across the table and wrapped his fingers around Erik's. "I like you. I want to get to know you better. And a little thing like seeing ghosts isn't going to change that."

"Good," Erik replied as the server brought their baklava. "I like you, too."

Ben had never considered baklava to be an aphrodisiac, but watching Erik move his lips over the flaky pastry layers and lick at the warm honey made Ben's cock uncomfortably hard. Erik met his gaze, winked, and licked the rest of the sticky fluid from his long fingers. Ben's quiet moan made Erik's smile broaden.

"I was wondering if you'd like to come up for a drink," Ben asked, feeling his heartbeat rise. "It's still early."

"I was hoping you'd ask."

They walked back a little more quickly than before, bumping shoulders and brushing fingers if not quite holding hands. Ben found his stomach tight with excitement and nerves. Under the streetlights, Erik looked even more beautiful, with a blush of color in his cheeks that excited Ben to think he'd put it there.

He nearly fumbled the key when they reached the door to his apartment. "Right this way," he said, stepping aside to let Erik enter. Just in case, he had spent some time tidying up, wanting to make a good impression. He decided not to look too closely at why Erik's opinion mattered quite as much as it did.

"Nice. More modern than I expected," Erik observed, taking in the living room.

"It's usually a rental unit, but Aunt Meg's letting me stay here for as long as I want." *Or until I decide to move here and get a place of my own.* "There's plenty of room, especially compared to what I was used to back in Newark."

He ushered Erik into the kitchen and opened a cabinet. "Not quite the selection they have at The Spike, but I've got wine, beer, and some whiskey, plus soda if you want to mix."

"Jack and Coke is good for me please," Erik said, and Ben mixed drinks for both of them.

He was surprised when Erik stepped up behind him, close against his back, resting hands on his hips. "I haven't been able to stop thinking about you, since we met," Erik murmured.

"Me, too," Ben confessed. He left the drinks on the counter and turned, finding himself face to face with Erik, confirming that their heights were perfect to fit their bodies together just right.

Ben lifted a hand to brush the backs of his fingers across Erik's cheek. Erik leaned into the gesture, maintaining eye contact, pupils dilated with arousal. Ben moved forward, Erik stretched up, and their lips met midway. Ben's arms slipped around Erik, while Erik placed one hand on Ben's lower back and the other on his ass.

The kiss started out light, tentative, but it deepened quickly when Erik opened to him, flicking his tongue across Ben's lips for good measure. By the time they came up for air, Ben's heart pounded and his erection ground against a very similar bulge in Erik's jeans.

"Is this okay?" Ben asked.

Erik smiled. "More than okay. What do you want?"

"You. Whatever you'll give me," Ben replied, surprising himself. "I'd like to see you again. So tonight can be as much or as little as you want. We don't have to rush."

"I'd like that," Erik said. "I'd like that very much."

Erik slid his palms up Ben's chest, while Ben let his fingers trace the muscles in Erik's back. Ben tugged Erik toward the couch, leaving their drinks behind on the counter. Then he backed Erik against the wall, reversing their positions.

Erik's rapid breaths made Ben wonder just how much his date enjoyed being pinned by his weight. He took hold of both of Erik's hands, lacing their fingers together and pressing them against the wall as he bent to capture Erik's mouth again. Erik tasted of honey and black coffee, and Ben felt a buzz from their kisses that had nothing to do with whiskey.

"Shirts," Erik panted. "Off. Please."

Ben let go of Erik's hands but did the honors of unbuttoning Erik's shirt, moving slowly and deliberately, keeping eye contact the whole time. When he had it open, he pushed the fabric off Erik's shoulders and took a moment to enjoy the view.

"So sexy," he breathed. A groomed smattering of blond hair grew darker as it tapered beneath the waistband of Erik's jeans. Ben leaned forward to lick one pink nipple, and Erik caught his breath. Ben didn't miss the way Erik trembled at his touch, and it was sexy as fuck.

He took his time, going back and forth between the nubs, licking, sucking, and teasing them with his teeth until Erik was grinding against Ben's thigh. Part of Ben wanted to lift Erik up, let the other man wrap his legs around Ben's waist, and fuck him against the wall. But more of him wanted to savor this first, because he could see from the fire in his partner's eyes that Erik intended to give as good as he got.

Erik reached out and helped Ben pull his shirt up and over his head.

"I'm kinda scratched up, from going through the window seat yesterday. Got a few bruises from it, too," Ben confessed.

"That's okay."

Ben caught his breath, because there was no hiding the bullet scars. He hadn't taken a real lover since Caleb left, since the bust. Just a few one-night stands, and he'd always made sure to keep his shirt on. But with Erik, he hadn't even hesitated.

Erik's gaze softened. He stretched out a hand toward Ben's chest, then stopped, with his palm hovering just above the round, pink marks. "May I?"

Ben just nodded, unable to find words. Erik's fingers ghosted over the scars gently, almost reverently. "I'm sorry," he whispered.

"Not your fault. Shit happens."

Erik leaned forward and pressed his lips first to one scar, and then the other. The touch wasn't sexual, although it felt to Ben like every inch of skin tingled. No tongue, just a brush of lips, and the heat of his breath, and Ben thought he might cream his jeans.

He had touched those scars hundreds of time in the shower, and he could have sworn the damaged flesh didn't feel anything. Ben had assumed the nerves were severed. He'd just been glad to be alive. Now, under Erik's lips, the scars became an erogenous zone.

Erik looked up at him, his blue eyes luminous. "I'm glad you're here."

Ben reached down and lifted Erik, and Erik wrapped his legs around Ben's waist. Ben kissed him again, like a starving man. He'd always thought verbs like "plundering" or "devouring" were cheesy to describe kisses, but maybe that was because he'd never had a kiss like this one. Now, they were the only words that came close to matching the intensity, the hunger.

He wasn't sure where to go. The bedroom seemed presumptuous. He wasn't sure he could get them to the couch—Erik was solid and heavier than he looked. Ben improvised, pivoting and setting Erik on the edge of the kitchen table.

In a heartbeat, everything changed.

Erik went rigid in his arms, face pale, eyes wide. He scrambled away from Ben like he'd been scalded, and for an instant, Ben saw utter panic in his face.

"No!" Erik's voice was a dry croak.

Ben stilled, hands raised. "I'm sorry. What—"

Erik huddled in the corner by the fridge, shaking, and now his head hung down. He looked so vulnerable, and all Ben wanted to do was take him in his arms and protect him, but he didn't dare move.

"Please, Erik. I'm so sorry. You don't have to tell me. I didn't know. I'd never hurt you."

Years of being a cop gave Ben far too many scenarios to choose from that might have prompted a reaction like that, all of them ugly, some worse than others. He was blindsided by the protectiveness that burned through him, something he'd never felt for a lover before. Someone hurt Erik, broke something in him, and in that moment, Ben wanted to take that son of a bitch apart, piece by piece.

"I...should go."

Ben's heart sank. "I wish you wouldn't. I promise I won't touch you again. Just please, stay. I don't think you should be alone."

He could almost see Erik pull himself together. The trembling stopped. Erik had wrapped his arms around himself tightly, and he only now seemed aware of it, letting them drop. Ben sensed that Erik relaxed by an act of will, shaking out his shoulders, slowing his breathing. Finally, he raised his head, and Ben saw so much pain and vulnerability in those tear-filled blue eyes that it broke his heart.

"I...overreacted."

"No apologies necessary," Ben said quietly. "But if you'd like a stiff belt for what ails you, the whiskey's already poured." He inclined his head toward the two glasses on the counter.

That got a bleary half-smile. Ben moved slowly, taking the glass with the Jack and Coke, then extending his arm to put it in reach. Erik took the glass and raised his chin, defying whatever memories had triggered him. To Ben's surprise, Erik knocked it back in one shot and held the glass out for more. Ben poured, straight whiskey this time.

He'd already decided that Erik shouldn't be alone tonight. Whether he agreed to sleep here, or Ben walked him home and sat up keeping vigil, or they stayed up all night talking, Ben had seen that kind of PTSD response in veteran cops, and he knew that once triggered, old ghosts took a while to re-bury.

"I'd like to sit down."

Ben nodded. "The couch is more comfortable. I'll keep my distance."

Erik's pained smile didn't reach his eyes. He moved stiffly, as if the motion hurt, squaring his shoulders and gathering his tattered dignity. Ben counted it as a win that Erik hadn't already fled. He stepped aside so Erik could go around him, into the living room, without touching, although Ben ached to comfort him.

Erik sat on the couch. Ben hesitated, trying to decide whether to sit facing him in a chair or next to him, with some distance between them. Erik patted the seat next to him. Ben tried not to read too much into the gesture, knowing that if Erik meant to talk, it would be easier not to have to make eye contact.

They sat in silence for a while. It didn't feel awkward; the only thing Ben cared about was helping Erik get through whatever it was that had triggered him.

"You didn't throw me out. That's…a good start."

Ben's head snapped up. "Why would I—"

"Nobody wants damaged goods." Erik's tone held a note of self-loathing that made Ben's throat tighten.

"I don't see you like that," Ben replied. "And…I've got my scars, too."

Erik seemed to come to a decision. He didn't look at Ben, kept his gaze focused across the room at the empty fireplace, and his voice was low when he started to speak.

"My last case was a Fabergé music box egg, owned by the Tsarina Alexandra, said to be cursed. It was the unicorn of the antiquities world—everyone had heard the story, but no one had seen it since the revolution. The Bolsheviks claimed to have destroyed it. But there were always whispers…"

Erik's tone stayed flat, objective. Ben recognized that defense from the voices he'd heard of countless witnesses, who needed to distance themselves from whatever horror they had seen, pack the pain away, so they could function.

"Interpol got word that the egg had surfaced in Antwerp. A private collector who seemed legit, but actually dealt in items with shady provenance. We knew the guy was dirty, but we couldn't get him dead to rights. Blood diamonds, arms deals, drugs, stolen cultural items—the people who trade in them have money and connections. This guy could have been the lynchpin to take down a whole network. All I needed to do was authenticate the musical egg."

Ben stayed still and quiet, not wanting to spook Erik further. When Erik had told him that he'd been involved stopping fraud and forgeries, Ben had pictured him telling people that their grandmother's "priceless" figurines were cheap fakes. Apparently, the truth was closer to James Bond than *Antiques Roadshow*.

"The buyer was a honcho with the Russian Mob. The collector was nervous. There'd been another offer, from one of the oligarchs, for even more money. Both of the Russians showed up with their guards. They were going to fight over the egg. We didn't expect that. I didn't get out before the shit went down, and our backup had to wait for more firepower."

When Ben first met Erik, he'd been taken by the man's good looks —his high cheekbones, full lips, and startlingly blue eyes. But as he watched Erik tell his story, pain written in every line of his features, Ben saw something else. A force of character and will that made the other man even more attractive.

"What happened?' Ben whispered when he feared Erik wouldn't continue.

"They talk about the 'fog of war.' I guess it was like that. Everyone shooting, deafening noise, and air that smelled like gunpowder. The collector got caught in the crossfire, riddled with bullets. Someone picked me up and threw me out of the way to get to the guy behind me. I slammed my head pretty hard. A bullet grazed my shoulder."

"Jesus."

"Pretty sure he wasn't there that night," Erik replied. "The mobster won the fight, and he was going to leave with the egg. He told his boys to take care of anyone who was left. I thought I was going to die."

Ben knew that since Erik was sitting right next to him, he'd made it out somehow. That didn't ease the tension in his chest or the grip he had on the couch cushion.

"All of a sudden, the lights went out. Except for one security bulb. And then the killing started again. Something found us in that warehouse. Something that wasn't human. Couldn't have been. It moved too fast, just a blur. Ripped the heads off half a dozen of the Russian Mob's best enforcers, or tore their throats out, and they never had the chance to react."

He paused again. "A man I'd never seen before picked me up and carried me out of there. Then the warehouse exploded."

Ben had a million questions, but he didn't dare ask. He waited for Erik to go on.

"I was in the hospital for a few days. That's when I decided I wanted out. So when I flew home, I was going to talk to my boyfriend about making a fresh start. But instead, I found him banging my personal assistant on our dining room table."

*Oh. Dining room table. That's what triggered it.* Erik's story had been so riveting that Ben had forgotten to listen for a connection to what happened in the kitchen. Betrayal on the heels of a near-death experience would do that.

"And the Fabergé musical egg?"

"It's never been seen again."

Ben wasn't sure what to say. The silence grew heavy.

"Anyhow, I'm sorry I freaked on you," Erik said as if he hadn't just told an epic tale. "And I totally understand not wanting to see me again."

*Wait, what?* Ben reached out without thinking and took Erik's hand. "I never said that."

"You don't have to. I'm too messed up to do this. I should have known that. You can do better."

"You know, there are plenty of places to have sex that don't involve tables, and if it was me picking you up... Well, we can work around that too."

Erik finally looked at Ben, with a stare that defied Ben to put his money where his mouth was. "Why would you still want to? I'm broken."

Ben held Erik's palm over the bullet scars on his chest. "So am I. Although mine was more *Serpico* than *Scarface*." Erik didn't move, so Ben took a chance. He leaned closer, and when Erik didn't pull away, he pressed a gentle kiss against his mouth. Erik moaned softly, and

Ben deepened the kiss, bringing his other hand to cup Erik's neck, drawing him in.

By the end of the kiss, Ben was holding Erik in his arms. "Stay," Ben whispered. "We can be just like this. No expectations. Just please stay."

Erik nodded, and Ben felt relieved. Now that the story was over, he decided he needed a slug of that whiskey himself. He'd known Erik had spirit, but he'd never figured him for a badass. The tale Erik had told highlighted just how different their worlds were. Ben knew he couldn't fit into that world, not over the long run. But maybe he could be what Erik needed for the summer, even if that was all it ever was. Because Ben already knew he wanted more than a fling.

"Come on," Ben coaxed, helping Erik to his feet without actually lifting him. "I've got some sweats you can borrow. The bedroom's this way." He paused. "Unless you'd rather sleep on the couch…"

Erik shook his head. He looked up at Ben, and his gaze was open and vulnerable. "No. Please. I don't want to sleep alone tonight."

Ben's arm tightened around Erik's waist. "I'm here. Let's go to bed."

NINE

ERIK

E rik woke, disoriented, in a bed that wasn't his own. Seconds later, memories from the night before trickled back. Making out with Ben in the kitchen. Being totally onboard with seeing how far they wanted to go. And then, that stupid table and the flashbacks to Josh's betrayal and to when a stranger had grabbed him in the midst of all the gunfire. His reaction, which made Erik's face flush with shame.

But Ben hadn't run. He hadn't told Erik to leave or gotten angry that the date was ruined.

And unless Erik was badly mistaken, the inked, muscular arm flung across his chest belonged to Ben, as did the morning wood poking Erik's ass through the fabric of his sweats.

"Good morning." Ben's voice was a sexy rumble. "It's okay. You're safe."

Erik wasn't sure about being "okay" because what happened the night before left him shaken. As for "safe"—there was nothing "safe" about risking a relationship again after how badly the last one had ended. But he had actually slept soundly, when he had expected his dreams to be dark. And waking up like this, on sheets that smelled like Ben, so close to him, was definitely better than "okay."

He shifted, pressing his back against Ben's chest. Ben tightened his arm over Erik, holding them together. Erik wondered if Ben would make a move on him and debated whether he wanted him to. Was he ready? Ben's hard cock dug against Erik's ass, and his own erection tented his briefs. But Ben just held him, close enough to reassure, loosely enough to let him know he wasn't restrained.

"How did you sleep?" Ben's mouth was right next to Erik's ear, and the whisper of his breath made Erik's cock twitch.

"Better than I expected. Thank you." *Oh, fuck. I'm not sure if I care if I'm ready. This is nice.*

"Any time."

They lay there together for a few minutes before Erik worked up the nerve to speak again. "About last night…"

"It's okay."

Erik shook his head. "No. It isn't. I didn't know I'd trigger like that. I…haven't been with anyone since Josh and I broke up." He didn't mention that it was less than six months ago—which probably made his reaction even stronger—or that his nightmares often combined it with the shooting.

"I meant what I said. Plenty of other options to explore. If you're still interested."

Erik heard the edge of nervousness in Ben's voice and felt bad that he had put it there. He turned to face Ben, tangling their legs together, lying face to face just far apart enough to see each other. "I'm still interested." He guided Ben's hand between them to feel his own rock-hard prick.

"I need you to show me what's okay and what isn't," Ben said. "I don't know where you are on…all this." Erik guessed Ben meant their fledgling relationship.

"I'm right here," Erik replied. He pushed down the sweats and his briefs, letting his cock spring free, and hesitated with his fingers at the waistband of Ben's. "This okay?"

"Definitely."

They were both hard and leaking. Erik ran his fingers up Ben's bulge and felt the pre-come soaking through the fabric. He pushed the cloth out of the way and took them both in hand. He couldn't get a good look at Ben's cock from this angle, but it was heavy in his hand, a bit thicker than his own. The feel of them together made him bite back a moan.

"There's no better way to say 'good morning,'" Ben said, closing his hand around Erik's. Together they set up a rhythm, letting the pre-come slick their palms, thrusting into the circle of their joined hands. It didn't take long. Erik came with a cry, and Ben followed seconds later. Their mingled spend coated their hands and spattered the sheet between them.

When Erik caught his breath, he realized Ben was watching him. "I think I could get addicted to watching you come," Ben murmured. "So sexy." He leaned in and kissed Erik, and Erik kissed him back.

"You look pretty amazing yourself," Erik replied.

Ben wiped them up with a corner of the sheet. "Shower with me?"

Maybe it should have felt awkward, waking up in the bed of a man he'd barely met, but it didn't. There was something about Ben that just felt right, felt comfortable. The room smelled of sex and Ben's after-shave, and Erik knew the two would be forever entwined in his memory.

Last night, all he'd had time to register about Ben's body was the bullet wounds, before everything had gone to hell. But now, in the early morning light, Erik could study the beautiful man lying next to him. Ben's chest and shoulders were as muscular as Erik's fantasies had supposed, based on the fit of his shirts, the way the cloth clung to his body. Defined abs led down to a sexy "V" and a beautiful cut cock. Powerful thighs and toned calves finished up a perfect package. Ben was a couple of inches taller and probably thirty pounds heavier than Erik, a difference that just added to the attraction.

An artfully laid-out assortment of symbols was inked across Ben's shoulders and upper arms, as well as one forearm. He knew enough folklore to recognize them as protective sigils, mainly Celtic. Just above the scatter of pink scars from the bullets was the Latin phrase *"Non tiembo mala." I will fear no evil.*

He realized that he hadn't answered Ben's question. "Yes to a shower. That would be good."

Erik had wondered if they'd both fit. The master bathroom in his Victorian house had a retrofitted claw-foot tub with a curtain, and for all its charm, it wasn't made for two grown men to use at the same time.

Ben's modern bathroom included a walk-in tiled shower with glass doors and a rain head, and plenty of elbow room. "Nice," he said, as Ben adjusted the water temperature.

"I know, right? So much better than my old place in Newark. The shower surround in that dump was crappy plastic, and the water pressure sucked."

They stepped in together. Erik felt suddenly shy. Last night's conversation had stripped him bare emotionally, and the intimacy of his confession, before they had really done anything physically, made him feel topsy-turvy.

"Just relax." Ben's voice had lost some of its morning rasp, but the low tone made Erik shiver as the water sluiced over his skin. "Let me take care of you."

Ben poured a puddle of golden shampoo into his palm, tipped Erik's head under the water to wet his hair, and then began to rub the rosemary-scented liquid down to his scalp, pulsing his strong fingers through the hair. Erik let out a little whimper of contentment and felt sure he was about to wake up from the best dream he'd ever had.

Ben's soap smelled of balsam and cedar. He lathered his hands and then ran them all over Erik's body, stopping now and then to suds up again. His strong fingers massaged the tight cords of Erik's neck and shoulders, slid down the planes of his back and across his pecs and belly, then—finally—down between Erik's legs, slicking his cock and balls.

"That feels...fantastic."

Ben chuckled. "That's the idea." He left one hand cupping Erik's groin, while the other slipped behind him, across the globes of his ass, one soapy finger sliding between them to tease at his hole before moving on.

"So important not to miss any spots," Ben whispered.

Although Erik definitely counted everything so far as foreplay, Ben didn't seem to have an agenda. He didn't try for a second round, although Erik had definitely started to plump at the contact and the feel of Ben's strong hands on his body. When Ben ran his hands down Erik's legs, first one and then the other, Erik wondered if Ben meant to turn him around and go down on him, but he didn't, and Erik found himself fighting disappointment.

"All clean," Ben murmured, shifting him to let the water rinse away the suds.

"My turn," Erik said, taking the bar. He met Ben's gaze, hoping his eyes could say everything he didn't trust his voice to speak. *Thank you. I want you.*

Erik took his time, even though he had to stand on tip-toe to wash Ben's hair. He loved the scent of the soap—another sense memory he'd never forget—and the feel of the lather as he took every excuse to touch Ben everywhere. He studied the tats, memorized the symbols, and let his fingers skim over the old scars, reassuring Ben that he didn't find them ugly.

The muscles in Ben's arms and thighs felt as good as they looked, as did his tight, dimpled ass and a well-hung package Erik hoped he would get the opportunity know better.

Cooling water reminded Erik he needed to finish the job. And although he wanted to go to his knees and give Ben the blow job he'd fantasized about, he knew this wasn't the time.

*Later. Please let there be a later.*

Ben chuckled and reached out to tip Erik's chin up so that their eyes met. "There'll be time for that." Erik blushed, but he didn't object to having Ben guess his thoughts.

They finally got out and toweled each other off. "I need to go open the office," Ben said with a sigh as he rummaged through his dresser for a shirt. Erik retrieved his cast-offs from the night before, figuring no one was going to notice if he was wearing the same clothes.

"I should go work on inventory," Erik replied. "And I promised Jaxon I'd stop back at the Arts Center." He was reluctant to leave, because for as badly as last night had ended, this morning was more than he'd hoped for, and Erik was afraid that stepping outside the apartment would somehow break the spell of what had just happened between them.

He followed Ben to the kitchen. "I've got toast and coffee to offer you," Ben said. "I'm not a big breakfast eater."

"That's fine." Erik stared at the table that had caused so much trouble last night. It was just a table, nothing more.

"Don't."

Ben's voice made him look up. He hadn't turned around from where he was readying the coffee maker. "Don't worry about what happened last night. I'm not. If we're going to do this, it would have come up sooner or later. It's okay."

"Thanks," Erik murmured, still fighting embarrassment.

"So…if you're not busy tonight, I might have some new intel for you on that clock," Ben said, changing the subject. "Assuming you'd be free for dinner again. We can try someplace different. There's a great seafood place at the marina."

"I'd like that." Erik knew they were moving fast, but his heart seemed to be on board. He didn't dare hope that Ben would change his mind about staying in town, but if he ended up leaving, Erik didn't want to squander a moment of memories.

"Great," Ben said. "Same time?"

"That works."

They ate quickly and walked down the stairs together. It felt comfortable and normal and so right that Erik's heart skipped a beat at the thought. *Maybe I'm not as broken as I thought…*

When they reached the bottom of the staircase, Ben pulled him in for a quick kiss. "Make sure you have a good appetite," he whispered. "You'll want to be hungry for tonight," he teased.

"I don't think that will be a problem," Erik told him. "I'll see you later."

———

Erik spent the morning on inventory, pausing only long enough to make himself a sandwich for lunch and grab a cookie from the container he'd bought at the bakery a few doors up from the shop until it was time to go back to the Arts Center. All morning he fought the pull of the box of memorabilia and consoled himself that he'd tackle it as soon as he got back.

He'd made sure to take gloves and his tools with him. Jaxon hovered as Erik examined the Ingraham clock. While Erik couldn't confirm it was owned by the Commodore Wilson or that it was the clock in the pictures, he did verify its authenticity as an Ingraham. The old clock wasn't hiding any other mysteries or clues. There were no impressions or visions – it seemed to be exactly as it appeared, an antique clock.

When he returned to the shop, he ignored the inventory and went right to the box of items from the cursed hotel. He tempered his guilt over avoiding his "real" work with the excuse of wanting news to share with Ben at dinner that night.

Erik forced himself to slow down and examine the box with the same trained observation he used on his old cases. The cardboard box showed its age, but any packing labels were long gone. Erik documented as he unpacked, taking photos as he removed each layer of items, then photographing the pieces themselves. From the odd assortment, Erik wondered if the box had been sold "as is," a grab bag of sorts. He'd seen auctioneers sell odds and ends that way plenty of times, and occasionally, the buyer netted a real find. More often than not, the mishmash was just junk or valuable only in the eye of the beholder.

Erik grabbed a tablet and started a running tally of the items as he laid them out across the break room table. Paper items on the top layers—menus, event programs, monogrammed napkins, and the like—had discolored, but those farther down were well-preserved. Collectors paid a pretty penny for "ephemera"—items that became valuable in their rarity because they were never meant to be saved. At the least, Jaxon might find a trophy or two for his exhibit.

He found a cup and saucer with the distinctive "CW" monogram as well as a single dinner knife, and a similarly etched "Baby Ben" alarm clock with a round face that probably dated from the 1930s. Beneath that was more paper—which he put to one side to go through later—a couple of metal fobs for hotel room keys, two ashtrays, and a few random pieces of barware, along with salt and pepper shakers.

Erik had been so focused on the Cafaro connection that he felt surprised when the box proved to be a time capsule of sorts, with pieces from the forties through the late eighties. He vowed to go back and read up on what happened in the years after the hotel slipped out of the Mob's grip. Erik thought he remembered Susan mentioning a shady televangelist, but he couldn't recall the details.

The old clock Ben had found might not turn out to be as mysterious as it appeared, Erik thought. Even if he was right about the insurance fraud, they were long past the statute of limitations—on everything except murder. But Cafaro was dead, and after all this time, so would the detectives who worked the case as well as any of Cafaro's associates. Even if he and Ben could prove something, it would be moot.

*But it sure could be fun*, he thought with a grin. And it gave him one more excuse to spend time with a certain sexy ex-cop who seemed to be enjoying the thrill of the hunt as much as he was.

Erik had dared to rummage through the box without gloves, almost challenging the items to show him visions and reveal their ghosts. He caught fleeting images skittering through his mind's eye, moments in time, but nothing that grabbed his attention or seemed more than just a faded memory of a long-gone era. Perhaps when he came back and handled the pieces more slowly, they would share more secrets, but he felt relief that he had avoided a psychic wallop.

Even the ghosts kept their distance. Erik sensed them and saw glimpses of movement, but if they retained enough energy or sense of self to manifest more clearly, they chose not to do so. Perhaps they were watching, waiting, to see what he intended. If so, they'd need to be patient, because Erik himself didn't have the answer to that.

On impulse, he went to his sales receipts and found the phone number for Justin Kramer, the man who had sold him the box. He called, not quite sure what he meant to say, but the phone rang until it went to voice mail.

He decided that he needed to know more about Justin's grandfather who had purchased the box and see if the old man had passed along any stories. Erik typed Justin's address into his phone, locked up, and got into his black Grand Cherokee. He'd bought the SUV when he left Atlanta, figuring that he needed the cargo room to pick up antiques from estate sales or auctions and that the four-wheel drive would come in handy for Cape May winters.

Police tape cordoned off the house at the address Kramer had given him. Erik parked a block away, and walked back, trying to figure out what prompted the crime scene markings. Then he saw the broken windows and soot streaks, as well as where part of the roof was gone. A chill went through him, and he wondered what had become of Justin.

Before he could second guess himself, Erik walked up to the next-door neighbor's house and knocked. A pleasant-looking older woman answered the door.

"Hi. I'm looking for Justin Kramer—he lived in the house next to yours. Do you know where I can find him?"

The woman gave Erik the once-over, and he hoped he looked trustworthy and non-threatening. "Justin's gone. I don't know where. Someone broke in and set the place on fire right after he left. So either Justin was very lucky, or he had reason to think his luck was going to turn," she added. "I knew his grandfather, God rest his soul. He was a nice man. Never any trouble."

She'd managed to imply, without actually saying so, that the problems that followed were somehow Justin's fault.

"Justin had called my store and asked me to come by and have a look at some antiques, give him an appraisal," Erik fibbed. "I'm the new owner of Trinkets. I finally had a chance to stop over, and well…" He gestured toward the ruined house.

"I don't know what that boy was thinking, bothering you like that," the neighbor replied. "I've been over there a time or two to give old Mr. Kramer a hand, and I doubt there was anything a shop like yours would be interested in. The furniture I saw might have been old, but not that old, and it got used, so it had wear on it. I'm not sure the consignment store would have taken it, to be honest."

"Still, it's a shame the house was damaged," Erik said, with complete sincerity. It had probably needed major renovations before the fire, but he hoped it could be restored. The house was a Queen Anne style and had good bones.

"That boy should have come around more than he did," the woman said. "Then again, I doubt Mr. Kramer asked for help, even if he needed it. And I did see the grandson working hard to clean the place out after the old man died." She shook her head. "And then to have a break-in, on our street…what's this world coming to?"

Erik excused himself and headed back toward his car. On a hunch, he kept walking. The Kramer house sat on a corner, so by going down the side street, he could get a good look at three sides of the building. The old house needed repair and looked as if it had skipped a lot of maintenance in recent years. The outdated windows wouldn't have been a challenge for even a rookie to break into, and Erik doubted there'd been a security system.

The real question is why a thief would bother.

*Was it just a coincidence? Am I just being crazy to think there could have been something in the box he sold me that a thief wanted? The box that's sitting in my break room.*

Erik found himself holding his breath when he went home, worried that somehow the people who had broken in at the Kramer's house would have already ransacked Trinkets, but to his relief, the store was as he left it. Following another hunch, he called Susan.

"I bought cookies at Crumble," he told her when she answered his call. "More than I should eat by myself. And I have questions—and coffee."

A few moments later, Susan knocked at the door. He welcomed her and turned the lock, leading her to the break room where the promised treats awaited.

"What's all this?" Susan asked after she had helped herself to a shortbread cookie and a cup of coffee.

"It's a treasure box—and it needs to stay a secret," he replied. "Seriously. I think someone might be looking for it and was willing to break into an old man's house to get it—although I don't for the life of me know why."

Susan finished her cookie and set her cup aside. "It looks like Commodore Wilson stuff."

"I bought it from a guy who was cleaning out his grandfather's attic. Said the old man bought it at the bankruptcy sale, and no one's really touched it since then." Erik gestured at the random assortment of objects on the table in frustration. "I can't see anything especially valuable, but maybe I'm missing something. And when I went over to ask the guy some questions, it turns out he's left town suddenly, and the house was broken into—and burned."

"Yikes. Does anyone know you've got the box?"

Erik shook his head. "Just you—and Ben Nolan. Unless Justin—the guy who sold it to me—told someone, or they saw him carry it in."

Susan chewed on her lip as she thought, walking around the table and peering at the objects without touching anything. "Probably good to keep it that way, at least until you can rule out it having anything to do with the break-in."

"I wanted to ask Justin if his grandfather had told him any stories about the Commodore Wilson. The old man worked there as a bellhop back in the day. I think that's what I need right now. Context. Maybe if I spoke to some of the old-timers, I'd figure out what I'm missing."

Susan peered at him over her glasses. "You sound like a character in one of those cozy mysteries I read. What's got you playing Nancy Drew?"

Erik smirked. "Hardy Boys, please." He didn't want to endanger Susan by drawing her into the Cafaro situation, but he needed her connections. "Jaxon Davies over at the Arts Center asked me to consult on his new installation, which is going to include some of the history of the Commodore. I'm trying to be helpful, but since I'm not from here, talking to people who had a personal tie to the hotel would help me get more of a feel for the place."

Susan nodded, still eyeing the pieces on the table. "If you aren't particular about the exact date, I know folks who worked there or just liked to party there regularly. They're all my age or older, obviously, and there's no one old enough to go all the way back to the start, but I can probably give you a list of people who can speak for the fifties through the time the place closed in ninety-five."

"That would be fantastic," Erik replied, grinning. "Thank you."

Susan helped herself to another cookie. "You're welcome. Thank you for the cookies. That bakery is bad for my waistline." That didn't stop her from finishing the treat. "How's the inventory coming?" she asked.

"Slowly. I'm making progress. Robert had an odd eye for acquisitions. I'm not sure yet whether he was an unsung genius or a closet hoarder."

Susan laughed. "Probably some of both. I used to go with him sometimes to estate sales and auctions. I figured he could use a hand loading and unloading his truck, and I needed to get out after Keith died. We made a regular outing of it and had a lot of fun. I never could find a pattern to the things we brought back with us, so I asked him one day why he bought what he bought."

"And what did he say?" Erik found himself genuinely curious.

"He said that he bought the pieces that spoke to him. He wasn't into collecting any particular kind of thing—jewelry, furniture, memorabilia. He said that he just knew when he saw or touched a piece that it was meant to be his, and that's what he bought."

Erik felt a chill go down his spine. Robert's comment sounded far too much like his own touch magic to be a coincidence. Had the old man had some of the Sight himself? Other than Simon Kincaide's cousin, Erik had never heard of psychic abilities being common among antique store owners. He'd have guessed the opposite, that being psychically null around objects that had witnessed all the good, bad, and ugly parts of other people's lives would be a blessing. Maybe not.

"Did Robert ever say anything odd about any of the items in the store? Like that maybe they were haunted, or something like that?"

Susan studied him for a moment before she answered. "Robert was a fascinating man. He'd been in the military and been posted around the world. I don't think I've ever met someone who was better read, and he read a wide variety of books—history, biography, myth, religion. Non-fiction, mostly, although he'd toss in a classic or a bestseller from time to time."

She looked wistful. "We used to get together for coffee at least once a week and talk about books, the garden, stuff like that. Sometimes there'd be some bit of local history that came up, and whenever it did—and ghosts were mentioned, as they often are—Robert never pooh-poohed the idea like some people do. He said that so many cultures have legends and beliefs about spirits, there had to be a grain of truth in it somewhere."

"Did he ever say he saw ghosts?"

"In Cape May, it's more rare to find someone who hasn't. I don't know that I ever asked him. But he did tell me that every object has a story to tell, if you're willing to listen."

"That's an interesting way to look at it," Erik said, although his heart skipped a beat.

He'd pounced on the real estate listing for Trinkets almost as soon as it had gone live online, something uncharacteristically impulsive for him, but he hadn't been able to resist. Robert had agreed to sell after a single conversation, handing off the shop and house at an extremely reasonable price. And from the time Erik had walked in the door, he'd felt that he belonged here.

If he didn't know better, he'd say it sounded like fate.

"Yoo-hoo. Erik?" Susan's prompt told him he'd zoned out. "I texted you the names of the people I can think of, off the top of my head, who would probably be willing to talk to you about the Commodore. If you can't find their numbers online, let me know, and I'm sure I can dig them up. They probably still have landlines, so I imagine they're in the phone book, if you can find one. Just tell them I sent you."

"Thank you," Erik said. "You're a lifesaver."

"I just want to hear the stories, maybe over another batch of cookies?"

"Deal," Erik confirmed, laughing. "I'll share all the juicy gossip."

"Speaking of which—there are a couple of people who should go to the top of the list. You've already met Jaxon. Most of the time, there's no scoop worth knowing that he doesn't know. Sherri and Jo, down at The Spike, have been here for about twenty-five years. They know everyone and hear everything, so that's a possibility."

She chewed her lip as if debating what else to say. "Alessia Mason runs the Spirit of the Sea gift shop. She's married into one of the old Cape May families, and she's also a witch."

"Come again?" Erik wasn't sure whether Susan meant that literally or was dishing on Alessia's personality.

"I'm not telling tales. She makes no bones about it. Alessia is a practicing witch, from an old Sicilian family on her mother's side. Head of the local coven—very preppy witches, but witches nonetheless."

"Interesting."

"And then there's Monty. Have you met him yet?"

Erik shook his head. "Short for Montgomery?"

"Nope. Montana. Monty Clark is the ranger at the lighthouse and a real-deal psychic medium. He's every bit as good as that local guy who writes all the books. Monty leads some ghost tours now and again, but mostly he does private readings. He might be able to 'put you in touch' with some other sources, if you know what I mean."

Interviewing ghosts for intel from beyond the grave hadn't crossed Erik's mind, but he wasn't about to rule anything out. "That's definitely someone I need to meet," Erik said.

Susan grinned. "Glad to help. And don't worry—I won't spill the beans about your box. In fact, I'm dying to know what all you've got there, so if you need a hand going through it, I'm happy to help. I work cheap," she added, grabbing a third cookie.

The offer was tempting, but a glance at his phone told Erik it was almost time to meet Ben. "I would love your help, but not tonight. I'm meeting someone."

"It wouldn't happen to be that hot new guy at the rental office, by any chance?"

Erik blushed, which he seemed to be doing more of lately. "Maybe."

Susan gave a little squeal and clapped her hands, sounding more sixteen than sixty. "Ooh! I knew it. I thought I saw you two walking toward town the other night."

That might also mean she saw Erik coming home that morning in the same outfit, a dead giveaway to where he'd been. He wasn't going to ask.

"It was just dinner," he said, although that certainly hadn't been all it turned out to be.

"You have to start somewhere," she replied with a gleam in her eye. "He's handsome. I totally approve."

"Yeah. He is." Erik felt his heart go a little fluttery, something that had never happened even during his best days with Josh. He might have wondered about it longer, but Susan started speaking.

"You know, I remember him and his cousin biking around here when they were teenagers. They were always going too fast, riding where they weren't supposed to, that sort of thing. Meg and Stewart— his aunt and uncle—are good people. So's Sean, their boy. I hear he wanted to run a restaurant or some such up in Wildwood. Probably why they brought in their nephew to run their business."

From a couple of the comments Ben had made, Erik wasn't sure that was as much of a done deal as Susan made it sound, but he couldn't help hoping that would change if things worked out. The fact that Ben brought out feelings Erik had never felt for anyone else—not even Josh—made him worried that he'd fallen too hard, too fast, for someone he might not even be able to keep.

*Maybe I'm imagining things and making stuff up that wasn't really there...or better yet, I'm not and can give him another reason to stay*, Erik thought.

"Don't you need to get ready? I don't want to make you late for your big date," Susan teased. She swiped another cookie and gave him a mischievous smile. "One for the road. And I'll bring some home-made chocolate chip cookies tomorrow, to sustain us as we delve into the mysteries of the box." She waggled her fingers at him and let herself out the door.

———

Ben pulled up outside Trinkets in a black Mustang and Erik's heart did a little flip. Having a gorgeous man with sexy tattoos pick him up in a rumbling muscle car definitely pressed all the right buttons.

"Still okay with seafood?" Ben grinned as Erik climbed in the car.

"Better than okay. I had a sandwich for lunch, and I'm starved."

Fisher's Seafood sprawled along the marina, providing a view of boats and the water. "You can get whatever you want here," Ben told him as they walked from the parking lot. "Broiled, fried, fancy sit-down, takeout, walk-up—it's all good, and everything's fresh off the boat."

When Erik headed for the walk-up counter, Ben caught his arm. "Nope. In here." He led Erik into the main restaurant, complete with candles and white tablecloths.

"Got us a reservation," Ben said. "I wanted to take you on a proper date this time."

Erik smiled. "I like the sound of that."

Their table in a quiet corner promised that no one would overhear them. Erik looked over the menu, finding it full of even more enticing options than the Greek place the night before.

"Everything looks really good."

"I've never had something here that wasn't," Ben replied. "I don't think you can go wrong."

They agreed on an appetizer of hot crab dip with toast points and crab-stuffed jalapeño peppers. Erik couldn't resist the lobster roll, while Ben went for linguini with clam sauce. While they waited for their food, Ben filled Erik in on the last round of properties he'd toured with Sean, and Erik caught him up on how the inventory had gone.

Once the food came, Erik paused to take a deep breath, inhaling the delicious scents of fresh seafood, butter, and cheese.

"Wow. If it tastes as good as it smells, I'm going to be in a food coma for days."

"It's pretty amazing. The owners have had forty years to perfect their game. The place is a legend."

Ben listened intently as Erik filled him in on the Kramer house and Susan's input. Erik didn't want to mention the box in public, and Ben must have picked up on the same vibes, because he didn't ask.

"So tomorrow I'm going to see some of the people Susan suggested," Erik said. "I've already called three of them, which is about what I can handle and still get the inventory finished."

"I've got to go do a walk-through on a unit we're remodeling, and work through some issues," Ben said. "Otherwise, I'd love to go with you."

"I wish you could. But they might talk more easily to one person instead of two." He grinned. "And if we both went, we'd have to come up with fake FBI names from seventies rock bands, like those guys on TV."

Ben laughed and Erik drank in the sound. He'd never been so thoroughly, dangerously, besotted with someone, and it both thrilled and terrified him. The high was so good, he didn't want to even consider how he'd survive if it crashed and burned. Tonight, Erik intended to push that thought from his mind.

"I guess you're right," Ben replied. "But I did get a look at the deed for the house where we found the...item. It really was in the same family all those years. But get this...one of the owner's daughters was married to the manager of the Commodore Wilson, around the time the item would have gone missing."

"So the real question is, was the husband in on the theft and scam, or playing a different game with what was stashed inside?" Erik asked.

"If his other game was blackmail, he picked a hell of a target." Vincente Cafaro wouldn't have taken a blackmail threat lightly, and Erik couldn't imagine a man like that paying. He'd have been much more likely to eliminate the threat. Maybe someone beat him to the draw.

"My friend Simon got his cousin to run that...item...through a database of insurance claims," Erik said. "It was reported stolen about six months before Cafaro died. Decently large payout, too. Not that the piece itself is that valuable, but there was some provenance about it having been owned by European royalty. Which means the big question is—when did someone switch out the real for the fake?"

"I called in some favors and got a few leads myself," Ben continued. "One of the guys I left on good terms with in Newark—one of the few —knew a cop up here who was friends with his dad. The guy's retired now, but he's still in town, and he'd be old enough to remember at least some of the Commodore's run. I'm meeting him for lunch tomorrow."

"I want to hear all about it," Erik replied. "And I'll catch you up on my meetings. Even if there's no one left to prosecute, it would feel good knowing we solved the mystery."

The sun was low in the sky when they left the marina. Erik was surprised when Ben turned right instead of left. "Where are we going?"

"Best place in Cape May to watch the sunset," Ben replied with an enigmatic smile.

Erik was really confused when Ben drove through the gates to the Lewes Ferry parking lot. "You want to go to Delaware?"

"Nope. My aunt told me about this place. They just built a brand-new terminal, and there's a bar downstairs where the locals hang out in tourist season to avoid the madhouse." He parked and waited for Erik to get out, then led him by the hand around the bar area to the other side, and climbed a set of outdoor steps to a balcony.

From there, they had a view of the harbor, and off to the right, a magnificent sunset.

"This is gorgeous," Erik whispered. The breeze ruffled his hair, and Ben wrapped his arms around Erik, keeping him warm. They watched the sun go down like that, with Erik's head on Ben's shoulder, hands clasped together in the front, Ben's solid body pressed close behind him. As the last of the light faded, Ben turned Erik in his arms to face him.

"Thank you," Erik said. "This was beautiful."

"You're beautiful," Ben replied, lifting his fingers to touch Erik's hair, and then his cheek. He ran the pad of his thumb over Erik's lips. "And I want to get to know you."

Erik's hand caressed Ben's cheek, and Ben leaned his face against it, turning to press a kiss to his palm. "I want to get to know you, too," Erik replied. *I care. More than I should. More than is safe. More than I can control. I'm in too deep already, but it's too late to back out now.*

"Want to come up to my place?" Erik offered. "Turnabout's fair play, after all."

"I'd like that." Ben's voice was husky. "I'd like that a lot."

Ben's phone shrilled with an odd ring. "Shit. It's the alarm company. I have to take this." Ben took the call, keeping Erik close against him.

"Mr. Nolan? The alarm at your office is going off. Police have been dispatched. We need you to meet them there."

Ben let out a long breath. "Okay. I'm on my way." He buried his face against Erik's hair. "Sorry, baby. I've got to go."

"I'll go with you."

Ben stilled, then shook his head. "I don't think that's a good idea." Erik started to protest. "Hear me out," Ben cut him off. "We don't keep cash in the office. The computers aren't new—they aren't worth stealing. So why break in? Unless someone knew I found the clock and thought they'd find it there. And if you go with me, it might make them take a second look at Trinkets."

"Assuming they don't already know we're together," Erik countered.

"Maybe. So I'm going to take you home and walk you to your door like a proper gentleman, and then go meet the cops. And I want you to lock up and put the alarms on." He kissed Erik on the lips, long and lingering. "This is probably going to tie me up for most of the evening. Can I take a rain check on coming over? I'd love to see your place. Maybe we can break it in properly," he added with a wicked smile that went right to Erik's cock.

"Definitely," Erik replied, returning the kiss far too briefly. "I'll hold you to that."

## TEN

## BEN

By the time Ben reached Nolan Resort Real Estate, the cops were in full swing. "I'm Ben Nolan. I was a little ways out of town when I got the call. What happened?"

"Your alarm company called us. Something tripped the system." The officer who responded was a tall black man whose name tag read: *Dorchester.* "By the time we arrived, no one was around. But the back door appears to have been forced."

Ben followed Officer Dorchester around back, where a few technicians were still taking photographs. "You're the only one who could say if anything's been taken," the officer continued. "Although they left the office computers and the TV monitor in the lobby."

Ben led them around to the front and let them in the main door, so they didn't disturb the technicians. "Did you check the upstairs door? That's my apartment. Did they break in there, too?"

Dorchester shook his head. "No. And there's no sign that they tried to, either. Do you keep anything valuable in the office? Petty cash, maybe? Keys?"

Ben shook his head. "No cash. Everything is either credit, checks, or direct transfer these days. As for the keys..." He pointed to the safe beneath the desk in the rear office, which remained bolted to the floor. "They're in the safe."

"What about sensitive records? Financial information on your clients?"

"The filing cabinets are all locked, and they'd need a crowbar or more to get into them. Seems like a lot of work to get a small number of credit card numbers. They'd do better scamming cards at a restaurant."

The cop gave him a look. Ben sighed. "Former Newark PD. If there's a way for someone to steal card numbers, I've busted them for doing it. Think I've seen it all."

"You're new in town? Any chance one of your old cases followed you here?" The officer sounded a little less friendly, and Ben chalked it up to a resort town cop who didn't like big city police encroaching.

"Doubt it. Been off the force for two years going on three." He didn't mention his investigator gig, deciding the cop didn't need one more reason to dislike him.

"Do you have any idea what someone might have been looking for?"

Ben shook his head. "No. My aunt and uncle have run this business for decades. They never had a problem. I haven't changed anything."

"So you're the new boss?"

A week ago, Ben would have made a quip about seeing how the summer went. But the more time he spent with Erik, the less the idea of leaving Cape May appealed to him. "Yeah. I guess I am."

"We'll see if we can get some prints from around the door, but if you can't confirm that there's been a theft, all we can charge someone on is breaking and entering."

Ben felt certain that the break-in had something to do with the clock, but he also knew the cop wouldn't care for his theories. "If you can find out who did it, I'll sleep better," he replied. "And even if it's just B&E, I'll press charges."

The cop shrugged. "We'll keep you informed. In the meantime, I've got some paperwork for you to fill out."

By the time the cops finally left, it was after ten and Ben was exhausted. He trudged up the stairs to his apartment, checked the door—just in case—and went inside.

The apartment still smelled of coffee and toast—and Erik. Ben dug out his phone and saw he'd missed a message.

*Everything okay? Call me, maybe?* A string of emojis followed, including a smiley face, a heart, and an eggplant.

Ben sat on the couch, remembering how vulnerable Erik had been the night before, and how good it felt to hold him tight and help him fight off his demons. Ben called, and Erik answered on the first ring.

"Are you all right? Is the shop okay?" The worry in Erik's voice warmed Ben's heart. Caleb had never bothered to worry about Ben, not even when he was on dangerous undercover busts, because he figured Ben could watch out for himself. He could, but that didn't mean he minded having someone who cared enough to be concerned.

"Yes to both," Ben replied. "They got in, but it doesn't look like anything was stolen. Which means I think we were right—someone was looking for the clock."

"It's in the safe at the shop," Erik replied. "And the Kramer box is locked in a steamer trunk."

"Good job," Ben replied. "So what are you doing with the rest of your evening, now that your date ended early?"

"Um…lying on my couch, thinking about what I wanted to do if you'd come over."

"Oh yeah?"

"Yeah." Erik's voice was low and seductive, and Ben realized this was a side of Erik he hadn't seen yet. *Maybe he's more confident because it's not in person? Interesting.*

"Why don't you tell me what I missed out on," Ben prompted. The tone of Erik's voice already had Ben hard, even though he'd thought he was too tired to do more than sleep when he climbed the stairs.

"Well, you haven't seen my place yet," Erik replied. "So I was going to show you around. Make a memory in every room."

"I like that."

"Do you? I thought I'd kiss you in the kitchen, take your shirt off in the living room and run my hands all over that fine body of yours, and get you out of your pants in the hallway. So by the time we got to the bedroom, I could get on my knees and see how you taste."

*Fuck.* Ben thought phone sex only happened on 900 numbers and in romcom movies. Caleb would have rather cut out his own tongue than try to be seductive over the phone. Ben didn't know what got him hard faster—listening to Erik talk dirty or knowing that he was fantasizing about Ben in such maddening detail.

"Uh-huh," Ben said, and his voice sounded breathy, even to him. His cock was already hard, and Ben unbuttoned his jeans and slipped a hand inside.

"Are you touching yourself?" Erik asked. "Because I am."

*Damn.* Ben pictured Erik sitting on a sofa, legs splayed, sweatpants pushed down to his thighs, slowly jacking himself. The thought made his own prick leak even more.

"So what would you do, on your knees?"

"Lick you," Erik replied. "Get you real wet. Taste you. And then go down on you like I'm starving for cock. I might not get you all in. But I'd be willing to give it a try."

Ben moaned, and his hand moved faster, slicking with pre-come. He and Erik only got as far as that one handjob in bed—was it only this morning? But if they'd gone home together tonight, Ben had intended to see if Erik would be up for blowing each other. Maybe at the same time.

Apparently, the answer would have been yes.

"I'd move my tongue over the top, swirl it all around, suck on you real good," Erik continued in a sultry tone that just made the words even sexier. "Then I'd put my hand between your legs and roll your balls on my palm, run my finger up your taint, and circle your hole."

"Erik—" Ben groaned, knowing he wasn't far from climax. "I'm gonna—"

"And then I'd take in everything I could fit, and swallow everything you gave me."

Ben cried out as his back arched and he shot, feeling his release explode through his body. He heard Erik shout his name a second later, and the mental picture of him coming like that sent an after-shock through Ben's body.

"Was that good for you?" Erik asked with mock innocence.

"Oh, baby. The only way it could be any better was if you were really here."

"At least you know what I think about when we're apart."

And didn't that just give Ben new material for his morning shower? "Really?"

"Uh-huh. Did I do okay?" Seductive Erik suddenly gave way to a much less confident version.

"You were fantastic," Ben assured him, reaching for a box of tissues to clean up. "Maybe the next time we get together, we could try that in person."

"I'd like that," Erik replied, and Ben found the shy note in Erik's voice to be just as much of a turn on. "Want to come over for dinner tomorrow? I picked up this recipe for arrabiata sauce in Rome that's easy and sooo good. We could eat in, for a change."

Left unspoken was the fact they could also babysit both the box and the clock.

"Sounds perfect, if you don't mind cooking."

"I actually like to cook, but it's less fun when it's just for one."

Ben was discovering all kinds of new things about Erik, and each one just reinforced the dangerous attraction. Dangerous to Ben's heart, that was. Because if Erik walked away now, deciding Ben wasn't good enough to keep for the long run, Ben knew it would hurt a lot.

"Same time?" Ben asked. "What can I bring?"

"Just yourself," Erik replied. "And a healthy appetite."

After they said good night, Ben took a shower to clean up, and slipped into a T-shirt and sleep pants. He could still pick up a faint trace of Erik's scent on the pillowcase. Ben wasn't sure exactly how it happened, but Erik was getting past his defenses, and working his way farther into Ben's heart than Caleb ever had been.

*I thought I was in love with Caleb. But it never felt like this. Oh, God. Does that mean?* But he already knew the answer. *I'm falling in love with Erik.*

———

The next morning, Ben went down to the office early to clean. The police had left a mess of fingerprint powder and footprints, and the would-be thieves had rummaged through the papers in the folders on the desks. He mentally cataloged everything as he straightened up, then ran the vacuum and wiped down the furniture until he had erased all traces of the invasion by both the thieves and the cops.

He had already decided not to open today, since the season still hadn't started, and gave Jenny, the office manager, the day off with pay. Anyone interested would call or email, and he could take care of both without having to be in the office. Very few clients just walked in, unless they were returning a key or reporting damage. They could leave the key in the night drop box, Ben figured. He needed today to figure out what the hell was going on.

Ben made a pot of coffee and ran through the messages, returned calls, and answered emails. They were already eighty percent booked for the summer and booked solid from Memorial Day through mid-July. Ben had to admit that his aunt and uncle had built a very solid business, and he was both humbled and a little scared that they trusted him enough to take it over.

He also indulged his investigator side, doing a web search on Erik Mitchell, which turned up a lot more than he'd expected. Ben spent the next hour reading articles about Erik's role in recovering stolen pieces and unmasking frauds. There weren't many pictures—no surprise, given the nature of his job—but in the few Ben found, he quickly recognized his new boyfriend. Only that Erik didn't look like his Erik. The Erik in the tuxedo at an event in Paris looked stiff and aloof, as if he was somehow separate from everyone else even while he was standing in the middle of the action.

Ben tried to square that stranger with the Erik he knew, the man who'd been in his bed, who'd talked dirty to him over the phone. The charming geek who blushed easily and laughed quickly. The damaged man haunted by past betrayals. Did Erik have some PTSD? Not unlikely, given what he'd survived. Ben had spent his own time in mandated counseling, so he wasn't one to judge. Those shadows never really went away, although you could learn to cope, compensate.

*If he'd been happy in his old life, he wouldn't have left. Buying a house and a store is a pretty big commitment. If the men he knew then were all bastards like Josh, then maybe—just maybe—he's ready for someone who isn't his usual type.* Christ, Ben hoped so.

By the time he needed to meet with the retired cop friend-of-a-friend, Ben had drained the coffee pot, confirmed half a dozen new rentals, emailed information packets to another eight potential customers, ordered some do-it-yourself surveillance cameras for the office, and paid the bills. A note on the door directed anyone who showed up to either use the key drop or leave a message. With that, Ben double-checked the locks, set the alarm, and headed out to Abbott's, a bar on the outskirts of town.

He pulled in and parked the Mustang, pausing to size up the joint. His cop instincts had served him well so far, and he didn't see a reason to change now. Tony Basalmo was one of the few Newark cops he still trusted, who'd earned that trust by sticking by him during the aftermath of the clusterfuck that had almost killed Ben. Tony believed Ben that the gang had been tipped off by an insider, although no one was ever caught. So if Tony thought his dad's buddy was a good guy, Ben trusted the intel.

Still, he'd learned a long time ago to trust—and verify. Everything he'd been able to find on retired Detective James Cooper—short of a full background check—panned out. Ben just hoped the man showed up.

Ben walked in and scanned the room. A few men were already at the bar, some eating lunch, others already nursing beers. None of them looked like tourists. In the back corner, a man who might have been in his early seventies was staring at Ben with an intensity that marked him as a cop. Ben strode over.

"Mr. Cooper? I'm Ben Nolan."

The older man's grip was firm. Cooper looked in good health. Maybe seventy was the new fifty.

"Basalmo said you wanted to talk to me. Have a seat." He had a voice that sounded like it had been honed by a pack a day and hard liquor.

"Tony said you knew his father."

Cooper nodded. "I did. Tony Senior was a good cop. We worked together in Newark, and then I moved down here with my wife. Got a promotion that I wasn't going to get anytime soon in Newark—you know how that goes. Found out the sea air did me good."

"You were on the force here in the seventies, eighties, and nineties, right?" Ben waved off the server who showed up with menus. Depending on how the conversation went, he'd either order later or grab something elsewhere.

"I retired in ninety-five," Cooper said. "That's a long time ago. Especially for you."

Ben nodded, trying not to react to the older man's jab about Ben's age or the edge of macho posturing in his voice. Marking territory, measuring dicks—Ben knew how to play the game, and still hated it.

"You would have been around when the Commodore Wilson was still in its heyday."

Cooper raised an eyebrow. "Debatable whether that snake-bit place ever had a heyday. I got here in seventy-seven, two years before that no-good preacher Hank Chason disappeared."

"You ever meet him?"

"Chason?" Cooper snorted. "Sure I met him. He'd throw a big retreat, bring in his faithful sheep from all over the country, and we'd have to work overtime to handle the traffic or keep the protesters away."

"Protesters?"

"Guy was a phony. Oh, he was slick, and he could talk real pretty, but I've seen eyes like that on every grifter I ever busted. Although I will say, he sure could put on a show."

Ben had done his homework. After Cafaro's death, Hank Chason bought the Commodore Wilson to help him make the jump from fire breathing radio preacher to TV evangelist. His mix of Red Scare politics and red-meat fundamentalism drew a faithful—and well-armed—

crowd, eager to hear a gospel that linked the End Times with their own paranoia.

"The locals hated the guy, by the way. But he brought in the crowds, and they spent money in the beach shops and at the bars—since Chason didn't serve alcohol at the Commodore, if you can believe that. The hookers made bank whenever he held a convention because the faithful weren't very faithful, if you know what I mean." Cooper took a gulp of his beer. "Chason wasn't any better. There were always rumors about whose wife—or husband—he was fucking. Guess it doesn't count if you pray afterward."

"Chason disappeared. Did anyone ever figure out what happened?"

Cooper shook his head. "Nah. I hadn't made detective yet when he pulled a runner. But it's true what people said. One of the maids found a sex dungeon in the basement. Chason snorted coke like he was taking communion. And he might not have served alcohol to anyone else, but he liked to wander the halls dead drunk, in nothing but a bathrobe."

Well. Those details hadn't been in any of the retrospectives Ben had read. "So he was losing his grip."

Cooper gave a cold chuckle. "Oh, he'd lost it, all right, toward the end. Chason made a mint fleecing his flock, but he didn't pay his taxes. More to the point, he didn't pay the construction company he hired to shore up the east wing. And the Mob doesn't take that kind of thing lying down."

*Another mob connection,* Ben thought. "So they never figured out what happened to Chason?"

Cooper's shrug made it clear he didn't care. "They had him on all the wanted lists, but he never turned up. Probably got a bullet in his head. Maybe he's bunking with Jimmy Hoffa under a parking garage."

Cooper reminded Ben of the older cops he'd worked with in Newark. Most were ex-military, and they policed like they were in occupied territory, not an American city. Some of them saw the Mob as a source of order in the midst of Newark's gang-fueled war zone chaos.

"What happened after Chason?" Ben accepted the glass of water the server brought and took a sip. Somehow, despite all the years of non-smoking laws, the smell of stale cigarettes still clung to the bar.

"This crazy long-haired hippie guru bought the place. Kendry Ambrose. He turned it into a goddamned celebrity playground." Cooper shook his head. "I was a detective by the time he finally burned out, and let me tell you, it was wild over there. Supposed to be some kind of New Age wellness retreat," he said, adding air quotes, "but what I saw looked more like sex, drugs, and rock and roll."

Ben remembered the picture of Ambrose he'd seen on the web, a model-handsome man hawking his bestselling self-improvement books to an audience that couldn't seem to get enough. For a while, Ambrose built an empire. But he couldn't keep his dick in his pants. Alimony, jealous mistresses, harassment lawsuits, and lavish spending meant bankruptcy—and maybe prison—had been in the golden boy's future.

"But that didn't last either, did it?"

"'Course not. That guy Ambrose was just a different kind of con man." Cooper took another slug of his beer. "Although I didn't think he'd have the stones to go out the way he did. Walked out on stage in front of a packed audience, shoved a gun in his mouth and pulled the trigger." He made a gun shape with his thumb and index finger. *"Bam."*

"Is there any reason that someone with a grudge against anybody connected with the Commodore might still be out there?" Ben asked.

Cooper tilted his head, giving him a look. "Meaning what?"

Ben had been debating whether to trust Cooper enough to tell him about the clock. He liked playing things close to the chest, but this wasn't his hometown, and he needed a lead. Cooper was his best bet.

"I found a clock hidden inside one of our rental properties—a new place we bought recently. I think it's connected to the old Cafaro killing. They never solved that one, did they?"

Cooper watched him with cop eyes, the cold, calculating stare Ben reserved for suspects. "No. They never pinned anyone for the bomb, but that was a long time ago."

Ben ran a hand back through his hair. "Yeah, that's what I thought. Then someone tried to break into my place last night, and there's no reason except for searching for that clock. And that fire, over at the Kramer house? Rumor had it the owner had some stuff he'd bought when the Commodore closed down."

Cooper sat back and let out a guffaw. "That's what's got your panties in a wad? My God, boy. Is that what passes for policing in Newark these days?"

"I didn't imagine the break-in. And the fire at the Kramer house—that wasn't my imagination, either." Ben leaned forward. "Yeah, Cafaro died a long while ago. But that wasn't the end of the Mob's ties to the Commodore. They had their hooks into Chason and Ambrose."

"Chason's missing. Ambrose is dead. It's over."

"Maybe someone is afraid that it isn't."

Cooper hunched closer, and Ben instinctively drew back. "Son, let me give you some advice. Those dogs bite hard. If they're sleeping, let them lie."

Ben walked out to the Mustang, torn between being annoyed at Cooper and angry at himself for expecting to find answers. Then again, guys like Cooper lived to be a ripe old age by being sons of bitches. If Cooper knew anything that linked the Commodore to the current Mob, he wasn't talking.

*And why should he? What's past is dead and gone. Maybe he's right.*

Ben's phone rang, and he recognized the tone. It belonged to Dan, the head of his remodeling crew. "What's up?"

"Boss, I need you over at the Weber house. There's something you need to see."

Ben pulled up in front of the gray Victorian house with the widow's walk on top. Sean had told him the house was a rental favorite, but it had gotten so much use that it needed a refresh. Right before Aunt Meg left on her permanent vacation, she'd scheduled Dan to handle freshening the place up. New paint, patched drywall, replacing tile, fixing all the little things that could go wrong. The house had been off the rental schedule for a couple of months and probably had at least another month before it was ready to have guests.

He hurried up the steps. Dan sounded a little freaked out, and that didn't square with the level-headed guy Ben had met.

"Dan?" he called when he got to the entrance hallway.

"Up here. Second floor, third room on the right."

Ben was surprised to find the rest of the crew gone. Dan was waiting for him just inside the empty bedroom.

"What happened? Someone get hurt on the job?" Ben hoped not, but construction could be dangerous. At least the company carried plenty of insurance.

"No. Nothing like that. But…" Dan was usually unflappable, but he looked spooked. "We had to go in and trace a water leak. When we opened up some of the wall to get to it, we realized that someone had covered over a closet. And, well—see for yourself."

He led Ben over to the hole in the corner. The crew had busted out enough of the wall to reveal the old closet. And the yellowed skeleton inside.

For the second time in less than twenty-four hours, Ben found himself talking to Officer Dorchester. Dan gave his statement and supplied the names of the guys who made the discovery. The cops were polite, but Ben knew from experience that their captain was probably already trying to make a connection between the break-in and the skeleton, because cops didn't believe in coincidences.

"Looks like the wall had been in place for quite a while," the police technician told Dorchester. "And the bones aren't new. If I had to guess, I'd say maybe thirty, forty years old, based on the clothing. Forensics will narrow it down."

"People don't wall themselves up in closets and die of old age," Dorchester replied. "Can you figure out what killed her?"

"Him," the tech said. "And cause of death isn't the hard part. Bullet to the back of the skull. Execution style. Definitely not a suicide. Off-hand, I'd say it was a hit."

———

Once again, red tape and paperwork meant Ben didn't get back to clean up for his date with Erik until the last minute. He had just enough time for a shower after he stopped to pick up a bouquet of flowers and a bottle of good wine.

On impulse, Ben had grabbed his messenger bag and gotten his Glock out of the safe. He had a concealed-carry license, but he rarely felt the need unless he was doing an investigation. The break-in had spooked him, and Cooper's warning still echoed in his ears. If anyone was watching him, they'd know about Erik. And given Erik's business, it wouldn't take much to suspect where the clock had gone.

The skeleton had raised the stakes in the game. Ben had no intention of becoming a victim—or letting anyone get near Erik. He tucked the gun into the bag, hoping he didn't need it, and wondering how he'd explain its presence to Erik.

Ben also second-guessed himself over the flowers. Caleb had been ex-military, not long out of the closet—or the footlocker, as he'd joked. Maybe it was armed forces macho bullshit or the way Caleb had been raised, but while he owned up to being gay, he was quick to take offense at anything that appeared to sleight his masculinity.

Flowers would have touched off an epic fight.

But Erik wasn't Caleb. Funny, but after he'd learned more about what Erik's past life had entailed, Ben put his money on Erik as the bigger badass over his hulky former lover. Somehow, they had managed to start with the sex and the broken parts and skip over the stuff normal people usually covered in the early days of a relationship. Favorite music. Funny childhood stories. Pets. Books. Video games. Movies.

*Relationship.*

Ben hoped that was what he and Erik were forging. The more he got to know Erik, the harder Ben knew it would be to ever let him go. He, at least, was well past "fling." And he looked forward to learning all those little details that partners knew about each other.

Like whether Erik would be offended by getting flowers.

*He likes art. There are lots of paintings of flowers. Go for it.*

By the time he got to Erik's house, he was still carrying the bouquet, and he either needed to present the flowers with the wine or ditch them in the bushes. He hung on to them and hoped for the best.

Erik met him at the door with a kiss. He smiled when Ben offered the flowers and wine. "Thank you." Erik bent to sniff the large pink and white Stargazer lily in the center of the bouquet. "My favorite. How did you know?"

Ben gave a sheepish smile. "Lucky guess."

"Good instincts," Erik said, leading him up into the apartment. Ben put his bag on a chair in the kitchen.

Ben had tried to imagine what Erik's home looked like. He had figured it would be full of antiques, maybe a little formal. Instead, the furnishings were modern and comfortable. A large leather sofa faced the TV, and Ben admired the media system housed beneath it. Another oversized leather recliner and a coffee table created a comfortable place to relax. Bookshelves covered the walls, filled with paperbacks and DVDs.

"Dinner's almost ready, so I'll give you the grand tour after we eat," Erik said. "The short version is that there are two bedrooms and a bath on the third floor, which are for guests, and two more bedrooms and the main bathroom here. One of the rooms on this floor I use for a computer and workout room, and the other is the master bedroom."

Erik's modern furnishings mixed well with the architecture of the old Victorian house. The framed prints decorating the walls were a mix of styles and periods, some of which looked vaguely familiar from long-ago museum field trips. The apartment was eclectic and off-beat, just like its owner.

"I like it. It's...very you," Ben said. He reached for Erik, but his boyfriend eluded his grip with a smile.

"Eat first, sex later," Erik said, heading for the kitchen.

The homemade sauce smelled so good, Ben hoped he wasn't drooling. That was doubly hard to avoid, watching the way Erik's jeans hugged his ass. Ben followed him into the kitchen. Erik wore a blue T-shirt that played up his eyes. He was barefoot, which somehow seemed even sexier. Smooth jazz played in the background, and Erik swayed as he stirred the sauce. The pot on the next burner bubbled and steamed, and Ben couldn't help thinking that he felt the same way.

Every time he was with Erik, he fell a little harder. He really hoped Erik felt the same way, but Ben hadn't exactly been good at reading signals with Caleb, and he was afraid to find out his feelings were one-sided. *Admit it. You're falling in love with him.*

Deep inside, Ben knew it was true. But did Erik feel the same? Or was this just a summer fling for him, safe because Ben was supposed to leave in the fall? A classic beach romance with the bad boy, never meant to be more?

Ben knew he didn't belong in a world of art museums, galleries, and billionaire collectors. If he had any place in that world, it was working security, invisible hired help. The realization stung, but that didn't make it any less true.

*Erik left that world. And maybe, an ex-cop and an antique store owner can make it work.*

Ben decided he'd do just about anything for a chance at that future.

"Ben?" Erik looked at him as if he'd been talking for a while. "Are you okay?"

Ben managed a smile that probably looked as fake as it felt. "I'm just off my game," he said. "I'll tell you after dinner."

Erik stiffened. "Bad news?" There was that vulnerability again.

Ben moved up behind him and nibbled on his ear, making Erik squirm. "Nothing that has to do with us. I promise. Just weird stuff at work. We're good. Better than good."

Erik relaxed, and Ben snuck another kiss to his neck. He didn't miss the way it made Erik shiver. "Can I help with dinner?"

"There's a bag of salad in the fridge and some croutons and fixings on the counter if you want to toss it all together," Erik replied. "The pasta should be done any minute, and the garlic toast is in the oven."

Ben opened cupboard doors until he found a serving bowl, and realized how comfortable he felt, not at all like someone visiting for the first time. He pushed that thought out of his mind and concentrated on the salad, then found a corkscrew and opened the wine.

"I hope you don't mind if we eat in the kitchen," Erik said, still facing away from Ben. "I don't have a dining room."

Ben winced, remembering. "This is fine. It's…cozy."

The table was already set. Erik fixed plates for both of them, while Ben carried the salad and wine over to the table, then pulled the garlic toast out of the oven. "This looks great," he said.

"I hope so," Erik replied. The shy smile was back. "I got stuck in Rome on a case and found this little restaurant in Trastevere where the food was so good, I ate there every night for two weeks. When I left, the woman who owned the place gave me the recipe for her sauce."

Now it was Ben's turn to feel insecure. "Never been to Rome," he admitted. "But there are some great Italian restaurants in Newark. That was what I figured I'd miss the most about leaving."

"So if the food isn't what you miss, what is?" Erik tried to make the comment sound off-handed, but it didn't quite fly.

Ben met his gaze. "Nothing. Turns out, I don't miss anything about Newark. Hadn't realized I'd find so much to like here in Cape May."

Erik smiled, and the hint of color that came to his cheeks told Ben the message had been received. God, he hated dancing around the elephant in the room like this, but he needed to be sure that Erik felt the same before he just went and blurted out "I love you" like some love-struck teenager.

Because if Erik hadn't gotten to that point yet, or didn't feel the same, Ben didn't want to know. And if they did stand a chance, Ben didn't want to scare Erik off. He'd seen how deeply that son of a bitch Josh had hurt Erik. He couldn't blame Erik for being cautious. And Ben had already decided to give Erik all the time he needed.

Should he tell him that he planned to stay in Cape May? Or would that make Erik feel pressured? Shit, Ben was bad at this romance thing. And if Erik was just counting on this being a summer fling, would finding out Ben intended to stay make Erik pull back? Ben wished to hell relationships came with a manual.

"Try the linguine. See if you like the sauce," Erik prompted.

Fuck, Ben had spaced out again. He was going to give Erik a

complex if he kept this up. Ben did his best to twirl a reasonably neat amount of pasta on his fork and managed to get it to his mouth without dropping anything on his shirt. Then the mix of flavors hit him, and his eyes went wide.

"Oh. My. God. That's so good."

Erik grinned. "Simple, too. The best things usually are." He reached out to cover Ben's left hand with his own, and Ben twined their fingers together.

"I'll drink to that," Ben replied.

They both dove into the food, and Ben had seconds on the pasta, while still doing his share on the salad and bread. They split the bottle of wine, and while two glasses weren't enough to give him a buzz, it did take the edge off a hard day.

"Can we wait a while before dessert?" Ben begged. "I'm stuffed."

Erik's eyes twinkled with mischief. "Sure. It's got whipped cream though. I had some ideas about how to serve it…"

"Hold that thought," Ben replied. "I like that idea."

Erik opened a second bottle, and they took their glasses into the living room. The leather couch was as comfortable as it looked, and Ben loved that Erik sat next to him, close enough for their thighs to touch, and leaned in when Ben slipped an arm around his shoulders.

"So…what happened today?"

"We found a skeleton in the closet."

Erik frowned. "You came up with some info on Cafaro?"

Ben shook his head. "No. My guys were doing some remodeling and found a real skeleton in a real boarded up closet. And here's the kicker—he'd been capped."

"Holy shit."

"Yep. I also got an earful from a retired cop who knew a lot about the Commodore Wilson. All the scandals. And I definitely got the feeling from him that there might still be some people around with reasons not to air that dirty linen."

Erik chewed on his lip before answering. "Do you want to drop it? Looking into the clock?"

"Do you?"

"No. At first, I thought it was just a harmless bit of history. But now, I'm thinking there might be more to it."

"Maybe we should turn it over to the cops."

Erik raised an eyebrow. "Would they believe us?"

Ben sighed. "Probably not. Right now, all we've got is coincidence. Even in Cape May, I doubt they're bored enough to go looking into decades-old mysteries without a smoking gun."

"Then I say we should keep digging," Erik replied. "Are you in the mood for dessert yet? Because I could go for some whipped cream." Erik licked his lips, and Ben felt his cock twitch in response.

"I think you'd taste good now," Ben replied, reaching to bring Erik in for a kiss.

The alarm shrilled, an ear-splitting siren, and both men jumped. Erik's eyes widened. "The store!"

They headed back through the kitchen. Ben reached into his bag for his gun. Behind him, Erik pulled something out of a drawer. They went down the stairs together, with Ben a step ahead. There was no way he intended to let Erik go first, unarmed.

They got to the shop door just in time to see a dark figure in a hoodie sprinting away.

"Stop! Police!" Ben shouted, raising his Glock.

In response, the figured turned, and Ben saw the motion before he saw the gun.

"Down!" he yelled, dropping and pulling Erik with him as a shot zinged over their heads and hit the wall.

By the time they got to their feet, the intruder was gone. That's when Ben realized Erik also had a gun in his hand.

"You know how to shoot that thing?"

Erik rolled his eyes. "Yeah. My old job didn't always introduce me to the best people. Seemed like a good investment. I'm decent at martial arts, too."

Before Ben could reply, two patrol cars pulled up, lights flashing.

"Put your weapons on the ground. Come out with your hands up."

"I'm the owner!" Erik yelled as he and Ben both laid their guns down. "Don't shoot!"

"Get on your knees. Hands behind your head."

Ben felt his heart thud. He'd been on the other side, and he knew how easily and quickly things could go to hell. He and Erik fell to their knees, hands laced behind their heads, as one of the cops retrieved their guns.

"Nolan. You again?" Ben looked up to see Officer Dorchester looming over them.

"Officer Dorchester. Good to see you. Erik owns the shop. We were having dinner, and the alarm went off."

"You have permits for those pieces?"

Ben and Erik both nodded. "Yes sir," Ben replied. "License and concealed carry."

"Me, too," Erik confirmed.

Dorchester gave a long-suffering sigh. He turned to his team. "Stand down. They're not the bad guys."

He looked back at Ben. "All this, after you find a skeleton in one of your rental houses earlier today?"

Ben licked his lips. "Yeah. I guess it's my lucky day." He didn't mention that this was the second time in two days he'd been cock-blocked by an alarm.

"All right, get up. Nolan here should remember how this goes. How is that you two come to town, and we get a freak crime spree?"

Ben didn't think any answer he gave would help the situation, so he kept his mouth shut. He stood by while Erik answered questions, and the team examined the door. This intruder had tried picking the lock instead of forcing his way in. That told Ben they were dealing with a motivated amateur, because a pro could have gotten around Erik's lock, and the alarm systems, too.

"The guns check out," a second officer told Dorchester after Erik had spent an eternity answering questions.

"Do you usually eat dinner armed?" Dorchester asked, cocking an eyebrow.

"I think we were both a little freaked out over the break-in at Ben's office," Erik replied. "I guess we were right to be nervous."

"We'll see if we can get any prints. But at least the thief didn't actually get into your store," Dorchester replied. "We've got all we need from you for now, but Captain Hendricks may want you to come down and give another statement or answer some more questions." He shook his head. "Two break-ins *and* a skeleton? This is not going to be good for his blood pressure."

The second officer returned their guns, and Dorchester and his team headed off. Erik and Ben watched them go. Ben tucked his gun into his waistband and reached out to take Erik's hand.

"You're just full of surprises," he said.

# ELEVEN

# ERIK

Erik shut the door behind Ben and locked it, then reset the alarm. He put his Sig Sauer P226 back in the drawer. Ben let out a low whistle.

"That's a serious gun," he said. "It's what the FBI uses."

Erik kept his back to Ben and nodded. "Yeah. That's what they trained me with." He had been putting off this conversation, afraid of how it would go over. Tonight had forced the issue.

Ben had left the police because he no longer trusted the Newark cops. Erik knew that the law enforcement agencies he'd cooperated with weren't totally pure. Would it matter? He'd left all that behind, come here to start over. Would those old connections cost him this relationship?

"Talk to me, Erik. Please?" Ben was behind him, and his voice was quiet.

Erik braced his hands on the counter and stared out the window. He couldn't look at Ben, not right now.

"I wasn't an agent, just a consultant. But I had a very specialized skill. I guess I was a little too good at my job," he said with a hitch in his voice. "I was already working with museums and the high-end auction houses to authenticate acquisitions. A big-name museum bought a very good forgery. I exposed it. That's what put me on the radar for the FBI and their buddies."

Erik saw his own reflection in the glass. He thought he looked tired and worn. What could Ben possibly see in him? "I guess I was naive. I didn't realize what I was getting into. Then again, I'm not sure I could have said no."

He hung his head, not wanting to see his face staring back at him. "Art thefts, black-market sales, relic misappropriation—it's not just about greedy collectors and entitled billionaires. It's also money laundering. Cartels. Russian Mob. Traffickers. The feds loaned me out to Interpol and some others like them. Because not many people could do what I did. I had a good eye. But I also had…intuition. Freakishly accurate intuition. The more successful I was, the more they used me, and the harder it was to walk away."

Ben stayed quiet.

Erik was afraid to turn around. He could come up with all kinds of reasons Ben wouldn't want to stay after he heard him out. Sure, Ben had seemed cool with the ghost thing. But visions from touching objects? That was freaky. And Erik had arguably made powerful enemies on both sides of the law. Walking away certainly hadn't made him any friends. Josh had never liked all the travel, but deep down, Erik knew that Josh hadn't liked the job. And back then, Erik *was* the job. Things were different now. *He* was different. But did he still come with more baggage than Ben would want to deal with?

"How did you get out?"

Erik couldn't read anything from Ben's tone. "I got hurt on the last sting. I told my handler that I wanted out. He said that wasn't an option. I didn't know what to do, but I did know that I couldn't be what they needed me to be anymore. I was desperate, and I knew Josh wouldn't understand. We hadn't broken up, but on some level, I knew things weren't good. So I called my friend Simon. I had nowhere else to turn. I couldn't tell him much—I'd signed some wicked NDAs—but we ran in some of the same circles. He didn't know what to tell me, but he knew some people who might be able to help. I really thought the only way I'd ever leave was feet first."

"What happened?"

Erik shook his head. "I'm still not sure. When I was ready to be discharged from the hospital, my handler came in. Looked like he had a real stick up his ass. He told me I was being let go. Didn't give me a reason, and I didn't ask. He wasn't happy about it, but he had the paperwork. Told me it meant I was on my own, and I'd better watch my back. And...I was free." He paused. "I was so excited, I came back to tell Josh that I was out, done, finished. He hated my job. And, well... you know the rest."

Erik didn't move. He braced himself to hear the door open and close behind Ben, hear his footsteps on the stairs for the last time. He blinked back tears. *My own stupid fault for getting close to someone. I don't do flings. I fall in love. And look what it gets me.*

Ben moved up and slipped his arms around Erik's waist. "I'm glad you got out. It's not the same, but I knew undercover cops who never were able to quit the life. Either they died working a case, or they went dark side and became the thing they were supposed to hunt. So...different level, but...I get it."

"It doesn't scare you? What I said?" Erik found himself holding his breath, cherishing the feel of Ben's arms around him, so afraid Ben was going to let him down gently. There wasn't any "gently" possible. Erik was already in too deep.

"What part? Knowing how dangerous your job was? Hell, yeah. I hate thinking of you around those scumbags. Finding out you worked for the feds? Not your fault. Sounds like they made you an offer you couldn't refuse."

Ben laid his cheek against Erik's head. "Knowing you might have some enemies out there? Baby, you do realize I busted gangs and mobsters and drug dealers and worse? Infiltrated their inner circle. Ratted them out. Hell, at one point a drug lord put a price on my head. So if you're worried about having a target on your back, understand I've got one, too. I'm not going anywhere. Unless you tell me to leave."

Erik laid his hands over Ben's and pulled him tighter. "And my intuition? That doesn't freak you out?"

"I don't understand it. And I'm guessing you don't fully, either. But it's part of who you are. So I'm okay with it."

After the whiplash of emotions, Erik felt a little weak in the knees. He relaxed into Ben's hold, and Ben steered him to the couch, pulling Erik down next to him and wrapping his arms around him.

"I know you aren't going to like it, but I think that you should keep your gun with you, until we know who's behind this. Because that guy tonight was armed. We were lucky he ran."

Ben stroked Erik's hair. "I feel better, knowing you've got martial arts training and can handle a gun. But please don't take any chances, Erik. Whatever's going on, it's a lot bigger than we thought. And they know who we are, so we can't walk away until it's finished."

Erik nodded, burrowing his head against Ben's chest. "I know. Same goes for you. Don't get dead. I'd miss you."

Ben leaned down to kiss the top of his head. "I'd miss you, too."

"Stay?"

Ben chuckled. "Baby, I was going to stay one way or the other. Either in here, with you, or in my car out front. And I know which way I'd prefer."

"Is it okay if we save dessert until tomorrow?" Oddly enough, being shot at dampened Erik's libido.

"You know, that's a rain check for each of us now. We're gonna have a real good time when we cash them in."

"I'm looking forward to it," Erik replied.

They sat up for a while, watching a cooking show because it was safe and brainless. Gentle shaking woke Erik, letting him know he'd fallen asleep against Ben.

"Come on, let's go to bed. You're going to have a crick in your neck if we sleep here."

"This isn't at all how I'd planned the night to go," Erik mumbled, half asleep.

Ben's low chuckle still zinged through Erik's body. "That's all right. We've got time to get it right."

They barely managed to get cleaned up and into bed. Ben curled around Erik, his arm over Erik's chest, pulling him close. "Go to sleep," Ben murmured. "I'm here. And I'm going to do everything I can to keep you safe. You have my word."

————

Erik slept better than he expected, something he felt sure was due to the handsome, inked man in his bed. He still couldn't believe Ben had heard his confession and stuck around, but if for once fate chose to smile on him, Erik wasn't going to turn down a gift.

He wished they could pick up with sexy times that got derailed the night before, but he'd made appointments with some of the people Susan had recommended, including Monty Clark, the medium. Ben must have felt him stir, because he opened his eyes and blinked a few times, looking adorably rumpled and sleepy.

"Going somewhere? I had plans."

Erik leaned over and kissed him, slow and gentle. "Unfortunately, I've got appointments. But I also have that cream pie, and I'm hoping to entice you to come back tonight."

"Told you, I'm staying until you throw me out," Ben said. "Not going to leave you alone at night." He stretched, arching his back, showing off all those muscles, and Erik had to remind his stiffening cock that they had work to do.

"I'm fine with that," Erik replied.

"Good to know." Ben rolled to his feet. "As it turns out, I have appointments, too. I need to find out when we can fix that closet. I can't rent the place if it's covered with police tape. And I really should spend some time in the office."

"When I get back to the store, I want to have another look at the papers that were in the clock. And the stuff in Justin Kramer's box. I think we've missed something. I just don't know what."

"I was going to work a few angles from the investigator side," Ben said. "Good thing I kept my license."

Much as Erik would have liked to shower together, his bathroom wasn't designed for that. They moved around each other with an easiness that surprised Erik, like they'd been doing this for a lot longer. He liked that, and decided to take it as a good omen.

"I'm out of eggs," Erik confessed when Ben joined him in the kitchen. "But I have frozen waffles."

"I ate too many of those growing up. I'll just stick with coffee." Ben glanced at the drawer where Erik had put his gun. "I was serious about carrying, until we know who we're up against."

Erik nodded. "I will. I hate it, but I will."

"It won't be for long," Ben said. He drank his coffee, washed out the mug, and left it on the counter. "Be careful today."

Erik stretched up to kiss him. "You, too." He tried to put all the feelings he wasn't quite ready to say into the kiss. *I'm worried about you. I need you. I think I love you.*

"See you for dinner," he said, walking Ben to the door. "Text me if anything interesting happens—like you find another skeleton."

"Believe me, if that happens, you'll be the first to know."

———

Erik's first appointment was with Mort Jenner, a retiree in his late seventies who had been hotel security for the Commodore Wilson during the Chason and Ambrose years.

"You want my opinion? They were both scum," Jenner said. "Cheating, lying scum. Just packaged a little different, you know what I mean? You can tell a lot about people by how they treat the little guys. Chason and Ambrose, they were all smiles and nicey-nice when the cameras were on or they had an audience. But behind the scenes, whoo-boy. Whole different story."

"What do you mean?" Erik wasn't taking notes. Afterward, he'd jot down the key points, a skill he'd honed in his past career. That left him free to give Jenner his full attention, which usually prompted better information.

"I mean, they grabbed the waitresses—and some of the waiters, too. Wouldn't take no for an answer. Drank too much, screamed at the staff if everything wasn't just so." Jenner shook his head. "And the drugs? You'da thought it was one of those fancy New York City nightclubs where the stars go. Pills, blow, pot—everything and plenty of it."

Erik knew it was easier to get away with all that before cell phones and social media. Before the internet bypassed media gatekeepers and made whistleblowing easier. Not that it still didn't happen, but it was harder to hide.

"So everyone knew, and no one did anything?"

Jenner shrugged. "There's a difference between 'knowing' and 'proving.' And both guys were mobbed up. People thought twice about crossing them. They paid off the cops. Made sure their conventions brought in lots of money for the town. Folks didn't want to rock the boat. Things were different back then."

"What happened when Chason disappeared?"

Jenner stared off into the distance and sipped his coffee. "Chason was an odd duck. Saw Commies under every rock. Told everyone the Ruskies were coming, and that it was part of the tribulations sent by God to punish the wicked. But his flock could make sure they and theirs were protected if they just gave him enough money."

He snorted. "And they believed that! He was so looney the feds yanked his radio license, so he bought himself an old barge and set up a station just outside of U.S. waters, where he could still broadcast, ranting and raving to his heart's content, and they couldn't stop him. He wanted to be a TV star, but there wasn't any Boob Tube, or whatever the kids watch these days."

"YouTube," Erik supplied.

"Yeah, that. Can't get my grandson to put down the damn phone long enough to go fishing, but he'll watching fishing videos all day long." Jenner's fingers twitched, like he was itching for a cigarette. "Anyhow, Chason spent money like my ex-wife. Expensive suits. Fancy cars. Diamond rings. And he dropped a boatload on trying to fix up that old place, but it was a money pit. I guess it all caught up to him. I heard he owed taxes, and he didn't pay his Mob construction buddies. So he skipped town. I imagine he's been down in Argentina all these years, laughing at the chumps he left behind."

Erik suspected Chason had stayed a lot closer to home, but he didn't say anything. "And Ambrose?"

"Geez. That guy. Drugs. Booze. Hookers. Orgies. And then he'd go on TV and be this understanding, soft-spoken guy with all the answers, when we'd all seen him throw plates at the housekeeper and pass out drunk on the patio. Just another phony. He got away with it for a while, but when it all started to close in on him, he checked out."

"The people Chason and Ambrose paid off—are any of them still around?"

Jenner shrugged. "I imagine some are. I'm no spring chicken, so they'd be around my age or older. I never knew who they were, just that payola had to happen, or anyone with eyes in their heads would have shut them down quick enough to make your head spin."

He looked Erik up and down. "So what's your game? You come to town and start digging up dirt? What for? Nothing good can come of it."

"Just interested in local history," Erik replied. "I'm in the antiques business. I figure pieces from the Commodore will turn up for sale sooner or later, and I want to know the story."

Jenner looked down at his coffee. "About ten years after the Commodore closed, there was a big shake-up with the police department. Never did hear all the details, but they got rid of a lot of bad seeds. Fired 'em or made 'em retire. That was around the time the feds came down hard on the Jersey Mob. Those guys never go away, but they know how to go to ground. As far as I ever heard, the town's been pretty clean ever since."

"That's good to know. Thank you for talking to me, Mr. Jenner."

"Eh, not many people want to hear an old guy ramble on about the past. Now git. I think I feel a nap coming on."

Erik knew when he'd been dismissed. He left a tip for the server and walked out of Crumble, carrying what remained of his latte. Jenner's stories had squared pretty well with what Cheryl Sparks had told him earlier that morning. Cheryl had been the head of housekeeping at the Commodore during the Chason and Ambrose years. She hadn't said anything about Mob connections, but she did talk about how both Chason and Ambrose had "rough" friends, men from the city who scared her. He'd wanted to go talk to Sherri and Jo at The Spike, but they couldn't fit him in for a couple of days, so Erik figured he'd talk with everyone else first.

*It's been almost twenty years since the Commodore got torn down. Why is all this stuff surfacing now?*

Erik glanced at his phone. Time to go see Monty Clark.

Cape May Lighthouse stood tall and proud, still a working navigational light after one hundred and fifty years. The white cylinder with its red top was a local landmark. Erik stood at the bottom and craned his neck to see the top. The wind whipped around him, stronger here at the tip of the cape, and the sea stretched toward the horizon.

Being the park ranger here wasn't exactly as isolated as the lighthouse keepers of old had been, but in a tourist town the job was probably one of the least social. Maybe that made it perfect for a medium, someone with reason to want a break from the chatter of the living and the dead.

The parking lot had only two cars, and Erik guessed the drivers were probably locals come for their daily walk or some birdwatching. They sure weren't here to picnic, he thought, pulling his jacket closed. The wind still had a bite to it.

He headed to the ranger station and knocked on the door. Erik wasn't sure what he had expected, but the large man who opened the door looked more like a pro wrestler than Erik's mental picture of a ranger or a medium. "Monty Clark?"

The man cocked his head to one side. "You're the guy Susan Hendricks sent over?"

Erik held out his hand. "Erik Mitchell. New owner of Trinkets."

"Come on in." Monty led the way into the cabin-style building that consisted of a large community room with a small office to one side. Erik studied Monty as he followed him. The guy had to be at least six-foot-four and he was built like a tank. Monty had short dark hair, but if he ever decided to grow it long and rock a beard, he'd have the biker look dead to rights.

"Mrs. Hendricks is a good lady. I grew up with her oldest son. We go way back. So if she vouches for you, that counts for a lot with me."

"Susan's been a godsend," Erik agreed. "I moved in and she kind of adopted me."

Monty laughed. "Yep. I believe it. Nice to know some things never change. So…how can I help you?"

Erik wasn't sure how to broach the topic. Would Monty mind discussing his mediumship while he was on the clock with his ranger job?

"Let me guess. You've got ghost trouble."

Erik nodded, relieved that Monty spoke first. "I can see ghosts, but that's it. I don't get messages from them, and I don't know if they can hear me. But I was handling some items that came from the old Commodore Wilson Hotel, and I saw the ghost of Vincente Cafaro."

Monty's eyebrows rose at that. "Well, well. He gets around for a dead guy."

"What do you mean?"

"His ghost showed up about four days ago. First time I'd seen him. Which is odd, because I thought I'd run into all of Cape May's dead residents," Monty replied.

"What would make a ghost suddenly appear like that?"

"Could be any number of things. An anniversary. Changing something the ghost was attached to. Handling an object that has resonance with the spirit. We'll probably never know."

"Did he…say…anything to you?"

Monty gave a rueful grin. "Just because I can hear some ghosts, doesn't mean that all ghosts try to talk. Some of them can't—there isn't enough left of who they were. Others have been dead long enough, they don't remember much about their lives except for the incident that caused their deaths, or whatever unfinished business binds them here. Cafaro's been dead for what, over sixty years? A ghost can fade as the years go by. Some do, some don't. I've never been able to tell what makes the difference."

"Did you sense anything from him?"

Monty shrugged. "Besides the fact that he was pissed someone blew him sky high?" He paused. "I don't think the apparition is dangerous. He didn't strike me as vengeful. Maybe more of a...warning."

"Have you had any other ghosts from the Commodore's past show up recently?"

Monty leaned back in his chair. "Funny you say that. I was just finishing up with a scout group that was here for a hike, and I saw this ghost that I didn't recognize. Then he turned around, and it's that preacher, Chason, who went missing." He chuckled. "I mean, it's been a long time, so it's probably not a stretch that he's dead. But he looked just like the pictures I've seen. Except..."

"What?"

Monty's expression darkened. "The back of his head was bloody. So I don't think he died of old age."

*Well, maybe that confirms whose bones were in that closet.*

"And no, he didn't tell me who killed him. But he looked seriously pissed. Can't say I blame him." Monty gave Erik a look. "Did he try to hurt you? Because I can try to send him on if he's dangerous."

Erik shook his head. "No. I haven't seen him. And at least now I won't freak out—quite so much—if I do. I just don't think it's a coincidence, Cafaro and Chason showing up like this."

Monty had been fiddling with a pencil while they spoke, a nervous habit. Erik wondered if the big man got jumpy around people or had a touch of social anxiety. If so, a job that let him be out in nature might be a perfect fit.

"I've lived here all my life," Monty said, still turning the pencil back and forth between his fingers. "Some local ghosts have always hung around. Like my own little spooky gang." The self-deprecation in Monty's voice told Erik that not everyone had easily accepted him or his abilities. "I didn't pick them, but they don't hurt anything, and they're not bad company. They don't usually say much. But lately, they've been around more than usual."

"Protecting you?"

"Maybe. Or scared. Cafaro and Chason weren't nice people when they were alive. People don't change after they die—they just get more so. Cape May's ghosts are a pretty stable bunch. Most of them have been here for a long time. They don't hurt anyone. They just don't want to move on. It's a nice place. I can't blame them." Monty's pencil twirled faster. "I keep an eye out when there's a violent death or a bad accident, and if I sense a vengeful spirit, I take care of it. Unofficially, of course."

"Of course."

"I don't know why Cafaro and Chason showed up. But whatever drew them back, I don't think it's a good thing. I'd take it as a warning if I were you," Monty said, growing very serious. "I am."

Erik shook his head. "I'm not sure what to do. A warning only helps if you know what you're being warned about. Someone tried to break into my shop last night. But I've got no idea who. So I wish the ghosts would quit with the charades. Aren't they supposed to be able to fog up windows and write messages?"

Monty laughed. "Only on TV. It would take a scary powerful ghost to do that. Be careful what you wish for."

Erik got up. "Thanks for seeing me. If any of your ghost buddies decide to start whispering, please call me." He passed Monty his card. "I'd really appreciate it."

Monty nodded. "I can't guarantee anything, but I'll get in touch if I find out something." He met Erik's gaze. "You have a gift. Not just the ghosts. Something else, too. It's real, and you have it for a reason. Don't hide from it. Opening yourself up to it might just save your life someday."

"I'm not sure how to do that, but I'm getting the feeling that I'll need to learn," Erik replied.

Erik had one more contact to meet, Aggie Fletcher, who had worked at the Commodore Wilson's front desk during the Ambrose years. As he drove the short stretch back into town, he kept thinking about what Monty told him, and what he'd learned from Jenner and Sparks. Chason and Ambrose had been dirty. Maybe in a different way from Cafaro, but ultimately all of them were in deep with the Mob.

They'd found a skeleton that might be Chason's. Erik had

suspected what Monty confirmed, and he didn't doubt that the crime lab would back that up. He had the clock linked to Cafaro, with the damning items inside. But so far, nothing from Ambrose had surfaced.

Then again, he hadn't finished going through Justin Kramer's box.

Erik wanted to go back to the shop and dig into the box, but he'd already set things up with Aggie and couldn't reschedule now. He'd arranged to meet her at Crumble, a good neutral spot where they could talk. All the nearby parking spots were taken, so Erik had to parallel park across the street. He checked both ways, then jogged toward the coffee shop.

Tires squealed as a battered white van bore down on Erik. Erik dove out of the way with seconds to spare, landing hard on the hood of a parked car and rolling across to the other side. He landed in a squat, ribs and back aching, just as the car alarm went off.

"Are you all right?" A woman helped Erik to his feet. Passers-by had stopped, and people started coming out of the coffee shop.

"I called the police," a man said. Erik's heart sank. So much for not calling attention to himself.

"You'd better sit down." The woman who had helped him off the ground accompanied him to one of Crumble's outdoor tables and pulled out a chair. Erik sat as the adrenaline hit him, leaving him shaky.

"That van was going way too fast," someone said.

"It looked like it was *trying* to hit you."

"What the hell is wrong with people? That driver needs to lose his license."

The small group of bystanders buzzed about the incident but didn't crowd Erik, for which he was grateful. He didn't think he'd broken any ribs, but he bet he'd have a hell of a bruise tomorrow. *It could have been so much worse.*

"All right folks, the show's over." The speaker had a note of authority in his voice. "If you actually saw what happened, stick around. I'll need to take your statement. If you have video, I want to see it. Otherwise, I need to ask you to clear the sidewalk."

The crowd parted, and Erik recognized the speaker. Officer Dorchester. The cop seemed to recognize Erik in the same moment.

"Seriously, Mitchell? What's with you and Nolan?" Dorchester asked. "This was a quiet little town until the two of you moved in."

"You'd have had a bigger mess if that van had run me over," Erik snapped. "Because that's what it was trying to do."

Dorchester listened as Erik told his story. "It happened so fast. I only got a glance at the driver. Hat and sunglasses. I couldn't even tell you if it was male or female," Erik concluded.

"Jesus. Did anyone know you were going to be here?"

"I did, officer. We were supposed to meet up for coffee. But I swear I didn't tell anyone." Aggie Fletcher had come to stand next to Erik.

"Meet why?"

"I'm a consultant for Jaxon Davies's retrospective on the Commodore Wilson," Erik replied. "And since I'm new in town, I thought it would be a good idea to talk to people who remembered working there, to get the vibe."

"This have anything to do with that break-in attempt last night?"

Erik shrugged. "No idea, officer." He hoped he sounded sincere.

"Stay put," Dorchester ordered. He moved away, toward the willing witnesses, and started taking names and making notes.

Aggie's hand rested lightly on Erik's shoulder. "Do you need a doctor?" she asked, looking at him with concern.

"I don't think so. Although I'm probably going to be real sore tomorrow."

"You're lucky you have good reflexes."

Erik stared down the road in the direction the van had disappeared. "Yeah. Real lucky."

By the time Dorchester finished talking to the witnesses, Erik had already rescheduled with Aggie. He just wanted to get back to the shop before he stiffened up and couldn't move.

"Any idea who tried to run you down?" Dorchester asked. "Because everyone who saw it said the van sped up and aimed right for you."

That sent a chill down Erik's spine. Bad enough to think that himself, but hearing it confirmed just made it worse. "No," he replied.

Nobody from his past should be anywhere close to Cape May. And for as much trouble as the old clock had caused, neither Erik nor Ben had made any connections between it and anyone still alive to care about old scandals.

"I'm going to drive you home, and you're going to let me," Dorchester said. "You can send your boyfriend down for your car. And until we figure this out, you need to assume someone wants to kill you, and act accordingly."

Erik was too sore to argue and was just glad Dorchester let him ride up front, so he didn't look like he'd been arrested. Susan must have seen the police car pull up, because she met him on the front walk.

"What happened? Are you all right?"

"Good to see you, Mrs. Hendricks," Dorchester said. "I think Mr. Mitchell here might benefit from a cup of hot tea."

"I can handle that, officer," Susan replied. She turned her attention back to Erik. "Come on. Let's get you inside."

"Thanks, Officer Dorchester," Erik said as he hobbled into the shop. He didn't even want to think about going up the steps to his apartment right now. He followed Susan into the break room, where she was already filling an electric kettle with water.

"What happened?"

"A beat-up white van tried to run me over outside of Crumble."

Susan looked at him, aghast. "Holy shit. Are you all right?"

Erik winced. "I didn't break anything, I don't think. But I bounced off a parked car. So I'm sore, and I imagine I'll turn all kinds of pretty colors."

He could almost see Susan going into "mom" mode. "Sit down. I can manage to make tea. Do you have ibuprofen?"

"There's a bottle in the cabinet."

Before long, Susan returned with two steaming cups and pushed one toward Erik. She slid a couple of caplets to him as well. "Here. It'll help. Do you need some sports cream? It might take the soreness out."

Erik shook his head. Bad enough he was going to move like an old man; he didn't need to smell like one, too. At this rate, he and Ben were never going to actually get to that rain check.

Susan frowned. "You said it was an old white van?"

"Yeah. Like a delivery van. But it wasn't in good shape."

"I saw an old white van parked down the street when I went for a walk last night. I figured someone was getting a late delivery."

"It's probably stolen. Whoever's involved would be stupid to use their own vehicle," Erik replied.

"Do you feel up to going through the box?" Susan asked. "Or would you rather go lie down?"

"I'm too wired right now to rest," Erik admitted.

"What about calling your sweetie?" she asked with a smile.

Erik shook his head. "Ben's coming over for dinner. He needs to be in the office. All the excitement is over. I'll tell him about it when he gets here." He'd already distracted Ben from his business, and if Erik wanted Ben to change his mind about leaving, he needed to let the man handle his affairs.

"You really like him." Susan's eyes glowed with interest.

Erik nodded. "Yeah. I do. Maybe…too much."

Susan tilted her head, confused. "Too much?"

Erik felt overwhelmed by the craziness of the past few days. "We haven't known each other very long. I mean—it's been less than a week? And there's been so much going on—"

"Isn't it good to have someone to see it through with you?" Susan asked in a gentle tone.

"I guess I'm just afraid. I don't have a successful track record when it comes to relationships."

"Well, it seems like he's already stuck by you through some scary stuff," she said. "I saw the police cars and heard a little about last night."

That surprised Erik. "How?"

Susan smiled. "This is a small town. I have friends on the force. My point is, have a little faith. Ben stuck around when someone shot at you. That's a good sign."

"I hope so. Because I don't think I've ever felt like this about anyone before." Erik didn't usually talk so openly about his private life. Maybe it was the near-death experience, or just the aftermath of a wild few days, but Susan was easy to confide in, and he had to admit he didn't mind a bit of mothering. Was thirty-five too old for that? He'd never really had much of his parents' attention, so he couldn't say. But right now, her friendly caring filled a void.

"Come on. Let's play detective. It'll take your mind off things. And I'll get you some ice for those bruises."

Erik and Susan both put on cotton gloves to avoid damaging any of the fragile paper items. Since he'd handled everything once already, Erik wasn't afraid of getting a vision, but he also didn't want to try his luck.

Anything that might suit Jaxon's retrospective, Erik set to one side. Items too damaged to be easily salvaged went in another pile. Pieces like the random dinner knife, china cup, and ashtrays needed to be appraised, so they were grouped together. By the time they neared the bottom of the pile, several hours had passed.

Susan paged through a magazine from 1977 with a feature article on the Commodore. Erik sorted through more cocktail napkins, menus, and event fliers. Given how large the old hotel loomed in the local imagination, he guessed there would probably be interest in the pieces. Thankfully, none of them seemed to have ghosts attached.

A sealed envelope at the bottom caught his attention. "Hold up. What's this?" he murmured.

"My last words," Erik read the handwritten address aloud. "By Kendry Ambrose."

Susan's head came up at that. "What?"

Erik stared at the envelope in his hand. Just with handling, the sealed flap had come loose. "Do you think it's the real thing?"

"You can get a handwriting expert to authenticate it. What are you waiting for—read it!"

Erik might have hesitated if the envelope had remained tightly closed. But since the old glue had failed, he didn't see the harm in having a look. Maybe when Susan wasn't around, he'd try handling the suicide note without his gloves, but right now getting a vision of Ambrose's bloody ghost was the last thing Erik wanted to deal with.

"Fuck you all," Erik read aloud. He raised an eyebrow. That hardly fit his impression of Ambrose as a serene, if debauched, New Age guru. "You're nothing but leeches and parasites, and you won't be happy until you've sucked away the last of my money and my life."

"A special fuck-you to my ex, Christine. Did you sleep with my lawyer before or after you won that big alimony payment? The laugh's on you—I can't pay you or him. So I hope you enjoyed his shriveled dick. Be sure you get tested—you're not the first mosh pit Molly he's banged."

Erik paused. "Wow. From here on down, he starts naming names. His drug dealer. His 'fixer' who made 'problems' go away. His 'crooked' accountant. His mistress. And the construction company he owed money to—that he said let the Mob get their 'hooks' into him."

Susan met his gaze, worried. "Ambrose shot himself in 1995–not really very long ago. Some—maybe most—of those people on that list are probably still alive. I think maybe you should turn that over to the police, and we'll forget we ever read it."

"Yeah," Erik said, tucking the papers back into the envelope, but not before he photographed the letter with his phone. "I think that might be a good idea."

Erik buried the letter under a pile of old menus. Susan rinsed out their mugs and insisted on helping Erik close up the shop. She refused to let him talk her out of helping him up the steps to his apartment. As soon as Susan left, Erik hobbled to the window to make sure she got home safely. Then he pulled out his phone and called Ben.

"Hi there, handsome. I was going to offer to pick up dinner, but I didn't know if you already had something planned."

Erik shifted and bit back a groan as sore muscles cramped. "Takeout would be fantastic. I don't care what. Just…come as soon as you can."

He didn't need to see Ben's face to pick up the change in his boyfriend's mood. "What's wrong?"

"Someone tried to run me over. I'll tell you all about it when you get here."

"Fuck. There's a good Chinese place that's fast. I'll call in the order and be over there in twenty minutes, tops." Ben hesitated. "Are you okay?"

"I will be when you get here." Erik hurt too much and felt too raw to play games. "I need you."

TWELVE

## BEN

"What happened?" Ben had barely made it through the door when he put the takeout bag on the table and stopped to look Erik up and down.

"I jumped out of the way of a van that tried to run over me, and ended up rolling off a parked car," Erik replied with a wince.

Ben felt a surge of anger and a jolt of protectiveness. His heartbeat sped up, and his mind presented ugly pictures of how it could have gone wrong. "Let's eat before everything gets cold," he said. "And then I want to hear all about it."

The food from Canton Festival was always good, fast, and cheap—a difficult combination to find. Since it had been up to him to order for both of them, Ben had stuck to basics. Chicken fried rice. Egg rolls. Beef and broccoli. And two servings of wonton soup, because nothing smoothed over the rough edges of a bad day better.

Ben felt gratified when Erik enjoyed the food and praised his choices. It didn't take long for them to demolish the meals, leaving no leftovers. He also didn't miss the stiff way Erik held himself, or the near stumble when Erik got up and sore muscles protested.

"How about if we go stretch out on the couch, and you fill me in," Ben said.

Erik flashed him an appreciative grin that made Ben's heart flutter. Dammit, how did Erik undo him like that with just a smile? And how was it possible to be so head-over-heels in such a short time?

They got comfortable on Erik's big leather couch, which if the back cushions were arranged just right was the size of a twin bed. Ben maneuvered so that his back was against the cushions and Erik lay fitted against him, safe in his arms. He could smell Erik's shampoo, the combination of scents that was so uniquely him, and pressed a kiss to the back of Erik's head. "Tell me."

Ben listened as Erik recapped the conversations he'd had with Susan's contacts, including Monty. He tensed when Erik told him about the van and its homicidal driver, and Dorchester's quick appearance on the scene. Susan's comment about having seen the van earlier filled Ben with misgivings. Finally, Erik told him about the Ambrose letter, and those misgivings turned to fear.

"Wow," Ben said. "I think we stepped in it, without meaning to."

"Yeah. I'm just not sure who to blame, because Chason and Cafaro died a long time ago."

"Ambrose didn't, relatively speaking. Susan was right—those people he named in the letter might have a lot invested in not being called to account."

"Running me over seems like a messy way to handle it." Erik shifted his weight and grimaced. "Sorry. Stiff—and not in a good way."

Ben gently peeled back Erik's shirt and caught his breath at the red skin just beginning to mottle in darker shades. "You really slammed into that parked car." Erik's bruises looked almost as bad as his own from hitting the window seat.

"Beats being roadkill. Although it means an extension on that rain check. I can't think of a position—top, bottom, or side—that wouldn't hurt."

Ben stroked his fingers through Erik's soft hair. "That's all right. I can wait. You're worth waiting for." When had he gotten downright sappy? With Erik, apparently, because Ben sometimes didn't recognize the words that came out of his own mouth.

"Sorry," Erik said.

"Shh. You're safe. That's what matters." If the van had hit Erik, they'd have had this conversation in a hospital room, assuming Erik was able to talk at all. Knowing that he'd almost lost Erik, before they really had a chance to get started, made Ben's heart ache.

"I don't know what to do," Erik said in a hushed voice. "I'm new in town. I don't know how much we can trust the cops. Dorchester—that guy shows up every time there's a problem. It's spooky."

"It's a small police force," Ben reminded him. "So odds are good you'd see the same cops over and over. It's not like a big city where there are precincts."

"I don't think he likes me."

"I'm pretty sure he doesn't like me," Ben replied. "It's been a long while since I was a beat cop, but we always were suspicious if the same people kept showing up. It usually meant trouble."

"I just feel like this is one of those times where you can't stuff the genie back into the bottle. We didn't start out looking to cause problems or dig up dirt. The dirt kinda chose us. But we can't un-know what we know. So if someone is afraid of old secrets coming to light, their best bet is shutting us up. Permanently."

If he hadn't heard Erik talk about his old job, Ben might have joked about him watching too much TV. But Erik had a point, Ben reluctantly conceded. He just wasn't sure how to keep them both safe.

"What are you doing tomorrow?"

"Inventory. And there's one more person Susan wanted me to talk with. She's got an…unusual…perspective."

"What kind of unusual?"

"She's a witch." Erik tensed as if he was waiting for Ben to laugh.

"You mean like Wiccan? My neighbor in Newark was in a book club with a couple of Wiccans. Or you mean rhymes-with-bitch?"

"According to Susan, more of the 'eye of newt' variety." Erik kept his voice low, although it was just the two of them. "In the art community, there were always pieces and relics that people said were cursed. Like the Hope Diamond. We'd have never admitted it to a reporter, but everyone who had been in the business for a while took those stories seriously. The piece that was being handed over in my last sting was said to have supernatural power. And look what happened."

"You think something we've found might be cursed?"

"Well, the clock is definitely haunted, and so is the skeleton. Given the Commodore's bad luck, I thought it wouldn't hurt to ask Alessia and see what she says."

Ben believed in ghosts. He didn't have to stretch his imagination far to accept that Erik could see things from the past when he touched certain objects. That was just like a different kind of haunt. But witches? Maybe it was his Catholic upbringing, but the idea made him uncomfortable.

"Do you think witches are real?" Ben asked.

"I think that some people have abilities that aren't easy to measure. Superstitious people slap labels on what they fear. But I promise to end the interview if Alessia wants to sacrifice a goat and read the entrails."

Ben chuckled. "Good. I guess there's no harm in seeing what she says. I'm more worried about you being out and about."

"I can't stay locked in here forever," Erik pointed out. "And even if I did—someone's tried to break in once. Next time, they'll know what to do differently. If they figure out I've seen Ambrose's letter, it'll be worse."

"Just...be careful. Take your gun. You said you had martial arts training. What kind?"

Erik shrugged. "I'm hardly a black belt. The agents taught me some self-defense moves. A little Krav Maga, a little Systema. I liked it mostly for the workout. The agents might have been straight—but they were hot."

Ben felt a flare of jealousy surge through him at the idea of Erik grappling with musclebound agents on sweaty gym mats. The response was so visceral, it took him by surprise.

"I trained with Tae Kwon Do and Systema. I had to be able to hold my own in a street fight," Ben admitted. "Undercover, you know? Can't say I'm competition-level, but I did okay when I needed to."

"Just...text me when you head over, and when you come back,"

Ben continued. "I have a meeting with the bank about the funding for our remodeling projects. But I want to know you're safe."

"I promise," Erik said. "And you need to be careful, too. Whoever's watching has to know we're together. Heck, *Dorchester* knows we're together."

Together. Ben liked the sound of that. *For how long?* a traitorous voice whispered in the back of his mind.

They watched TV and cuddled on the couch, until both men had fallen asleep. "Come on," Ben said when a loud theme song woke him. "You'll be even stiffer if you sleep here. Let's go to bed."

Erik might not have woken completely, but he managed to walk with Ben's guidance. Ben got him to the bed and gently stripped off Erik's clothes, angry all over again when he saw the bruising. He rolled Erik onto the mattress and covered him, then cleaned up in the bathroom and crawled in next to him. At least this time, he thought as he drifted off, he'd remembered to bring a change of clothes.

---

In the morning, Ben woke up spooning Erik, not quite touching but close enough he could inhale the smell of soap, fabric softener, and shampoo that made him think about the new man in his life. He resolutely ignored his morning wood and leaned over to kiss Erik on the cheek.

"How about you get some rest? I'll bring you some water and Advil, and get the coffee started. Then I'll let myself out, and you can sleep in."

"Dinner?" Erik mumbled, bleary-eyed with sleep.

Ben kissed him again. "Sure thing. I'll get takeout again. How about lobster rolls?"

"Just want you," Erik's drowsy voice and tousled hair was adorable.

"Want you, too," Ben told him. "See you tonight."

He got a quick shower and rubbed one out, imagining having Erik writhing beneath him while they fucked. Or feeling Erik drive into him, over and over. Both fantasies got him going, since imagining a flip fuck tripped all the right triggers. He came, doing his best to muffle the way he called out Erik's name. The real thing would be so much better, and Ben hoped their streak of bad luck and interruptions would end soon and let them cash in those rain checks.

Ben double-checked that the door was locked as he closed it behind him. His phone rang before he made it to the car. To his surprise, it was Cooper.

"Didn't expect to hear from you," he said as he got into the Mustang. He'd driven over, because the Chinese restaurant was too far to walk.

"Heard about you finding that skeleton. A friend downtown tells me it matches Hank Chason's dental records. So congrats on solving an old cold case."

Ben should have felt more excited than he did, but having had both Erik and Monty confirm the identity already took the punch out of the big reveal. "Huh," he replied. "Well, didn't see that coming. And you can't say it's solved. What's open is who killed him."

"Everyone thought the SOB was living the good life down in the islands. Turns out he never left town."

"Life's a bitch."

"Ain't that the truth," Cooper agreed. "I might actually have a lead on who killed Chason."

"There had to be a connection to the house," Ben replied, putting the phone on hands-free as he drove back to the rental office. "Hard to hide covering over a closet if you were just renting the room. But so far, I can't connect Chason to the owners."

"It's the remodeling company," Cooper told him. "I pulled building permits around the time Chason went missing. And there was a permit out for remodeling at that address by a KTR Construction Company. It wouldn't be difficult to sell the owner a line of bullshit about needing to box in some water pipes or some such and have an excuse to seal up the closet with Chason inside."

"Hell of a smell, though."

"Maybe the owners weren't going to be back for months. That happens around here a lot," Cooper said. "But here's the kicker—KTR

Construction also had contracts with the Commodore, and the 'R' stands for Rugieri, as in Al Rugieri, who was big in the Jersey Shore Mob at that time."

"You think Rugieri had his hooks into Ambrose as well?"

"Since KTR had done work in the past for the hotel, I'd say almost certainly."

"Where's Rugieri now?" Ben asked as he turned into his lot and parked.

"Got put away for racketeering in 2002. Died in jail a year later."

Ben drummed his fingers on the steering wheel. Cooper's information tied all three murders up with one bow. That should have been cause for celebration. But if Rugieri was dead, then who was behind the break-ins? Or the van that tried to run down Erik?

"I wanted to pass that info along as soon as I heard about it, because I know you're out of the game now, and figured you'd want to get back to business."

"Yeah. Sure. Thanks."

"And, I've got a tip for you, but you didn't hear it from me."

"Sure. What?" Ben asked.

"You know I've still got some friends downtown. So I was out at Abbott's having a couple of beers with my buddies, and one of them lets slip that they're investigating that new guy, the one with the antique shop? Apparently, he ran out on a murder rap over in Antwerp—wherever the hell that is—and the European feds have been looking for him. Dirty as all get out, but a good con man. They think he was behind a slew of art thefts. The murder rap was just the icing on the cake. I guess he figured he could con the folks in a little place like Cape May and we'd never be the wiser."

"I've got to go," Ben said, getting out of the car and nearly dropping his keys with the way his hands shook. "Let me know if you hear anything else." He ended the call before Cooper had the chance to respond.

Ben let himself in through the back door to the rental office, barely waved to Jenny at the front desk, and closed the door to his private space. He sat at his desk, dizzy and cold all over.

*No. That can't be true. That's not the way Erik said it all happened.* Erik, an international art thief? A killer? He didn't want to believe it. His heart refused.

*I've known him for what, a week? Took me a lot longer than that to find out what Caleb was really like.* Ben felt like he'd had too much to drink, but not in a good way. More like a bad drunk, where nightmares came true and nothing was as it seemed.

Ben hadn't had any problems with the idea that Erik could see ghosts, or even glimpse an object's past. But his easy acceptance of magic, witches, curses…that was out of Ben's wheelhouse. Normal people didn't believe in that kind of stuff outside of TV shows—did they? Ben's head spun and his gut pitched. Had Erik played him? And all this time, Ben had been falling in love.

Ben's phone buzzed, and he saw a text from Erik. *Going to see Alessia. Can't wait for dinner.*

Ben started to respond on reflex and stopped. He needed time to think. God, he wanted to find a way to disprove everything Cooper had told him. Ben wished to hell he'd never picked up the ex-cop's call. Then he could have gone about the day trading flirty texts with his boyfriend, had a cozy dinner and maybe some sex later.

*If Cooper's telling the truth, it was all going to crash and burn some time. Maybe it's better to find out before I get any deeper.* Deeper? Fuck that. Ben had already fallen in love with Erik. And he'd thought Erik felt the same way.

Was it just part of a con? A cover to hide from either the European agents or the Russian Mob?

Ben realized he was holding his breath and made himself breathe while he tried to get control of his emotions. Whoever had been behind the attempted break-ins, Ben knew it wasn't the Russians. They were pros. They'd have been in and out without leaving a trace. The van attack also seemed sloppy for the Russians. If they wanted someone dead, a sniper would make it happen. Or poison. They seemed to like that. Maybe someone was sending Erik a message.

Something didn't fit, but Ben no longer trusted his ability to be objective. He'd only intended to have a bit of summer fun, a tumble in the sack with a handsome guy. Instead, he'd lost his heart, and maybe, his mind.

"Think, Nolan," he muttered. "Treat it like a case. Don't go haring off on one informant's tip. Dig a little deeper. Validate. Work your network."

Ben still had resources as a licensed investigator. That included being able to tap into "most wanted" lists from law enforcement agencies around the country—and all over the world. It didn't necessarily clear Erik if Ben couldn't find his name on a list; an investigation at that level could be confidential. But it was somewhere to start.

His phone buzzed with a new text. It took effort not to respond, but Ben needed distance. *Just for a while,* he told himself. *If I'm lucky, I can prove Cooper's wrong, and have it all straightened out by dinner. And then I'll beg forgiveness for not answering.*

He didn't want to think about what the outcome would be if he found out Cooper was right. No matter how much Ben liked Cape May, he couldn't stay, not if it meant running into Erik and not being with him. *If Cooper's right, Erik probably wouldn't be here. He'd be in jail, somewhere in Europe.* Just the thought of that made Ben's chest tighten.

Ben thought it had hurt when Caleb left him—and it had. But now he could see that he and Caleb had been drifting apart for a long time. Too many undercover assignments, gone too long from home without being able to stay in touch, too many lonely nights. It shouldn't have been a surprise that Caleb walked out. Almost all the undercover cops he knew were either divorced or never-married. Straight or gay, they got by on one-night stands and hookups. It was a lone wolf existence.

If Ben had been a lone wolf at one time, he'd finally decided he wanted a mate. A pack. And wouldn't it be just like fate to dangle what he wanted and jerk it away?

*Focus. The sooner you know, the sooner you can deal with it—either way,* the voice in his head told him.

Keeping busy kept Ben from feeling the pain. He ran a background check on Robert Pettis, the old guy who had owned Trinkets, and one on Erik. Just for the hell of it, Ben ran a check on Cooper, too. After all, he'd only had Tony Basalmo's word that Cooper was a good guy.

Then Ben remembered the conversation this morning, and did a search on Officer Dorchester, too.

The reports would take a few hours to process. Ben resisted the urge to pace. A news update dinged on his laptop, and Ben glanced at the headline, then stopped and stared.

*"Cape May man found murdered in gangland hit,"* the crawl at the bottom of a grainy video clip read. Ben turned on the audio.

"Justin Kramer of Cape May was found dead by authorities in Wildwood, who say the man's death may be gang-related," the anchor said. The video showed a dark parking lot by what looked like an abandoned shopping mall. "Police haven't released details, except to say that Kramer did not appear to be the victim of a random robbery. If you have any information—"

Ben toggled off the audio and stared dumbfounded at the screen. Justin Kramer had sold the box of Commodore Wilson memorabilia to Erik. Right before his house was broken into and set on fire. No wonder Justin ran. But whoever was chasing him had apparently caught up.

He did an internet search on "Justin Kramer" and found plenty of hits, all of them completely mundane. The man's Facebook page had a collection of memes, funny videos, and pictures of the beach. Justin hadn't posted often, but his most recent posts had talked about coming to Cape May to deal with his grandfather's house. None of his photos in the past year showed Justin either with friends or a date.

*The guy just couldn't get a break. Got stuck with the short end of the stick, cleaning out the old man's house, tried to sell off a little junk, and got whacked for his trouble.*

One of the search results was a link to eBay. The auction listing was for a *"box of assorted memorabilia from the Commodore Wilson Hotel."* Justin had posted a minimum bid at one hundred dollars. Bad photos didn't make the box's content look appealing or valuable. The listing had closed without any takers.

*That's got to be the same box he sold to Erik. Justin never went through it. So he wouldn't have found the Ambrose letter. Nobody should have guessed that letter was in the box. Back in the day, people must have carted stuff away by the truckload at the bankruptcy sale. But if somebody was tracking down loose ends, anyone with a search engine would know about the auction.*

Did Justin sign his own death warrant when he uploaded the listing?

Thankfully, Jenny seemed to be dealing with the phone calls and whatever walk-ins came through the front door. Ben knew he couldn't handle any of that. Not until he knew for sure whether Erik was for real.

Ben ate at his desk, scarfing down the protein bars he kept in his drawer without actually tasting them. He didn't have an appetite. Usually he drank the coffee from the welcome area, but today he dug into the stash of Mountain Dew that he kept under his desk. He felt like he was back in Newark, in the bullpen, tracking a case.

Only this time, it was personal.

Little by little, the Most Wanted lists trickled in. Even with a large monitor, the crowded fields of names and aliases made Ben's eyesight blur. He washed down another bite of protein bar and felt the sugar and caffeine ricochet through his nervous system. One foot tapped continuously, and he caught himself biting his bottom lip, an old habit.

A few more texts made his phone buzz. Ben didn't have the nerve to read them. He wanted things to work out, wanted Erik to be exactly who he claimed to be. But Ben couldn't handle connecting with Erik, not until he knew for sure. He might have been able to go undercover for weeks or months at a time and fool criminals and drug lords, but Ben knew Erik would realize right away that something was wrong. Ben didn't want to lie, and he couldn't very well tell the truth.

*It's only for a day,* he told himself. *I should have everything in a few hours. And then I'll know.*

Maybe just the fact that Ben doubted was enough to fracture Erik's feelings for him. After all, wasn't *trust* part of being in a relationship? Then again, Erik had trusted Josh, and Ben had trusted Caleb, and they'd both gotten screwed over. He and Erik hadn't exactly had a normal getting-to-know-you kind of beginning. Checking into someone's background before getting serious was just a part of the modern world. Careful. Prudent. But no matter how hard he tried, Ben didn't believe his own justifications.

*If Cooper was telling the truth, then Erik's got Interpol—or worse—on his tail. What if he's innocent? Who else is going to try to clear his name? Maybe the mobsters who didn't get what they wanted in Antwerp smeared him for revenge. He got away from them once. Maybe they really want to get rid of a witness.*

Thinking that Erik might have lied to him, used him, hurt like a mofo. Envisioning Erik being the target of a mob conspiracy was even worse. The Russian Mob had deep roots in New York City and New Jersey. If they wanted someone in the U.S. discredited or arrested on false charges, they were masters of disinformation. Hell, they learned from the best. They could frame Erik and make it stick. Or they could pull a Jack Ruby and make sure the witness didn't talk.

The shifting light in Ben's office made him notice the time. *Shit.* There was no way he could go to dinner and spend the night pretending everything was all right. And no way he could confess his need to "trust, but verify" without causing the very problem he hoped so desperately to avoid. Erik would be justifiably angry that Ben doubted him. Ben would argue that he needed to be sure, that he was protecting Erik. They'd fight. Erik would come to his senses and realize Ben was too much of a Jersey cop and throw him out.

They'd be through before they really got going.

Ben pulled out his phone. He saw half a dozen unanswered texts, all from Erik. They were the flirty, fun exchanges they'd been doing all week. But by the last one, Erik seemed to realize something was wrong.

*Ben? Is everything okay? Are we still on for dinner?*

That was an hour ago. Ben checked the time. He was due at Erik's in forty minutes.

With a heavy heart, Ben typed the text that was probably going to ruin everything. *Trouble at the office. Nothing dangerous, but need to handle it. Have to miss dinner. I'm really sorry.*

He sent the text, feeling like he had a lead weight in his gut. Erik would have every right to be angry at being stood up. He'd worry. He'd doubt. And if the intel on Erik turned out okay—and God, Ben really hoped it would be okay—Ben would have to win him back. He just hoped Erik would forgive him.

The reports were coming in, a deluge of information it would take hours to sift through. If this was a real case and Ben was still a real cop, he'd at least have a partner to divide the work with, maybe a team. There was no one he could trust to help him now, which probably meant pulling an all-nighter.

*I do have a partner. I'm supposed to be having dinner with him, making love on the couch, sleeping together in his bed. Dammit—please don't let me get this close and not be able to keep him.*

Ben barely registered Jenny coming in to say goodnight. He heard her key turn the lock in the door and dug out a packet of peanuts that were probably past their expiration date. Then he called up the next batch of reports. Ben wasn't going to let Erik go without a fight. He was going to consider his research to be protecting Erik from a false accusation, prove him innocent instead of looking to verify his guilt. And if Ben could do that, save Erik from being arrested, extradited, imprisoned—or killed, then it would be worth it. Because Ben had never been more sure about how he felt about someone than he was about loving Erik.

Even if it turned out that Erik didn't love him back.

THIRTEEN

# ERIK

The pang Erik felt as he heard the door click behind Ben that morning surprised him. In the years he'd been involved with Josh, Erik had relished having the best of both worlds. When he was home, he had a companion and lover. When he traveled, sometimes for weeks at a time, he had independence and freedom.

Then Josh had cheated, left him, and Erik understood what that old song meant about freedom and nothing left to lose.

He'd learned a lot about himself after Josh left, and plenty about loneliness. So when Ben had wandered into his life, Erik had been up for the challenge, even if Ben didn't intend to stay around. But Erik hadn't expected to fall so hard, so fast. What he felt toward Ben seemed completely different than his feelings for Josh. Because Erik couldn't imagine wanting to be away from Ben for weeks. Just the hours until dinner seemed too long.

Sure, Erik figured some of that was infatuation, the blissful first stage of a new relationship. But he also knew it was more. What he'd felt for Josh—what he thought was love—had been affection, fondness, a comfortable habit. Even in their early days, the attraction had never been this strong, like lightning in his blood. This was what love must feel like, as carried away as it seemed after only a week together. Erik could only hope that Ben felt it, too. That he'd stay.

Erik swallowed a couple of Advil and limped to the bathroom. One glance in the mirror revealed bruises that had bloomed in blue, black, and green across his hip, shoulder, and ribs on one side. From the way his leg throbbed, he'd also twisted his knee funny, too.

Which meant he moved more like seventy-five instead of thirty-five.

He turned on the shower and ran it hot, hoping that would loosen sore muscles. Taking care of his morning erection gave him time to fantasize about what it would be like when he and Ben finally—finally—made love.

He assumed Ben would want to top—a muscular ex-cop with tats was the alpha stereotype romance novels were built on. If so, that was fine with Erik, although he actually preferred to switch things up now and then. Josh had been a top-only, and Erik had resented that, as if Josh were suggesting that Erik was somehow inferior for preferring to bottom. So if Ben was open to experimenting, Erik had plenty of ideas.

He came hard, free to cry out for Ben with his release since no one was home to hear him shout. Erik finished his shower and got dressed, letting the post-orgasm release of endorphins blunt the pain of his injuries better than any pills.

Ben had left a full pot of coffee, and Erik poured his into a large insulated container to take down to the shop with him. He waited for his frozen waffle to toast, and decided he needed to expand his break-fast options, especially with Ben sleeping over.

That thought made Erik smile. He liked waking up in bed with Ben, bumping into him in his sleep, catching his scent during the night. Ben was handsome, but first thing in the morning with bed-rumpled hair, he was also adorable. Just thinking about him like that made Erik's heart skip a beat.

God, he hoped Ben was on board with having a relationship and not just a fling. Erik had realized he was well past "fling" when he'd dodged out of the way of that speeding van, when he was more afraid of not seeing Ben again than of dying.

*I'm in love. I'm actually in love with him.*

Erik carried his coffee downstairs and let himself into the shop. He needed to finish the inventory so he could open for business, and write several new blog posts to get *Treasure Trail* off the ground. It wouldn't hurt to check his email and see if there was any news about the TV proposal. Those should have been his priorities. Instead, he pulled out his phone to call Alessia Mason, hoping he could ask her about magic and curses.

He'd looked up the woman Monty and Susan both believed to be a witch, and read everything he could find online. Alessia Mason's gift shop was a local favorite, and she seemed to have her finger on the pulse of Cape May's social life, especially the events that catered more to the year-round residents than the tourists. No doubt she and Jaxon Davies ran in the same circles. But he'd only found a few references to being a follower of the "Old Ways," and nothing at all about a coven.

Then again, there were plenty of reasons not to shout that sort of thing from the rooftops.

Before he could place the call, a knock at the door interrupted. A dark-haired woman stood on the other side of the glass, and Erik recognized Alessia Mason from her pictures.

"May I come in?" she asked when he unlocked the door. Erik stepped aside to let her enter, then locked the door behind her.

"You're Alessia Mason? I'm Erik Mitchell. We're not open yet if that's what you came to see me about." Erik didn't usually babble, but Alessia's appearance seemed like too much of a coincidence.

"I'm Alessia. I know who you are—and who you've been. And I came to talk with you because my coven and I are pleased to see a potential ally come to town. We've fought to protect Cape May largely on our own."

Erik was glad he had put away the box of Commodore memorabilia so the table in the back was uncluttered. He led Alessia to the break room and offered coffee. She declined, but he poured a refill for himself. Erik suspected he'd need the jolt to get him through the day.

"I'm not sure I understand," Erik replied. "What do you mean, 'protect Cape May'?"

Alessia smiled. She appeared to be in her early forties, with olive skin, black hair, and dark brown eyes. Erik sensed a power beneath her attractiveness which he wasn't sure whether to attribute to confidence, insider knowledge, or something…more.

"Do you believe in witches, Erik?"

Erik sighed. "I'm not sure. I think there's a lot I don't understand about how the world works, and people have different talents that attract all kinds of labels."

She gave him an appraising glance. "Very diplomatic. You have some talent of your own," she added, eyes narrowing as she assessed him. "Mostly raw, untrained, but with definite potential."

Her intense focus made Erik want to squirm. "What does believing in witches have to do with anything? I'm an antiques and art guy."

There was that enigmatic smile again, an expression that Erik read to mean Alessia knew more than she was telling. "I'm betting that with the kinds of pieces you've dealt with, there have been oddities. Things you can't explain. Experiences that don't quite make sense."

"Maybe." As he'd admitted to Ben the night before, art and museum people were a superstitious lot. They knew the myths and legends, the stories of curses and hauntings, and most learned the hard way to take such warnings seriously.

"I'm the descendant of a long line of Sicilian witches—*strega*, we're called in Italian. It's a powerful bloodline. I married a man from a prominent, long-time Cape May family. That affords some protection —for me and mine as well as for the town," Alessia said. "Over time, we've drawn other individuals here who have psychic and magical abilities. I believe you've met Monty. And Jaxon."

"Jaxon?"

Alessia raised an eyebrow. "His kind of charisma is just shy of being a glamour, an inherent magic that makes those around him besotted with his presence. Interestingly enough, his partner Arjun is immune. Their pairing is a real love match."

"I haven't met Jaxon's husband. I've only barely met Jaxon himself,"

Erik said, retreating behind his coffee cup as he studied his visitor. Susan and Monty had both vouched for her, and Erik didn't *disbelieve*, but that wasn't quite the same as being fully onboard with the idea that witches and magic were real.

Then again, Erik already knew that ghosts and visions—and the ability to get glimpses of the future and past—were real. So it wasn't going to take much of a shove to convince him. Ben, on the other hand…

"How does this have anything to do with me, or protecting Cape May? Are you saying that your coven is some kind of supernatural neighborhood watch?"

Alessia full-out laughed at that, as if it was the funniest thing she'd heard in a long time. "You're not completely wrong," she said. "Although I can't say we've ever seen ourselves exactly in those terms."

She grew serious. "The land beneath Cape May is not completely solid. Gravel, silt, and sand make it somewhat porous, and subject to the tides. In magical terms—energy terms—it's a liminal space."

Erik recognized that term from the folklore classes he'd taken long ago in graduate school. "A place where the veil between one realm and another is thinner?"

Alessia looked pleased. "Exactly. Usually it's a dividing line between two things—a shoreline, the mouth of a cave, the edge of a forest."

"Or it can be invoked, in a ritual space," Erik said, meeting her gaze.

"Yes. All that. Liminal space is powerful," Alessia said. "Because the veil is thinner, energy is stronger, but it also fluctuates more. And that power attracts people and creatures with the ability to see it and use it —both good and bad."

"So your group keeps out the supernatural riff-raff?"

Alessia leaned back and folded her hands on the table. "You make it sound very judgy. But essentially, yes. We keep watch to deter anyone or anything from misusing the natural energies, causing harm."

"Begging your pardon, but whoever was on duty during the Commodore Wilson years dropped the ball."

Alessia nodded. "The man who built the Commodore was already under a curse—or perhaps, a crossroads deal—when he arrived. The hotel was the reason we originally organized, although it was such a nexus of dark energy that we've always been playing defense, even twenty years after it's gone."

"Can't you cleanse it?"

She gave him a look. "Don't you think we've tried? Over the years we've invited practitioners from every tradition we could think of to try to break the curse or banish the evil. Priests, ministers, witches, shamans, root workers, mystics—they've all taken a shot at it. Nothing worked. A lot of the people who tried came to a bad end."

"I've seen postings online from paranormal investigators and urban explorers. What happened to them?" Erik had scoured the internet and found plenty of blogs and photographs documenting the exploits of groups who had braved the old hotel during the times it was abandoned.

Alessia wrinkled her nose in distaste. "Some were lucky. Some weren't. There were also vandals, and a few raves thrown, or so I've heard. They didn't end well. The Commodore was always a dangerous building. Bloodthirsty."

"Wasn't there a reality show that tried to dare people to live there for a while, outlast each other?" He'd seen articles about the ill-fated show but wasn't sure how to separate the hype from the facts.

"Twelve residents, over six weeks, and the last one to leave won a million dollars," Alessia replied. "Back in 2005. One overdosed, one had to be hospitalized for severe anxiety. Another got hurt pretty bad falling down the steps, and one attempted suicide. They stopped the show at that point, but tragedy befell everyone involved even so— including the producer and director."

"How did the curse outlive the building?"

Alessia leaned closer. "When the preservationists found out that there was too much damage to the Commodore to be able to save it, a group of us tried to place a containment spell on the building so whatever evil was in its bones didn't go elsewhere. In hindsight, I'd say we were not completely successful," she added, with a self-deprecating note in her voice. "Even the demolition went sour. Freak injuries and a fire no one could explain. But the ghosts never left, and the dark essence remained. So, we try to limit the damage."

"Why are you telling me this?" Erik still cradled his mug.

"Because you have abilities that can help us protect this town. And because Robert was one of us."

"A witch?"

"A man with psychic abilities, much like yours. You'll find that Trinkets can be a magnet for items that have energies of their own. Whenever Robert found pieces that were dark, cursed, or haunted, he made sure they were handled."

*Well, that explains the spooky closet full of weird stuff. I guess he didn't finish dealing with the last batch.*

"I don't think there's anything very special about what I can do, but I'm all for helping to keep the place safe, since I'm living here," Erik replied. "But right now, I'm hoping you can help me. The ghosts of Vincente Cafaro, Hank Chason, and Kendry Ambrose are back—and they're riled up. Apparently, so is someone else—because I've had an attempted break-in, been shot at, and nearly run over. So…you help keep me alive, and I'll be around to help run off the undesirables."

Alessia watched him in silence, with the kind of intensity that made him feel like she could see down to his bones. "Your store already has very strong protective wardings."

"It does?" Maybe that explained why Erik felt immediately at home the first time he'd stepped inside. And perhaps it had something to do with foiling the attacks.

"Old magic. I suspect they've been part of the store since it was founded. Robert must have had a source to renew them now and again. I don't know anyone local with that kind of power."

"Huh. That's interesting." Erik toyed with his mug as he thought. "I think that the ghosts have come back because they've got unfinished business. If I had to guess, I think they want a shot at whoever caused their deaths. So…what can you do to keep me safe while I try to figure out how to lay the ghosts to rest?"

Alessia reached into her purse and withdrew two medallions on leather strings. "One for you…and one for your soulmate."

*Soulmate?* His surprise must have registered, because Alessia's brow quirked upward.

"You didn't know? Or do you make a habit of falling in love practically at first sight?"

Erik was torn between feeling gobsmacked at the idea that Ben was his *soulmate* and feeling invaded that this stranger seemed to know something about him that he didn't know himself.

"What does that even mean?"

"It means that you're supposed to be together. Destined. Made for each other. However you want to put it."

"That's really a thing? I thought it only happened in fan fiction."

"Oh, it's a 'thing' all right," Alessia assured him. "It doesn't happen to everyone. But I'm betting you can think of some people you know whose bond seems so strong it's a little spooky."

Erik could think of several couples who seemed like two halves of a coin. He'd always envied that a little, but figured it was like striking gold or winning the lottery—a one in a million bit of luck. *Maybe not. If Ben is my soulmate, does that mean he'll want to stay?*

"What does the medallion do?" Erik accepted the amulets hesitantly, waiting for a vision or some reaction from his gift. He didn't see any images, but a sense of peace and well-being came over him.

"It can protect you from some supernatural evil and enhance your own gifts. It won't turn you into Gandalf, but your abilities have a defensive aspect, as well as a practical one. This should help you access that with more ease."

Erik didn't know what Ben would make of the necklaces, but Erik resolved to bring it up over dinner. "Thank you," he said, slipping one of the amulets over his head and the other into his pocket.

"As for the ghosts, it sounds like they want justice, however long overdue. Help them get that, and I suspect they'll move on."

"Why now? They've all been dead for a long time. So what brought them back now?" Erik could not contain his curiosity.

Alessia shrugged. "Artifacts are powerful. If their ghosts are bound to items that have recently come to light, that could be enough. Especially if they felt that someone could champion them." She gave him a look that made her meaning completely clear.

"Is there anything else I need to know?"

Alessia winked. "More than we have time to cover today," she assured him as she got up. "But being part of a community means there are people who can help you learn. Welcome to Cape May."

She held out her hand, and Erik shook it. A tingle of energy ran from their joined hands up his arm, like hitting his funny bone.

"What just happened?"

"Think of it as the energy equivalent of texting each other phone numbers. A circle of practitioners is a powerful thing. This is how we stay connected." With that, Alessia let herself out.

Erik wasn't sure how he felt about either the amulet or the mystical connection. He pulled out his phone and texted Ben. *Interesting morning. How's yours going?*

Much as he wanted to hear Ben's voice, Erik knew his boyfriend needed to take care of business. Dinner seemed like a long time to wait, so he resolved to keep himself busy.

Erik avoided the "spooky" closet, resolving to tackle it last. To his relief, few of the other items he cataloged prompted any visions. Some of the pieces had a trace of ghostly connection, but the energy was faded, more of a repeater. Certainly nothing like he'd experienced with the Commodore pieces.

Throughout the day, Erik snapped pictures of odd items and sent off-handed observations to Ben via text. The entire morning had passed before Erik realized that Ben hadn't responded to any of his messages.

That was strange. Ben usually responded within minutes. Then again, Erik had been monopolizing Ben's time when he was just getting settled in at his new job. Not that Ben had seemed to mind, but if Erik wanted Ben to stay, he needed to succeed, and that meant letting Ben take care of business.

Still, Erik fought a niggling doubt. He tamped down on the insecurity, telling himself he was making far too much over things. *Ben could be in meetings. His phone could have died. He might be out walking properties. Or he could just be really busy. Chill out.*

Erik skipped lunch, happy he was closing in on finishing the inventory. When he was down to one last set of shelves, he decided to take a break. A glance at his phone told him that Ben still hadn't responded, and Erik fought the urge to call.

*No one likes a clingy boyfriend, "soulmate" or not. Get a grip. It's only been a few hours. It'll be dinnertime soon.*

Instead, Erik called Simon, who answered on the first ring. "Hi, Erik."

"Good guess. Was that from caller ID or Psychic Friends Network?"

"Funny. What's up?"

"Do you have a few moments? I can call back if you're busy."

"Pete can handle the store. Something I can help with?"

"How permanent is bad juju?" Erik asked. "If a place has seriously bad energy—maybe even cursed—is there a way to fix it?"

Simon was silent for a moment. "It depends. Curses and haunts are certainly real. Usually, there's a way to dispel them, although it may take a practitioner with unique skills in a difficult case. Some places are just born bad."

"What do you mean?"

"Ever hear the term 'genius loci'? It means 'spirit of a place,'" Simon replied. "People have gotten vibes about places being especially good or particularly bad throughout history. Sometimes it's not because of anything that happened, but because the energy is either very healthful, or twisted and malicious. If it's twisted, the best you can do is cordon it off—keep people away. Why?"

Erik told Simon everything that had happened since their last call. Simon heard him out, and it made Erik nervous when his friend didn't react right away. "Simon?"

"I need to do some digging," Simon replied. "It sounds like you've got a dark genius loci, so simply getting rid of it probably isn't an option. There might be more that can be done to contain it than your new friends have been able to do. Let me look into the lore and make a few calls. Just…be careful. That kind of bad energy isn't anything to fool around with. And neither is the Mob."

"Yeah. I know." Erik raked his fingers back through his hair. "Believe me, I'm playing it safe. And I've sent emails to the folks I'm still in touch with from the art world to see if any of the people I helped put away got out. Just in case this is really about what I used to do, instead of the Commodore."

"You think that's possible?"

Erik shrugged, then remembered Simon couldn't see him. "Maybe. I don't know which is worse: thinking one of those scumbags put out a hit on me, or believing it's the local Mob tying up old loose ends."

"There's something else bothering you." Simon didn't make it a question.

Erik hesitated, then sighed. "Your boyfriend Vic is a cop, right?"

"Homicide detective."

"How did you win him over? I mean, Ben understands about seeing ghosts. And he's cool with the images I get from pieces—at least, he says he is. But he sorta freaked when I started talking about mediums and witches." Erik dropped his voice. "I don't want to lose him, Simon. I think he could be it for me."

"Well…" Simon drifted off. "I'm probably the wrong person to ask for advice. In our case, I almost died. That kinda forced the issue. It's not a dating technique I recommend."

"I'd rather not try that. Two close calls in one week are enough for me."

"I don't have any psychic insights into your love life," Simon said. "Although Ben sounds like a good guy. Maybe he just needs time. You haven't known each other very long."

"Can you see anything? About the future?" Erik hated the lack of confidence in his voice.

"About you and Ben? No. And remember, the future is always in motion. Everything we do makes changes. So predictions aren't guarantees." Simon let the silence play between them. "The only thing I see is an old warehouse, and I get a strong sense of danger. So…stay away from big old abandoned buildings."

"I think I can promise to do that." Erik felt oddly dejected that Simon hadn't said anything that confirmed Alessia's "soulmate" comment.

"Don't overthink things," Simon said.

He'd known Erik long enough that his advice probably came from understanding how Erik's mind worked as much as it did any psychic abilities.

"Trust your gut. I believe in you."

"Thanks. I'd better let you get back to work. Say 'hi' to Vic for me."

"Come visit a real beach, where it gets warm enough to actually swim," Simon teased. "Always good to hear from you."

Erik stared at his phone for a moment when the call ended. He'd almost hoped that a text or call from Ben would have interrupted his conversation with Simon, but it hadn't. There was still an hour before Ben was due for dinner. Erik debated whether he needed a second shower or just a change of clothing.

Susan tapped at the glass, and Erik saw she had a tray from Crumble. He let her in and inhaled the smell of coffee, vanilla, and nutmeg.

"I thought you could use an afternoon pick-me-up," she said, handing off one cup to him. "I know I can!"

Erik gave her a tour of the more interesting items he had cataloged, and they joked about the odd pieces. By the time he had finished showing her everything and had savored the coffee, his mood had lifted considerably.

"I should probably go change clothes," Erik said. "Ben's bringing takeout."

"I'm so happy you two hit it off," Susan replied, patting his arm. "He seems like a good guy."

Erik's phone buzzed. He grabbed it a little too quickly, and read the text, expecting something snarky and sexy in response. Then the words registered, and he felt the bottom drop out of his stomach.

Susan stepped closer. "Erik, what's wrong?"

Erik swallowed hard, re-reading the text to make sure he hadn't misunderstood. "It's Ben. He's standing me up for dinner."

"Oh, Erik," Susan said. "I'm sure that's not—"

Erik forced himself to ease his grip on the phone before he snapped it in two. "Something's been wrong all day. We usually text, and he hasn't responded to anything. And now…"

"Did he give a reason?"

"He said 'something came up at the office' and he's sorry." Erik knew Susan could hear the hurt in his voice.

"And that's probably true," Susan returned. "You know how easy it is to misinterpret an email or a text. It's probably nothing more than what he says it is."

"I've just had this feeling all day, like the other shoe was going to drop," Erik said. "I didn't expect him to ghost on me."

"Well, his missed opportunity is my good fortune," Susan replied, brightening. "Because I happen to have a roast chicken in the oven, complete with stuffing. And now I won't have to eat it all by myself."

"I…"

"Of course you can!" Susan took his elbow and gently led him toward the door. "I insist. So lock up and come with me. You can help me with the salad. We'll make an evening of it." When Erik hung back, Susan gave him what he could only describe as a "mom" glare.

"Come on. Otherwise, you're going to stick around here and mope and make the whole thing into something bigger than it deserves to be. Things come up. Schedules change. I'm sure there's a good reason. In the meantime, you can have a good meal with a fascinating companion," she added, with a joking pat to her hair, "and we'll watch a movie. You'll feel better with a full stomach and a little wine."

Erik let her lead him to the front and locked the door without really thinking about it. "Thank you," he said, remembering his manners in spite of being preoccupied.

"I raised sons of my own, you know," she said. "I'm experienced."

Erik appreciated Susan's kindness, and he did his best to push his fears to the back of his mind, trying to be good company. They chatted as they worked together to get the meal ready, and Erik found that the wonderful aromas made his stomach growl, when he thought he might be too keyed up to eat.

Susan pressed a glass of wine into his hand. "You only have to walk across the driveway, and it goes well with the chicken. Enjoy life a little."

"I'm trying." Erik wanted to keep Susan talking. "Tell me about your kids. They're all grown, right?"

"My youngest went into the military a few years back, and the oldest went into law enforcement," she said as she wrapped up her tales. "They're good boys, and they come over when they can, but they've got their own lives, and that's what's supposed to happen. It's nice to have you next door. Like having another son."

Erik knew Susan missed her late husband. Photos of the two of them and of their family were scattered throughout her comfortable living room. Susan seemed so full of life, practically bursting with enthusiasm as she told him about her new yoga class and the week-long getaway she'd had recently with a group of old friends from college. Erik couldn't imagine bouncing back like that after losing a partner after decades together, especially since the fond tone in Susan's voice told him that she and Keith had been very close.

*You can't lose what you don't have. Ben isn't here. He ghosted.*

Susan seemed to sense the shift in Erik's mood. "You know, when Keith and I first started dating, we danced around each other before we both knew what we wanted. I know times were different, but maybe not that different. People are people, after all. And I think what spooked both of us was that we realized this wasn't just another date. We knew it could be the real deal, and as much as we wanted that, it was a little scary. It took time, I guess, for both of us to work up our nerve."

Erik took a sip of his wine. The meal had been fabulous and filling, the homemade cookies were warm out of the oven, and he had enjoyed himself much more than he expected. Still, worry about Ben's intentions dragged him down.

"I would really like this to work out with Ben," he confessed. "I've never fallen for someone like this. The way he makes me feel when we're together…I didn't think I'd ever find a guy like that. And I know we've been moving fast, but I don't want to lose him."

"A little advice, if you don't mind, from someone who was happily married for forty years," Susan said. "Don't invent stories in your mind to explain things the other person does or doesn't do. If you do that, you're usually wrong, and you can work yourself up into a tizzy. Before you know it, you've got your partner tried and convicted in your head, and then you blast them, and it might be you've had it all wrong."

"Did you and Keith ever do that?"

Susan smiled wistfully. "A few times, early on. Until my grandmother took me aside and told me what I just told you. She and Grandpa were married for seventy years, and they were still sneaking kisses and copping feels like teenagers. When we stopped writing those scripts in our minds, we stopped fighting. We started asking and listening and explaining. So…give Ben a chance before you come to dire conclusions."

Erik nodded. "You're right. It's just that…my last relationship didn't end well."

"Which isn't Ben's fault. It never works to keep fighting the last war. Don't worry—no matter how smitten you both are, there will still be plenty of things to disagree about!"

They watched a couple of episodes of a remodeling show and finished off the bottle of wine. Erik started to drowse and realized it was going on eleven. He set his empty glass aside. "I'd better head back. Thank you. You were right—this was just what I needed. I hope I wasn't bad company."

Susan grinned. "You did me a favor, helping me eat that chicken dinner! And you've been excellent company. Someday I want to hear more about all the interesting places you've been and those fantastic museums. But there's time for that. So go get a good night's sleep, and things will look better in the morning."

He saw himself out, insisting that Susan stay curled up on the couch to watch the end of the episode. As Erik walked across the driveway toward home, he resisted the urge to check his phone again for a message from Ben.

*If Alessia is right, then we'll find our way to each other. And if she's not, and we have to build a relationship the regular way, I'm willing to fight for that.*

A gray SUV pulled up in front of Erik, blocking his route to the house. At the same time, a man wearing a ski mask stepped out of the bushes and leveled a gun. "Get into the car."

"What the—" Erik spun toward the man, forcing his gun hand away, and slammed a fist into the gunman's jaw. He brought his knee up to the groin, hard, and his heel down on the instep, hearing the crunch of bone.

He heard the slides on two more guns and another voice. "Get in, now, or we'll drop you right here."

Erik's self-defense training didn't make him an action hero. He thought about resisting—better to die quickly here than face a worse fate somewhere else. But self-preservation overrode, and he let them herd him into the SUV. All three men wore masks. The vehicle was already moving as one attacker held a gun on him while the other zip-tied Erik's wrists and pulled a cloth bag over his head.

"You've got the wrong guy," Erik protested.

"Don't think so," the man next to him said. "Now shut up."

Erik tried to remember the route, but without being able to see, he quickly lost track of the turns. The bag made it difficult to breathe, and Erik fought panic to keep his breaths slow and regular.

*Oh, God. The warehouse from Simon's vision. This is what he meant. They know about the Ambrose letter. I'm doing to die.*

## FOURTEEN

## BEN

Ben throttled his guilt at standing Erik up for dinner by diving through the reports as they came in, reading until his vision blurred. He felt relieved when Erik's name didn't show up on any of the Most Wanted lists—U.S. or foreign. That was a step in the right direction, but it only proved that Erik hadn't been put on a public list. Some investigations were handled in secret. Still, the results crossed off one set of items on his list.

Robert's check came back clean. He'd been in the Army's CHARON division, a group Ben didn't recognize. After he left the service, Robert's background included a long stint as "private security" for the Brigg's Society, another unfamiliar name. He left security work to buy out the previous owner of Trinkets, taking over the reins of a store that had been in Cape May since the town's early days. Puzzling, but clean.

That left the reports on Erik, Dorchester, and Cooper yet to come in. Ben rubbed his eyes and guzzled his soda. Even after going through reams of data, he knew the sticking point really had to do as much with the idea of witches and magic as it did with Mob connections and old vendettas. For that kind of thing, there was only one person Ben knew he could trust. He decided to call and hoped it wasn't past his contact's bedtime.

Ben hadn't called the number in a long time. For all he knew, the man could have moved on or passed away. He crossed his fingers as the phone rang.

"This is Father Pavel, with St. Thomas the Doubter Church. Please leave a message."

Ben closed his eyes as the beep sounded. "Father Pavel? It's me, Benny Nolan from St. Aiden Catholic School in Newark. I need your help."

He was about to end the call when he heard a familiar voice. "Ben? Ben Nolan?"

"Father Pavel! I wasn't sure you'd still be at that church."

"I don't plan on going anywhere else, my son. My work is here now. Tell me why you've called. I'm pleased to hear from you, but I doubt you're calling to catch up on old times."

Father Pavel had been in his thirties, one of the younger priests, when Ben was in eighth grade at the Catholic school he had attended. Ben had never told his mother, but it was Father Pavel who had encouraged him to follow his heart. And as Ben looked back on their conversations, he was certain that the priest had meant to be truthful about his orientation as well as his lack of a calling for the priesthood.

They'd stayed in touch—just an email now and again—and Ben remembered when Father Pavel had left the school for a small parish in a poor neighborhood in Pittsburgh. The priest would be in his fifties by now, but Father Pavel wasn't the type to retire. Not if he thought he could make a difference.

"No, Father. I remember when you taught the class on defending ourselves from the Darkness. I had the sense that you really believed what you were saying. Some of them didn't, you know."

A wry chuckle on the other end of the line confirmed agreement.

"I see ghosts. I've always seen them. Is that a sin?"

"No, my son. But thank you for trusting me enough to finally tell me."

Ben stared at the phone, unsure of what he'd just heard. "You knew?"

"I knew that you could see the spirits that clung to that old school building and the abbey. I hoped that you would come to accept that about yourself."

"What about magic? And witches? Are they real? Are they evil?"

He heard Father Pavel let out a deep sigh. "Before I answer, Ben, I have to caution you. Once you know a thing, you can't un-know it. There is no reclaiming innocence once it's gone."

"Please, Father. Someone I…love…is in danger. I need to know what I'm dealing with."

"Very well. We don't speak much of the supernatural anymore, because most people don't wish to know. They're safer, perhaps, not knowing. But it's real. Magic, witches, demons, creatures. And there are people who stay in the shadows, fighting monsters, to keep the rest of us safe."

He paused. "As for magic and witches—they're not by design bad or good. It depends on where the power comes from and how it's used. The Church doesn't like to talk about it, but they've allied with witches and other beings many times over the centuries to overcome a common threat."

Ben recounted Erik's wild tale about what happened in Antwerp, realizing only belatedly he had surely outed himself in the telling. Then he gave Cooper's alternative story. "I don't know what to believe," Ben admitted.

Father Pavel had listened without comment.

Ben waited for his response.

"The story Erik told you is possible. Such things can happen. I can't speak to the Antwerp incident myself, but I know someone who might be able to set your mind at ease. I'll give you his number."

"Wait!" Ben said. "I appreciate that. And I'll call your friend. But first—I remember that you told us in class that you had been called in from time to time to send away the Darkness. Back then, I thought you were putting us on. But if we've really got ghosts of dead mobsters floating around, how do we protect ourselves?"

"Silver, iron, and salt work well," Father Pavel replied as if the conversation hadn't taken a Twilight Zone twist. "Do you remember the Latin from your catechism?"

"I, uh, haven't been real regular in church," Ben replied. "But yeah, well enough."

"I'll email you a short incantation—more of a prayer. It won't send the ghosts on to their final rest or drive out a demon, but it can help you hold a clear space around you or disrupt an attack."

"It doesn't require celibacy to work, does it? I haven't exactly renounced the pleasures of the flesh."

Father Pavel laughed. "You were never meant for the priesthood, Benny. There is no sin in accepting the gifts of the bodies God gave us."

Ben wrote down the phone number. "Thank you, Father. It means a lot."

"You're very welcome, Ben. You don't have to be in mortal danger to call or email. It's nice to hear from you. And I will keep you in my prayers tonight. Don't doubt what you know to be true."

Ben took a moment to gather his wits after he ended the call. Then he dialed the number, knowing how crazy he was going to sound to the man who answered the phone.

"Travis Dominick. St. Dismas Mission."

"Father Dominick—"

"Just Travis."

"Travis. Father Pavel gave me your number. I need to know what happened in Antwerp last year. There was a cursed Fabergé musical egg, and something went wrong—"

"Who are you?"

Ben took a deep breath. "I'm Ben."

"Why do you want to know, Ben?"

"Because Erik Mitchell is in danger, and I need to know if he told me the truth about what he saw in Antwerp."

Travis was quiet for a moment. "I wasn't in Antwerp when it happened. But I know people who were. The Fabergé egg wasn't just haunted—it was cursed. Two of the enforcers with the Russian Mob weren't human. Neither was the man who fought off the Mob goons, rescued Erik, and made sure the egg is somewhere it will never hurt anyone again."

"What do you mean, 'not human'?" Ben echoed.

"I can't tell you anything else. I've said more than I should. But I knew of Erik Mitchell, and people I respect spoke well of him. Just because something is hard to believe doesn't make it untrue."

"Thank you," Ben said quietly. "I'm sorry to bother you."

"I hope you can protect Erik. He's one of the good guys," Travis replied.

"Yeah. He is." Ben stared into space for a few moments, trying to digest what he'd heard. He'd seen TV shows where someone found out that monsters are real and then did something stupid, like screaming and running off into the woods only to get eaten. Ben felt as if the world had slipped its axis, tilting just enough to make everything look different. The world hadn't changed, but he had. It would take a while to unpack how he felt about finding out everything he'd believed was founded on secrets and lies.

That could wait until tomorrow. Tonight, he needed to clear Erik's name.

While Ben was on the phone, the last of the reports came in. So did the email from Father Pavel, which Ben printed and tucked into a pocket. His phone buzzed three times, calls from a local number he didn't recognize, and since it wasn't Erik, he didn't answer as he plunged into reading the new intel.

Dorchester was clean, he thought with relief. Commendations, spotless record. Erik's background check came back with odd redactions where names, dates, and places had been blacked out. But what remained showed no charges against Erik, no record of any allegations or investigations at home or abroad. His clearance level alone was a powerful endorsement.

Which left Cooper.

Ben had a sinking feeling even before he scanned the contents of the email. "*Investigated for possible ties to criminal activity,*" "*suspected of perjury in the disappearance of Hank Chason,*" "*has in the past been tied to known associates with links to organized crime."* And the final nail: *"Insufficient evidence to prosecute still resulted in Cooper being given early retirement from the Cape May police force."*

Ben felt pole-axed. *Cooper lied to me. Played me. Fucked with my head to make me doubt Erik. Whatever's going on, Cooper's part of it. I've got to warn Erik. I'll beg forgiveness later—right now, I just need to make sure he's safe.*

Part of the report on Cooper showed his interest in several local businesses. Odd, since Cooper had given Ben the impression he was retired. He was a part-owner in a car wash, and a liquor store, as well as a lawn service. *Classic businesses for money laundering.* The lawn service owned a warehouse on the edge of town, which was the only real estate other than his house that Cooper wholly owned.

The last email was from Tony Basalmo, his friend with the department in Newark. *"Should have told you this sooner knowing your gift for pissing people off, but be careful up there. The Cape May PD cleaned house back in the early 2000s, got rid of a lot of cops suspected of being on the Mob payroll. That doesn't mean they got them all, or that those guys aren't still around. So tread lightly until you know the players."*

Ben ran up to his apartment, grabbed two necklaces with silver saint medallions, and put them on. He had his gun in a back paddle holster, but as he swung through the kitchen, he snagged a canister of salt. Ben glanced wildly around the apartment for the last thing he needed, and spotted the fireplace tools on the hearth. He grabbed an iron poker and headed downstairs, intending to lock up the shop and go over to Erik's place.

Instead, he found Erik's neighbor pounding on the front door. "Mrs. Hendricks?"

"Three men pushed Erik into a van and drove away. I've already called the police. But if you want to be part of the cavalry, you'd better hurry."

"What?"

"Erik's in trouble. I tried to call you and finally came over here. You love that boy. And he loves you. So you'd better go help save him."

"The police…Cooper worked for the Mob…how do we know who to trust?"

"Start by trusting the chief of police. He's my son."

*Captain Hendricks. Of course.* "How did you know how Erik feels? How I feel?"

She rolled her eyes. "I'm Erik's neighbor. I'm his friend. And I'm an empath. Now can we please get this rescue on the road?"

———

"I know who took Erik Mitchell, and I think I know where he is." Ben burst into the Cape May police department with Susan Hendricks on his heels.

"Who are you?" The man in the captain's uniform was taller and more broad-shouldered, but he definitely resembled Susan. His gaze flicked between Susan and Ben, not hiding his annoyance.

"Ben Nolan," Ben said it at the same second as Officer Dorchester, who had moved up behind his captain.

"What are you doing here?" Captain Hendricks demanded.

Susan pushed her way to the front. "Scott, you need to listen to him."

Ben saw a muscle twitch in the captain's jaw. He sort of pitied the guy, having his mom bust into his headquarters. But since Erik's life was on the line, Ben's pity didn't last long.

"I'm Ben Nolan. Former Newark PD, New Jersey investigator—and Erik Mitchell's boyfriend."

"We've sent two squads to the Mitchell place," Dorchester interrupted. "Your mom called in a possible kidnapping, chief."

"Nolan, like Nolan Resort Real Estate? The guy who found the bones?" Chief Hendricks asked.

"Yeah. Hank Chason's skeleton."

Hendrick's head snapped up at that, and mistrust showed in his expression. "We didn't release that."

"And I'm not old enough to have capped him. Bullet to the back of the skull. I know who took Erik. James Cooper. He's one of yours—

retired—and he's dirty as fuck. We have to find Cooper and save Erik. Now!"

Hendricks raised a hand. Everyone in the bullpen stilled. "Whoa. Back up. Want to explain what the hell you're talking about?"

Ben wanted to rage and remind him that Erik's life was in danger, but at least he knew officers were already at Erik's. He'd been a cop. If Ben wanted to help save Erik's life, he needed to get Hendricks to trust him, not throw him in a cell.

He talked fast. "I found an old clock hidden in one of our houses. Took it over to Trinkets, and Erik discovered it was part of an insurance scam, back in the day. It had some ledger papers inside that implicated Vincente Cafaro for cheating on his taxes, and a photo of Cafaro shooting someone. Old blackmail goods. Then someone tried to break into the real estate office, and when they didn't find what they came for—the clock—they tried to break in over at Trinkets. Shot at Erik and me. And someone tried to run over Erik."

Hendricks glanced at Dorchester, who nodded. "I don't know anything about papers inside the clock, but the rest squares up."

"Go on," Hendricks said, returning his attention to Ben.

"Erik and I figured that the link between Chason and Cafaro was the Commodore Wilson. A friend from back in Newark gave me James Cooper's name, said he'd been on the force here before the old hotel was torn down. So I reached out to Cooper and asked him what it was like working there in the Chason and Ambrose years. I told him about the clock, but that was before my construction guys found the skeleton—and before Justin Kramer's house burned down and Justin turned up dead."

"What did you think you were playing at?" Hendricks snapped.

"We thought it was just chasing down clues on an old scandal, too old for anyone to care about. Provenance," he muttered, remembering the arty word Erik had used. Ben knew he was already wearing out Hendrick's forbearance. He told the abbreviated story as best he could without mentioning ghosts or Erik's visions. Giving a recap was already eating up too much precious time.

"A guy from Newark ought to know better than to poke the Mob," Hendricks said.

"We thought it was just the Cafaro incident, from the fifties," Ben retorted. "Old news. Listen, if you won't help me, I'll just—"

"Or maybe, you were muckraking fodder for that TV show that was in the news this morning, featuring Erik Mitchell, the guy who busted up international art theft rings? Jesus, could you paint a bigger target on your backs?"

Susan paled. "Oh my God, Scott. That's it. Someone knew about the Ambrose letter and thought Erik would go public about it."

The police captain turned to her.

"What Ambrose letter?" Hendricks demanded.

"I was helping Erik get the store ready," Susan said, lifting her head like she dared Scott to fault her. "When he bought that box of odds and ends from the Commodore Wilson, Erik asked me to help him go through it, because he didn't know the history. Most of it wasn't valuable. But down at the bottom he found Kendry Ambrose's handwritten suicide note, and Ambrose named names of all the people who pushed him over the brink."

"Where's that letter now?" Scott looked ready to bust a gusset.

"In Erik's safe at the shop," Susan replied. "Along with the clock."

Captain Hendricks reached up to pinch the bridge of his nose as if he were staving off a migraine. "Of course it is. Did either of you tell anyone about the letter?"

Susan shook her head, as did Ben.

"All right," Hendricks said. "When this is over, both of you are going to come to the station and give us a very detailed statement." He glared at Ben and Susan. "But if you're right about Cooper snatching Mitchell—and that makes sense, because we knew Cooper was dirty, we just couldn't make charges stick—then where did he take him?"

"Emerald Lawn and Gardens has a warehouse out on Route 109," Ben said. "Run by Cooper's brother, but Cooper's part owner, too. Out of all of Cooper's properties, that's the most likely."

The look on Hendricks' face promised that the two men were going to have words when this was said and done. Ben was fine with that, as long as they got to Erik in time. Because if Cooper thought Erik intended to do an exposé, Cooper had no incentive to let Erik live.

*Please don't let us be too late.*

Hendricks glanced to Dorchester, who shook his head. "We don't have anything better. Sounds legit."

"All right, let's move out," Hendricks said. When Ben headed toward the door, Hendricks grabbed his shoulder. "Where do you think you're going?"

Ben lifted his chin. "I'm a licensed PI, and I've got a license to carry. I'm an ex-cop. You don't have a big force, and you don't know what you're walking into. I can help."

Hendricks gave him an icy look. "All right, but you stay back, and you take your orders from me. Got it?"

"Yes, sir."

Hendricks turned to face Susan. "And you. Stay here where you're safe. We'll talk later," he added ominously.

"Be safe, and bring Erik back," Susan said. "Ben, too."

Hendricks muttered something under his breath and pushed his way into the lead. Ben jogged to keep up. He followed the cops in his own car, glad that the police came in quietly—no sirens, no flashing lights. If Cooper had Erik in the warehouse, they didn't need to tip him off, especially since Susan had told them there were at least three men in the SUV that took Erik.

Ben had the salt canister and the iron poker on the front seat of the car. The silver medallions were warm against his skin, gifts from his grandmothers for birthdays and his long-ago confirmation. He hoped he didn't need the incantation Father Pavel had provided, but it was in his pocket, just in case.

*Erik wouldn't have been alone or outside if I'd have been where I promised. I stood him up, and that left him vulnerable. If Susan hadn't seen them take him, Erik would just have vanished, and we'd have no clue.*

Would Erik forgive him? Betrayal by his ex already loomed large for Erik. And while Ben had nurtured his doubts privately, and for less than a day, he had still let Erik down. Erik would be within his rights to blame Ben for what happened to him tonight. He'd also be reasonable to wonder whether this attraction between them was just a fling, instead of something far more serious.

*First, we save his life. Then I'll do whatever it takes to win him back, prove I love him, that he can trust me. God, I've made a mess of things.*

When they pulled into the lot near the warehouse, Ben felt a chill he knew had nothing to do with the spring night. Whether Cooper had somehow called to them or not, Ben could see the ghosts of several brawny men outside the building, a spectral goon squad that might not be able to actually stop the police from entering, but could cause havoc and alert the men inside.

*Shit.* Hendricks already wanted Ben's guts for garters. If he saw Ben sprinkling salt on a parking lot and hacking at ghosts with a fireplace poker, he'd call the psych ward. That meant trying the invocation, which Ben felt certain would work perfectly for Father Pavel, but not so much for a guy who couldn't remember the last time he'd been to either Mass or confession.

He read over the Latin prayer, glad that he remembered enough from his long-ago catechism to manage the pronunciation with a vague sense of what the words actually meant.

*Powers of light, life, and creation, I call on thee to banish from this place all darkness, death, and chaos. Drive out those spirits that intend harm, scatter their energy, and take from them their power. In the name of the Father, Son, and Holy Spirit, Amen.*

When Ben looked again, the angry spirits were still visible, but they had faded. Hendricks and his team were suiting up in riot gear—something Ben doubted they had much call for in Cape May—which bought him a few extra minutes.

This time, Ben poured salt into one palm, and wrapped that hand around the iron poker, while he held tight to the silver medallions in the other. He pulled from his memory the most spiritual image he could think of, the way the light through the stained glass in the church he'd grown up in fell on the statue of the Virgin Mary during morning mass. Then he read the Latin one more time in the glow of his phone, trying to infuse the words with all of his love and protectiveness for Erik.

The ghosts vanished.

*For how long?*

Father Pavel said the incantation was only temporary. Ben dumped the salt into his pocket, shoved the fireplace poker back in his car, and tucked the incantation away for future use, then ran to join the cops who were about to enter the warehouse.

"Nolan. Stay behind us, stay out of the line of fire, and try not to shoot anyone," Hendricks ordered.

"Got it," Ben replied, keeping an eye out should the ghostly sentries return.

"Porter and Kent, go around to the right, try to find another way in. Stay in radio contact. Dorchester, Sanders, Thompson, you're with me. Nolan—stay out here until the shooting stops. Without gear, you're a target and a liability."

Ben didn't like Hendricks' assessment, but he knew the captain was correct. "Just bring Erik out alive."

"That's the goal," Hendricks responded.

They waited a few tense moments until Hendricks nodded to a comment heard through his earbud. "Porter and Kent are in position. Let's go—and be careful."

Ben felt his heart thudding in his chest. Help was on the way. But would they be too late?

# FIFTEEN
## ERIK

"I'm telling you, you've got the wrong guy. Look—I haven't seen anyone's face. Just let me go, and I'll walk home. I can't identify you. No harm, no foul," Erik bargained as two of his captors manhandled him out of the van.

"Shut up!" A fist connected with the side of Erik's face, and he would have fallen if the men on either side of him hadn't had a good grip on his arms.

"That's enough!" a new voice snapped. "We need to find out what he knows. Can't do that if you break his jaw."

Erik stumbled across what felt like a parking lot, then tripped on the threshold of a door, and felt smooth concrete beneath his feet. There were lights, because he saw a glow even through the bag that covered his head. He could smell freshly-mowed grass and motor oil.

His captors pushed Erik into a chair with his wrists still zip-tied in front of him. *If this were on TV, there'd be dramatic music. I am so screwed.*

A man he didn't recognize yanked the bag free. Erik blinked at the light. His heart sank. *If they're letting me see their faces, they're going to kill me. I was dead when I got in the car.*

The man in charge bent to look Erik in the face. "You're a lot of trouble. We had things taken care of, everything under control, and then you come to town and start kicking up dust."

Erik stared back, figuring that bravado was all he had left. He could play for time, in case anyone saw him get abducted. But deep down, Erik figured he was on his own.

"I have no idea what you're talking about."

His interrogator stood, then backhanded Erik hard across the cheek. "Don't lie to me. What do you know about Hank Chason, Kendry Ambrose, and Vincente Cafaro?"

Erik glared at his questioner. The man was probably in his seventies, but still trim and strong. He carried himself like a cop. Erik knew he'd never seen the man before.

"They're all dead. Been dead for a long time. Why does it matter?"

That earned him another slap, which snapped his head to the side. "Answer the question."

Erik licked his split lip. "Were you one of the cops on their payroll?"

The interrogator's eyes narrowed. "Sure was. And it was good money, too."

"So you're afraid I found something that ties you to them? After all this time? Is that what this is about?"

The man rubbed his knuckles as if he were weighing whether to strike Erik again. "There are a bunch of people left from back then. We didn't make it this far to go to jail now."

The warehouse was still in use, with plenty of pieces of lawn equipment and bags of supplies. There were an awful lot of ghosts at the edge of the lit area. Maybe his captor had been using the warehouse as a private killing ground for many years. The dark stains on the concrete bore out his guess.

"Hank Chason owed money to the wrong people," Erik answered. "Mob contractors, the IRS. His past was catching up to him. And then someone shot him, execution-style, and walled him up in a closet. Nice touch."

"Fuck with a construction company the Mob owns, and they fuck you over," the man replied. "How do you know about Chason?"

"A construction crew just found him. Turned the skeleton over to the cops. Hole in the back of the skull made it kinda obvious how he died." Erik smirked defiantly. "His ghost was pissed off."

"Ghost, huh? You think I'm stupid?" The flat of his hand connected with Erik's cheek.

Erik glared. "I see ghosts. Cafaro. Chason. Ambrose. They're angry."

"Yeah? Well that ain't doin' them any good now, is it? 'Cause they're still dead." He put his hands on his hips. "Cafaro's ancient history. But the Chason and Ambrose cases might cause people some trouble if anyone went poking around. So...who'd you tell? That washed-up Jersey cop?"

Erik felt a chill. He had to be talking about Ben. *Shit. How did he know?* "Who?"

That earned him another smack, hard enough to rattle his teeth. "Ben Nolan. A buddy of mine in the Newark PD put him onto me. My buddy didn't know about my extracurricular activities," he added with a grim chuckle. "So Nolan meets me and tells me about an old clock that showed up. Nothing about bones."

"Then I guess he didn't know about the bones," Erik replied, hoping he could trust the poker face he'd used on art busts. He had no expectation that he'd get out of this alive, but if he could save Ben, he could make peace with dying.

*Ben.* Erik hated the thought that he would never see Ben again. Was Alessia right about them being soulmates? Erik wouldn't get the chance to find out.

"Don't expect Nolan to ride to your rescue," the boss man said. "I fucked with his head about you. Convinced him you were wanted by Interpol. Art thief. He'll probably be relieved when they find your body." He shrugged. "Although, we'll have to see. If he causes trouble, he'll need to disappear, too."

*Please don't kill Ben.* "He's nothing to me," Erik lied. "Stood me up for an appointment tonight."

"What's the big deal about the clock?"

Erik hoped that the truth might put his captor off balance. "The clock was a cheap replica. It had been reported stolen. Cafaro probably sold the real one when he needed cash, then stole it himself and got an insurance payout."

The man laughed. "That's how it's done! That's a guy who knows how to work all the angles."

"Yeah, see, but he didn't," Erik said, playing a risky game. "Because whoever hid the clock hid a little insurance policy of their own with it."

"Meaning what?"

Erik shrugged. "There was a photo of Cafaro shooting someone. And pages from a ledger showing payments and receipts that probably didn't make it into the official books. Names. Amounts. Some of those companies might still be around."

The man's jaw set. "Where are those papers now?"

"Gave them to the cops," Erik replied, with his best look of wide-eyed innocence. "Civic duty and all that."

"You rotten snitch!" The big man's hand closed around Erik's neck, and Erik wheezed for breath.

"Don't...you...want...to...know...the...rest?" he managed.

His interrogator released his hold just as Erik thought his eyeballs would pop from their sockets. "The rest of what?"

"Why did you go after Justin Kramer? You're the one who broke in and burned his place down, aren't you?"

"Killed him, too, once we traced the little rat to Wildwood," the man bragged. Erik thought he might be sick to his stomach. "Then we found out he sold a box to you."

"So you tried to break in."

"Yeah, and we gave you a warning, but you wouldn't back off."

Erik guessed that was the shot that missed him and the car that tried to run him over. *What we have here is a failure to communicate.*

"Ambrose's ghost showed up after I bought the box," Erik said, hoping his voice held steady. "Couldn't figure out why. Then way at the bottom of the box was an envelope—Ambrose's long-lost suicide note. Damn, that man named names and kicked ass. I gave it to the cops, too."

"You're lying!"

"Call it 'insurance,'" Erik returned. "Because now, when they find my body? They'll know to go looking at old cases."

"Then they ain't never going to find your body," the man assured him. "Not so they'll know it's you, anyhow."

Erik struggled to breathe. He had no doubt that the dirty cop could make good on his threat. He'd just disappear. His parents might not have been the most supportive, but Erik knew they'd grieve his death. And Ben…

Among his regrets—and there were plenty—his biggest would be not seeing Ben again. Even if Ben had only wanted a fling for the summer, it didn't make Erik's feelings any less valid, or his hope any less real that they could have become more to each other.

Erik couldn't bear to think about Ben right now, not if he wanted to keep his tormentor talking. He saw the ghosts move forward from the shadows as if they were intrigued by the spectacle. He couldn't hear their voices or command them to attack—although he really wished that he could—but he might be able to use his limited abilities to buy himself more time.

The temperature in the old warehouse had fallen, cold enough that Erik shivered. He saw the goods shift from foot to foot, trying to warm themselves.

"Guess I'm not the first person you brought here, right? Like that girl, dark hair, big eyes, cute little sundress? Was she a witness or just an inconvenient one-night stand?" He did his best to describe the young woman with a slit throat who had moved close enough for him to make out details of her murder.

"How'd you know about Debbie?" the man demanded. Erik took pride in the fact that his inquisitor had paled.

"Because she's standing right next to you. Looks like she'd like to do unto you what you did to her."

"Stinking liar!"

"Am I? How about the short, pudgy guy with the bashed-in head? Witness? Snitch? Or maybe he just didn't pay up?" Erik didn't dare stop. Maybe he'd goad his captor into a heart attack. Or more likely, piss him off enough to at least give Erik a quick death.

"How about the tall guy, short dark hair, skinny, with a bullet in his forehead? Or the blond lady with the crooked neck? Or that old guy who looks like you threw him a necktie party?"

"Shut up! Shut your fucking mouth!" the man surged forward, and his fist shot out, hitting Erik on the cheek hard enough to rock his chair.

Erik spat blood. One eye was swelling shut. If the guy intended to kill him, Erik sincerely hoped it was with a gun instead of beating him to death.

Would Ben mourn him? Did Ben care enough to grieve for him? Erik wanted to believe he'd been important enough to miss, but his experiences growing up had taught him he was invisible, easily replaceable. Maybe it would be for the best if Ben's feelings hadn't run deep. That way, he wouldn't be hurt.

The ghosts gathered in a thick cloud around Erik's tormentor, and the temperature in the old warehouse grew even colder. The goons who had forced him into the SUV might not be able to see the ghosts, but they had to be aware on some level, because they had taken several steps back, away from Erik and away from the boss. Their breath made white puffs in the air, unusual for late spring. From the looks on the goons' faces, they were starting to get nervous.

*Sic 'em!* Erik thought at the ghosts, who didn't show any sign that they understood.

The boss raised his handgun, pointed at Erik's forehead. "As much as I've enjoyed our little chat, I need to be going. And so do you."

A *zing* like an electric shock shot up Erik's forearm. The ghosts suddenly surged forward, swarming the boss, and forcing his arm to the side, so his shot went wild.

That's when the lights went out.

Erik scrambled from his chair, not sure how long he'd have the dark to help him hide. He heard the men scream and had no idea whether his wishful thinking had prompted the attack or if the ghosts had decided to get vengeance on their own, but they had saved his life.

He tried to move quickly and quietly, fearing that he'd fall over something and give himself away. Sheer terror and adrenaline overcame the pain of his stiff, bruised muscles. His calf brushed against a solid object, and his bound hands made out cold metal, like the fender of a large riding mower.

Erik turned right and felt his way down a line of parked lawn tractors that smelled of grass and oil. He figured his luck was about to run out, so he wedged himself between two of the machines and hunkered down against their huge tires. Maybe it would be more heroic to go down in a blaze of glory, but Erik had never fancied himself a hero.

Shots echoed in the cavernous building, followed by shouts and curses.

*Is it too much to hope that the ghosts suck their souls out and leave nothing but shriveled husks, like in the movies? Probably.*

Still, the thought inexplicably made him smile, a bit of gallows humor. Erik huddled in the dark, trying to make himself as small and quiet as possible, and tried to still his thudding heart.

*I've had a good life. Traveled the world. Met interesting people. Fell in love. I'm not ready to leave yet, I don't want to die, but...I've had a good run. Everyone dies.* He just wished he could have said good-bye to Ben.

The lights snapped back on, blinding him. "Police! Drop your weapons!"

Erik heard running footsteps and a scuffle.

"Erik! Erik Mitchell! Where are you?" That was Ben's voice.

Ben was here with the cops? Erik hesitated a moment longer, then carefully eased out of his hiding place. Ben spotted him from a row away and started running.

"I've got him!" Ben shouted. "He's over here!"

All the fear and disappointment Erik felt over the missed dinner took a back seat to the relief that flooded through him. He was alive. Ben came for him. And Cooper was in custody. The nightmare was over.

"You're alive." Ben's breathless voice told Erik just how worried the other man had been. Ben pulled Erik into his arms, holding him against his chest, and burrowing his face in Erik's hair. "I'm so sorry. I let you down. I love you. Please forgive me."

Erik leaned against Ben, drawing comfort from his strong arms and the warmth of his embrace, breathing in the burnt orange tang of Ben's aftershave and the cedar scent of his soap. "I love you, too. I didn't think I'd see you again. I thought I was going to die."

Ben drew back, taking in Erik's injuries. "We need to get you to a hospital," he said, releasing his hold. "And get those zip ties cut." He looked around and spotted an old set of pruning shears. "Hold steady." The blades snipped through the plastic ties, and Erik shook out his hands to get the blood flowing. Ben reached for him and twined their fingers together as they walked toward Hendricks and the rest of the team.

Captain Hendricks looked Erik over as they approached. "Mr. Mitchell. Looks like you had a rough night. An ambulance is on the way. Let's let the medics have a go at you, and then I'll need statements from both of you."

"Thank you," Erik said, addressing Hendricks and giving Ben's hand a squeeze. "How did you know I'd been taken?"

"My mother reported it," Hendricks replied in a droll tone. "She was watching out the window to make sure you got home safely. Seems she thinks a lot of you."

Erik smiled. "I think a lot of her, too."

Ben walked Erik out to the ambulance that was pulling up in the parking lot. Erik's lip was split, his cheeks were red where he'd been struck, and one eye would likely be black by morning.

"Have I managed, at least, to get that roughed-up action hero look?" Erik asked when the medics were through with him.

"Definitely," Ben assured him. "Not that you weren't already perfect just the way you are."

SIXTEEN

## BEN

After a trip to the ER where Erik was treated and released, Ben and Erik spent the next three hours at the police station giving their statements. Police coffee was just as bad as Ben remembered it, worse without a doughnut chaser.

Hendricks waited until the formal statements were finished to call them into his office. "Part of me is pissed at both of you," he said, glaring first at Ben and then at Erik. "Especially you, Nolan, because you should have known better."

For once, Ben kept his mouth shut.

"On the other hand, you cracked open three cold cases and helped us get enough evidence to put away a bad cop and a murderer. You each have unique skills that may be useful from time to time, considering Cape May's 'special circumstances.' If you're willing, I'd like to be able to call on your expertise on a case-by-case basis. Unofficially, of course."

Ben and Erik exchanged a glance, then both men nodded.

"Thank you," Erik said.

"I'm in," Ben replied. He looked at Erik. "Since I'll be staying on permanently in Cape May, with the rental business." Erik's smile and

201

the glow in his eyes gave Ben confirmation that he'd made the right choice.

They still needed to talk. Ben knew he owed Erik an explanation and an apology, and intended to earn back his trust. But for now, it was enough that Erik was alive, that he still wanted Ben, that he returned Ben's feelings.

"This is not an open invitation to stick your nose into police business," Hendricks cautioned. "I feel I need to say that for Nolan's benefit." He added a stern look in Ben's direction.

Ben did his best to look the picture of innocence. "Understood, Captain," Ben said. Hendricks' eyes narrowed suspiciously, and then he rolled them skyward.

"Somehow, I doubt that," Hendricks muttered. He turned to Erik. "This television show you're considering…given your prior work, have you thought about the consequences?"

Ben glanced at Erik, unsure of his boyfriend's reaction. He'd had similar reservations once he realized just how dangerous Erik's old job used to be. And while he didn't want to stop Erik from pursuing a project that could boost his business, he also didn't want to do anything to attract Erik's old enemies.

"I'm going to ask my agent to table the idea, for now," Erik replied. "If there's a way to revisit it without putting me in the spotlight, I might consider it. But I think I'll have my hands full with getting the store open and my blog running in time for the start of the season."

Ben gave Erik's hand a squeeze, silently showing his support.

"That sounds like a good idea," Hendricks replied. "Now go on. Get out of here. Get some rest. You've been through the wringer."

They walked out of the station toward Ben's Mustang, still holding hands. Ben had expected to get the side eye from some of the cops—that certainly would have been the case back in Newark—but to his surprise, no one seemed to care.

A dark-haired woman stood next to Ben's car. He tensed, but Erik shook his head. "It's okay," Erik said quietly. "Alessia," he greeted the woman. "I didn't expect to see you."

Alessia Mason. Ben recognized the name. The witch. She smiled at Ben, as if she guessed his thoughts.

"I came to make sure you were all right," she replied. "I got your message."

Erik looked confused, then his brows furrowed and he looked down at his right arm. "Message? You mean that 'connection' you mentioned?"

Alessia's smile broadened. "I told you we watch out for each other here. I gathered our folk when I knew you were in trouble. Monty rallied his troops, so to speak. We handled the little problem with the lights," she added. "And added a distraction spell to help you hide."

The witch's comments didn't make sense to Ben, but Erik seemed to understand immediately. "Thank you. That made all the difference." He dropped Ben's hand for a moment and ran his left palm up and down his right forearm. "I felt it," Erik told Alessia. "I just didn't know what it was."

"Just return the favor when the time comes," she told Erik. "I'll let Monty know you're okay. And I'll count on your help dealing with our local genius loci. But for now, enjoy the win and recover. Don't be a stranger." She walked back to where she'd parked a black Yamaha motorcycle at the edge of the lot. A moment later, she roared off.

His phone buzzed, and Erik looked down, then chuckled. "Better late than never, I guess. Simon Kincaide, getting back to me about genius loci, and one of my old contacts from the FBI saying nobody I busted got out recently." Erik took Ben's hand again. "I promise, I'll explain."

"I'm the one who owes you an explanation," Ben said.

Erik lifted a hand to touch Ben's cheek. "We'll talk. Tomorrow. I think it's the adrenaline crash, but I'm ready to fall over."

"And the fact that it's nearly four in the morning," Ben pointed out.

"That, too."

"I'll drive you home," Ben said, opening the car door for Erik. He didn't presume that included an invitation to spend the night. Not after the crap he'd pulled earlier.

"Stay?" Erik asked as Ben got behind the wheel.

"I wasn't sure you'd still want me to," Ben admitted, looking down. He didn't want to see disappointment in Erik's eyes.

Erik reached out and gently turned Ben to face him. "I was angry and hurt about dinner, but I don't think you just blew me off. You had a reason, and I'm betting it had to do with the case. Cooper said he lied to you to make you think I was a criminal. I'm guessing you needed to check that out. You can tell me later. Right now, I want to fall asleep beside you, knowing we're both safe and alive."

"There's nothing I'd like better," Ben told him, pressing a kiss to Erik's palm before he put the car in gear and headed out.

When they got back to Erik's apartment, Ben refilled the ice bag the medic had given them and dug out more Advil. "It'll help the swelling," he coaxed.

Erik accepted the bag and the pills with a sigh of resignation. "I'm not looking too good tonight. Sorry about that."

"Are you kidding?" Ben echoed, gently taking Erik by the shoulders and turning him so they were facing each other. "You're alive. The damage is superficial. That's the best thing I could have hoped for."

Ben tried to find a middle ground between hovering and being attentive. No one had ever brought out his protective streak the way Erik did, and Ben decided he liked that. Not that Erik wasn't a total badass, capable of taking care of himself. He'd already proven that. But protecting each other—that's what people in a *relationship* did, wasn't it? Ben could get used to that.

When the lights were out and they had both slipped into bed together, Erik turned to face Ben. "Thank you for coming after me. And thank you even more for bringing backup, so you didn't get yourself killed."

"Of course I came after you," Ben replied. The moon's glow through the window shades gave him just enough light to make out Erik's profile. "As for bringing backup, thank Susan. She had already called the cops before she told me you'd been taken."

"Still, thanks." The note of wonder in Erik's voice made Ben's heart ache. Did he really doubt that Ben cared enough to save him? Or had that bastard Josh and Erik's upbringing just taught him that he wasn't important enough to notice? Either way, Ben resolved to make sure Erik never doubted him again.

"We keep having rain checks," Erik murmured, barely awake.

"We're together. That's good enough for tonight," Ben assured him. Erik rested his head on Ben's chest, and Ben wrapped an arm around him, gently stroking his hair. "Tomorrow's another day." As he drifted off, he thanked whoever was listening for keeping Erik safe and giving them another chance to make this thing between them work.

Ben woke up from the sexiest dream he'd had in a long time. He dreamed he was in bed with Erik, and Erik was giving Ben's morning wood a slow, delicious handjob—

When he opened his eyes, he saw Erik watching him with a mixture of mischief and lust, his very real hand gently stroking Ben's achingly hard cock.

"I'm done with rain checks," Erik declared, looking beautifully disheveled in the morning sun. "I want to make love to you. That is, if you want me to."

"Oh, there's really no doubt about that," Ben said, with a glance at his stiff and leaking cock. Erik's grip and the friction of his palm against Ben's most sensitive skin felt amazing.

"Then fuck me," Erik said, meeting Ben's gaze. "I almost died last night. I need to feel you, everywhere. Need you to make me yours. Make this real."

Multitasking wasn't Ben's strongest suit, especially when that meant talking while being jerked off. "You're hurt," he managed in a breathy voice that had to let Erik know how much he got to Ben.

"Like you said last night, the damage is superficial. I might be too sore to ride you right now, like I want to," he said with an extra tug that made Ben arch off the bed, "And I'd rather not be on my hands and knees. Blowing you is also, unfortunately, off the table until my jaw stops aching. But that leaves us plenty of other options."

Erik let his thumb catch a bead of pre-come and swirl it over the head of Ben's cock, making Ben catch his breath. "You sure know how to negotiate." Ben's voice sounded husky and sexed-out, even to his own ears.

"I promise to only use my superpower for good instead of evil," Erik replied, and this time, he let his thumb slide through Ben's slit, evoking a desperate moan.

"Yes. God, yes. You're okay with me topping?" They'd never really discussed that, though Ben's fantasies had given him plenty of inspired ideas.

"I like to switch it up. But right now, I want you in me. We have lots of time to try all the variations." Erik's voice was low and seductive, and Ben loved seeing this side of his boyfriend.

"I think that can be arranged. You have supplies?"

Erik nodded toward the nightstand. "I kept hoping we'd get lucky. Didn't count on all the rain checks."

"We'll start cashing those in, right now," Ben promised.

Erik reached over and opened a drawer, then dropped some lube and a string of foil-wrapped condoms on the bed.

"Ambitious, aren't you?" Ben joked. "I'm not a teenager anymore."

"Consider it incentive," Erik said with a naughty smile. "Let me get you started." He opened one of the packets, took out the condom, and rolled it onto Ben's stiff dick. Then he flipped onto his back and drew his knees up with his feet flat on the bed, baring himself to Ben. "Your turn."

Ben leaned forward, kissing Erik gently, careful of his swollen lip. He worked his way down Erik's body, stopping at the hollow of his throat, enjoying the gasps and moans that his mouth and tongue elicited as he explored. Ben noted the bruises and scrapes, carefully avoiding them, trusting Erik to let him know if anything hurt. Erik's nipples were already hard, but as Ben sucked and licked at them, Erik bucked beneath him.

"Keep that up, and I won't last," Erik panted.

"Mm. Then I'd just have to get you off again, wouldn't I?" Ben murmured. He mouthed his way down the sprinkle of reddish-blond hair that ran from Erik's navel to his trimmed pubes and flicked his tongue along the creases where thigh met groin.

"Ben—" Erik growled.

Ben spared a swipe of his tongue against the head of Erik's cock before swallowing him down, and Erik cried out, grabbing fistfuls of the sheet to keep himself on the bed. Ben bobbed once, twice, then pulled off, knowing how close Erik was. Ben used both hands to spread Erik wide and kept exploring, running the tip of his tongue down Erik's sensitive taint, then flicking it ever so lightly against his exposed hole.

"Oh my God! Ben—"

In response, Ben redoubled his efforts, licking and sucking as Erik trembled and moaned, loving the tremors his attentions sent through Erik's body, lost in the scent of his musk and the taste of his lover. As Erik's tight furl unclenched, Ben eased a spit-slick finger past the ring of muscle, still licking the tender skin.

"Come on. I want you inside me."

"Not going to hurt you." Ben's own painful erection rubbed against the comforter, reminding him that foreplay had a time limit before they both spent. He added a second finger, working Erik open, guessing it had been a while. *That makes two of us.* The idea that he was ending a long dry spell made Ben happy. They couldn't be each other's firsts, but first-in-a-long-while was maybe even better.

"Please, Ben. Fuck me now. I need to feel you."

Ben knew when he'd reached the breaking point for both of them. He slicked up his cock and lifted Erik's calves, placing them on his shoulders, then lined himself up with Erik's entrance and eased in.

"Yes. Please. Ben. More."

Ben felt just as desperate as his lover, but he forced himself to go slowly, giving Erik time to adjust. There would be other times for fast and hard. But not now. Now, Ben wanted to say with his body what he'd tried to convey with his words.

*I was worried about you. I'm glad you're safe. I love you. You can trust me.*

When he was finally fully seated and felt his balls slap against Erik's ass, Ben leaned forward to kiss him. Then he met Erik's gaze, gripped both hips, and started to thrust.

Erik bucked up to meet him, hungry to take all of Ben, over and over. Desire made Erik's pale skin flush beautifully, and the look of sheer, naked *want* on Erik's face, the open mouth and blown pupils, nearly pushed Ben over the brink.

As much as he wanted this first time for them to last forever, Ben knew he didn't have that much self-control. Not with Erik's hot, tight channel clamped around his own aching cock, or the sexy, incoherent sounds Erik made as he twisted and writhed, or the sight of Erik's own engorged prick leaking a steady, sticky stream of pre-come onto his belly.

"Together," Ben rasped, moving one hand to grip Erik's cock, matching his strokes to the rhythm of his hips. Once, twice, and he felt Erik stiffen and clench beneath him, even as his own orgasm closed in like a freight train and his thrusts grew quick and hard, chasing release. Erik shot white ropes of come, spattering his own belly and cascading over Ben's fist. Ben's climax followed seconds later, ripping through him and whiting out his vision.

He fell to the side, still inside Erik, who turned with him to keep them connected. Ben couldn't find his words yet, and neither could Erik, but the look in Erik's eyes told Ben everything he needed to know.

"Best rain check ever," Erik said when he could catch his breath. "Mighty fine painkiller, too."

"Definitely going to enjoy cashing in the rest of those rain checks —and earning some more," Ben replied. He kissed Erik again, a gentle touch after the wave of passion that had swept through them. Erik responded with fervor, promising a repeat performance.

Ben reached between them and held the condom in place as he pulled out, knotting it and tossing it into the garbage can by the bed. "That was…"

"Yeah. It definitely was," Erik agreed.

"Let me get us cleaned up, and we can rest before round two," he said. Ben padded to the bathroom and returned with a warm, wet cloth, wiping down Erik's belly and then gently cleaning off the spunk between his legs. Making eye contact as he did it almost seemed more intimate than the act itself, and Ben knew, as if he ever doubted, that he was truly and thoroughly besotted.

He tossed the cloth onto the floor and gathered Erik into his arms. "Just so you know, I intend to be exclusive."

Erik smiled. "Just so you know, so do I."

"Good. Very good," Ben said, feeling another layer of insecurity dissolve. He and Erik still had a lot to learn about each other, but as Erik snuggled into him and he pulled his lover into his arms, Ben thought they were getting off to a great start.

───────

When they finally got out of bed, after dozing in a post-orgasmic haze, Ben and Erik showered and headed to the kitchen. "So does that mean you're part of their coven?" Ben asked, lingering at the table over coffee and the last of the frozen waffles. "I'm new to witchy stuff."

"So am I," Erik replied. "Part of the coven? No. But there appears to be a loose confederation of people in town who have certain talents. Alessia and Monty helped save my life back there. I'll have to give back when the need arises."

"That makes sense," Ben said. "But why didn't Monty's mojo work on the ghosts outside the warehouse?"

Erik frowned. "I don't know for sure. But if I had to guess, I'd say he was focused on getting the ghosts on the inside to attack Cooper and keep him from shooting me. If they hadn't rushed him and spoiled his aim, I'd be dead."

Ben shivered at the close call and reached across the table to take Erik's hand. "I'm glad it worked."

Erik tilted his head, looking at Ben as if he were figuring out a puzzle. "So that incantation Father Pavel gave you, it drove off the mobster ghosts outside?"

Ben nodded. "I don't know where it sent them, or if they'll come back. All that mattered was that they didn't do something to alert Cooper or attack us from behind."

"Sounds like something handy to hang onto."

"Don't worry—I've got it on my phone, and I put the original in the safe," Ben assured him.

Erik had listened as Ben explained about Cooper's lies, Ben's frantic research, and his conversations with both Father Pavel and Travis Dominick. To Ben's relief, Erik accepted his apology and forgave him for doubting.

"So you're all right with magic, and the ghosts?"

Ben nodded. "I'm still getting used to the idea, but it saved your life, so I'm fine with it."

"I called Corinne and told her I wanted to rethink the TV show, take the focus off me," Erik said, getting up to pour another cup of coffee. Ben held out his cup for a refill as well. "She wasn't exactly thrilled. It'll mean pitching the new concept. But I think we can do something that's more about the history, legends, and yes, scandals, without having me on camera. It's just brainstorming at the moment. We might even go web-only and do a YouTube series instead. We'd have more control that way. So, we'll see. I'm plenty busy with the store and the blog."

"How likely is it that any of the people you helped put away might come after you?" Ben asked, worried. He'd made plenty of enemies himself with his undercover work, but Erik had tackled a whole different class of bad guys, people who had the money and means to destroy anyone who got in their way.

"No way to tell. I'm going to deal with things one day at a time."

"Now that Hendricks has the Ambrose letter and the papers and photo from the clock, plus the intel on Cooper as well as Chason's bones, he should have enough to tie up all those loose ends, and Justin Kramer's murder, too," Ben said. "I'm hoping that scares off anyone else from the old days who might have thought about taking care of the Commodore Wilson's unfinished business."

"Not to mention that Jaxon is giddy to have some new, really juicy tidbits and items for his exhibition," Erik added. Ben knew Erik had passed along the best items from the memorabilia box, and while the papers from inside the clock were in police custody,

Hendricks had agreed that the insurance fraud—even if it could be proven—was too far in the past to be an issue. That meant Jaxon added the clock to his exhibit, with a slightly redacted story to go along with it.

Erik suddenly dug into his pocket. "Oops! I forgot this." He held out a silver pendant to Ben. "Alessia gave it to me. She said it would help ward off bad magic. She made them for both of us."

"How did she even know about me?" Ben couldn't help his curiosity.

Erik blushed. "She's a witch, remember. And she said we had a special connection."

Ben had the feeling there was more to it, something Erik wasn't saying. That was okay. He'd find out when the time was right. After all, Ben was very good at getting sources to talk. "So it didn't stop Cooper, because he wasn't using magic."

Erik nodded. "Yeah. Just my luck. But if she thought we'd need the charms, I think we should wear them. There's always next time."

Ben lifted the leather strap and lowered the necklace over his head. He still had the two saints medallions on from the night before. Should he keep Alessia's amulet and one of the saints, to hedge his bet? Since the medallions didn't spontaneously combust on contact, Ben figured whatever sources of power they aligned with had declared a truce.

"I hired Susan to help me with the shop four days a week during tourist season," Erik said and sipped at his coffee. "That'll give me more time to get the blog going, which will reach a wider audience and should help even out the income during the winter, when the tourists go home. And I've already called my friend Simon to see if he knows what to do about the closet full of pieces with dark mojo. He said he thought he knew someone who could help."

"Sounds like you're in the home stretch to having everything worked out," Ben replied, finishing off his drink.

"Almost everything." Erik met Ben's gaze. "You're sure about staying?"

Ben reached out to cup his face. "If you want me, I'll stay."

"Of course I want you. But...are you going to be happy in Cape May?"

Ben had thought about that, and the real answer was *it depends.* If he and Erik had a chance at building a long-term relationship, then Ben was onboard with staying. And if it didn't work out...he'd be devastated, but he'd take it as it came. "I like the town. I'm getting to know the business. And I love you."

Erik leaned in for a kiss. "I love you, too. I just want you to be happy." The warmth of his lips and the passion in his kiss underscored his words and made Ben believe.

Ben slid his hand around to Erik's neck. "I know we haven't had a lot of time together yet. It's all new, and we've been moving fast. Anything could happen. But I know what I want to happen. I want a lot more than a fling, Erik Mitchell. I want to see where this goes between us, all options open. A real relationship. Maybe forever."

"Yes," Erik said, as Ben moved to kiss him again. "Yes to everything."

# EPILOGUE

## ERIK

Erik turned the sign on the door to *"Closed,"* marking the end of the first day of the new tourist season. Trinkets had been busier than he'd ever imagined, and he was so thankful that Susan had convinced him to hire her, because even with the two of them, they had been swamped.

He knew that every day wouldn't be like this, but if the store could have more days like this than not, Trinkets would be a financial success. That thought made Erik happy. It banished the last of his uncertainty over taking the bold step of uprooting his life and leaving his old job, and it honored all of Robert's hard work and that of the shop's owners before him.

Best of all, Ben would be coming over later with takeout from Fisher's Seafood, which meant lobster rolls, hush puppies, and secret recipe coleslaw. Erik's stomach growled, just thinking about it.

Ben had to work late, handling a sudden influx of rental requests, but Erik didn't mind. That just helped to secure Nolan Resort Real Estate's future and gave Ben one more reason to stay in Cape May permanently.

Erik had plenty to do before Ben came over, including straightening up the shop for the next day and refreshing the display in the window. The time flew, and the long twilight darkened to night.

A knock at the door made Erik jump. He turned, puzzled that someone would ignore the sign, and walked over. His eyes widened as he saw the man in the doorway.

"You're him. The man from Antwerp, the one who saved me," Erik said when he opened the door.

"Invite me in," the stranger said.

"Please, come in," Erik replied, stepping aside to let his unexpected guest enter. "How did you find me? And why are you here? For that matter, what exactly happened that night?" Erik needed answers. Ben told him what Travis Dominick said, which opened up even more questions than Erik had before.

He took a look at his rescuer. The man appeared to be in his mid- to late-twenties. His blond hair had a stylish cut, and he was dressed casually, but in clothing brands that were deceptively expensive. Yet it was his gray eyes, like the color of the sea before a storm, that transfixed Erik.

"My name is Sorren. I'm Robert's contact to get rid of any... problem pieces...you've come across."

"I have plenty for you to take," Erik replied. "But not until I know why you were in Antwerp, and what's going on. Thank you again for saving my life."

Sorren nodded. "You're welcome. As for the other part...I'm with the Alliance, a group of mortals and immortals who work together to keep dangerous magical items out of the wrong hands...and stop supernatural threats."

"Immortals?" Erik had been prepared to find out that the man who had saved him that night was a powerful witch. But this—

He caught his breath as he saw just the tip of fangs between Sorren's lips. *That's not possible.*

Then again, there'd been several impossible things that night in Antwerp. The unusual strength of the Russian goons who tossed him out of the way as if he weren't a full-grown man. The speed of the attack that left the mobsters dead and bleeding on the floor. And the way Sorren had picked him up as if he weighed no more than a child and carried him to safety. Maybe even the unlikely explosion that served to destroy the evidence of anything out of the ordinary.

"Magic is real. Supernatural creatures exist. Those of us who know do our best to eliminate paranormal threats and keep the world safe—and happily none the wiser," Sorren replied. "I helped Robert's ancestor open the original version of this shop back in 1614. It's been in his family ever since, although the building and location have seen a few changes over the years."

"But that would mean—" Erik's head spun as he did the math. *Immortal.*

"Robert didn't have an heir. I promised we would find a suitable successor. That's you."

Spotting the "For Sale" ad for Trinkets as soon as it went live online. Having his bid for the store and property immediately accepted, although it was lower than the asking price but the best Erik could offer. The way the ad seemed to be tailored specifically for him, as if someone knew his work and his extra abilities. *A suitable successor.*

"So you and Robert somehow chose me?" Erik stammered, knowing in his heart that it was true, even as he spoke the words.

"You always had a choice," Sorren replied. "But yes, you were the favored candidate. And I'd say you've proven us right."

"What does it mean for me, being part of this Alliance?" Erik thought of Alessia and her coven, of Jaxon and Monty and Susan, even Ben with his ability to see ghosts, and the way they had all found each other.

"Robert used his ability to sense which objects were haunted or cursed, or laced with dark magic. Dangerous. He intercepted them—and sometimes, went looking for them. I make sure they're destroyed or neutralized so that they can't hurt anyone ever again."

"I can do that." It wasn't too different from the way he'd used his knowledge to spot frauds and stolen art, and in the process, helped to shut down bad guys who would have used their proceeds to do terrible things.

"Sometimes, if there are creatures beyond what the human authorities can handle, the Alliance also steps in to take care of the problem."

"So you're a bunch of supernatural vigilantes?" Then again, what he and Ben had done with the Cafaro case hadn't been too far from the mark.

Sorren's lips quirked into an almost-smile. The fangs had vanished. "You're not the first to put it that way. A bit dramatic, perhaps, but not incorrect."

Erik thought about his training, not just with art and antiquities, but in folklore, mythology, and legends. Not to mention what he'd learned from the feds about fighting and weapons. *And Ben's an ex-cop. He could hold his own, if it came to that.*

He'd never liked the idea of destiny, and stories about people who were the "chosen" one never ended well for that person. But Sorren didn't seem to be asking him to fight the powers of darkness by himself. After all, "alliance" suggested a team. He already had a start on that, with his local friends who had a hint of "something extra."

Erik had already suspected that, given what he'd done before Trinkets, trouble might keep looking for him. One of the things he'd found most satisfying about his work with the authorities had been stopping people who took advantage of their position and power to hurt others, and getting a measure of justice in the bargain.

Maybe this was how he could still fight that fight, in a slightly different way.

"What about Ben? We're a team or there's no deal. It's not negotiable." Jesus, he was bargaining with a vampire. Could his life get any weirder?

"The bond between you strengthens both of you, and helps protect you," Sorren replied. "We have no problem with that. I really hope to work with both of you."

Erik licked his lips nervously. "I need to talk to him."

Sorren nodded. "Understood. But Travis Dominick has already

made Ben the same offer as I've made to you. And he is similarly intrigued."

"Can I let you know, when we've had a chance to discuss it?"

Sorren nodded. "I'll take your problem items with me now, and you can call me when you've made your decision." He handed over a card. *Trifles and Folly—Antiques and Curios*. The shop had a Charleston, South Carolina, address. "I look forward to hearing from you."

# ALSO BY MORGAN BRICE

**Witchbane Series**

Witchbane

Burn, a Witchbane Novella

Dark Rivers

Flame and Ash — *Coming Soon*

**Badlands Series**

Badlands

Restless Nights, a Badlands Short Story

Lucky Town, a Badlands Novella

The Rising

Cover Me, a Badlands Short Story

Loose Ends — *Coming Soon*

**Treasure Trail Series**

Treasure Trail

# AFTERWORD

Cape May is a beautiful resort town at the tip of New Jersey. It's a lovely place full of well-maintained Victorian houses, fantastic restaurants, and gorgeous beaches. It's also said to be very haunted by resident spooks that never wanted to go home when their earthly vacation ended. I made up the ghosts that Erik and Ben encounter, but if you want to read more about the *real* ghosts of Cape May, I'd recommend the excellent books by local ghost-whisperer Craig McManus.

The Commodore Wilson Hotel and its sordid history are completely the work of my imagination. But the building and a few events are based on the old Christian Admiral hotel, which was demolished in 2005. Photos of the grand old structure are easy to find, as are accounts of its history, which unfortunately included being rather unlucky for its owners.

You'll be seeing more of Erik and Ben and their friends in more Treasure Trail books, coming soon! And if you're intrigued by Erik's friend Simon Kincaide, he stars in his own series of urban fantasy MM paranormal romance, the Badlands books set in Myrtle Beach. Likewise, you can find more about Travis Dominick and Father Pavel in the Night Vigil series (first book is Sons of Darkness), and about

Sorren in the Deadly Curiosities series (first book is Deadly Curiosities), both written under my Gail Z. Martin name. And while you're waiting for the next Treasure Trail book, check out my Witchbane urban fantasy MM paranormal romance, with plenty of spooky chills and sexy thrills!

## ACKNOWLEDGMENTS

It takes a village to bring a book to life. Thank you to Larry N. Martin, my partner and co-author, for all the behind-the-scenes work that got this book ready to share. Thanks also to Jean Rabe, our editor, to our beta readers: Ashby, Chris, Donald, Laurie, Lisa, Mindy, Susan, and Terri, and our launch team: Amanda, Amy, Andrea, Anne, Anthony, Barbara, Candi, Carra, Cheryl, Cheryl, D'Niche, Darrell, Jessica, Jocelyn, Karolina, Kathryn, Kristy, Lee, Olga, Raven, Scarolet, Shakera, Shannon, Sharon, Sherry, Stacy, Terry, Vickie, and Wendy. Thank you also to my Shadow Alliance and Worlds of Morgan Brice street teams, who share the journey and the jokes along the way. And most of all, thank you to my readers. Because you read, I write.

# ABOUT THE AUTHOR

Morgan Brice is the romance pen name of bestselling author Gail Z. Martin. Morgan writes urban fantasy male/male paranormal romance, with plenty of action, adventure, and supernatural thrills to go with the happily ever after.

Gail writes epic fantasy and urban fantasy, and together with co-author hubby Larry N. Martin, steampunk and comedic horror, all of which have less romance, and more explosions.

On the rare occasions Morgan isn't writing, she's either reading, cooking, or spoiling two very pampered dogs.

Watch for additional new series from Morgan Brice, and more books in the Witchbane, Badlands, and Treasure Trail universes coming soon!

**Where to find me, and how to stay in touch**

Join my Worlds of Morgan Brice Facebook Group and get in on all the behind-the-scenes fun! My free reader group is the first to see cover reveals, learn tidbits about works-in-progress, have fun with exclusive contests and giveaways, find out about in-person get-togethers, and more! It's also where I find my beta readers, ARC readers and launch team! Come join the party! www.Facebook.com/groups/WorldsOfMorganBrice

Find me on the web at https://morganbrice.com. Sign up for my newsletter and never miss a new release! http://eepurl.com/dy_8oL. You can also find me on Twitter: @MorganBriceBook, on Pinterest (for Morgan and Gail): pinterest.com/Gzmartin and on Bookbub https://www.bookbub.com/authors/morgan-brice

Enjoy two free short stories, set in my Badlands series. Read *Restless Nights* here: https://claims.prolificworks.com/free/js6x0fq8 and *Cover Me* here for free: https://claims.prolificworks.com/free/iwZDEP9Z

Also check out the excerpts at the end of this book. In the Witchbane series, Seth Tanner and Evan Malone team up to stop dark warlocks who have been carrying out a century-long killing spree. If you like shows like Supernatural, Vampire Diaries or Buffy, this is your kind of story!

And you can explore the supernatural side of Myrtle Beach with psychic medium Simon Kincaide and skeptical homicide detective Vic D'Amato as they track a supernatural killer in Badlands!

**Support Indie Authors**

When you support independent authors, you help influence what kind of books you'll see more of and what types of stories will be available, because the authors themselves decide which books to write, not a big publishing conglomerate. Independent authors are local creators, supporting their families with the books they produce. Thank you for supporting independent authors and small press fiction!

# EXCERPT | WITCHBANE

## SONNY

"Hey, Sonny! Did we get the new shipment of Jack?"

"Yeah, I haven't unpacked it yet." Sonny looked up from behind the bar at Tredegar's—Treddy's to regulars. "You need me to get you a bottle?"

"Nah. Just checking to see if it came in." Liam, the bar manager, stood at the end of the counter. "Didn't want to pay for it if it hadn't arrived." Muscular, red-haired and with a thousand watt smile, Liam was the reason so many singles in Richmond—gay and straight— found their way to Treddy's.

"I'll check it out. Need to restock, and I'll put the rest away."

Treddy's took up three stories of what had once been an old tobacco warehouse. The unfinished brick walls and exposed wooden beams gave the place history and authenticity missing in newer build- ings. Sometimes, Sonny swore he could smell tobacco, and when he looked up, it wasn't difficult to imagine bundles of broadleaf hanging from the rafters to dry.

The first floor had the main bar and restaurant. The second floor boasted a dance floor and a DJ, and the third floor was mostly for catering and events. Sonny held court at the first-floor bar, a job he'd held since he came back to Richmond two years ago. Just one more stop on his long journey to shed his past, his family, and his stalker. Sonny hoped this time would last. He'd been bouncing around for seven years since he graduated from high school.

"It's a bar, not a mirror," Liam joked, as Sonny polished the heavily varnished wood. The counter and backbar had come out of a swanky club from the late 1800s. Rumor had it the chandeliers used to hang in ritzy Paris townhomes before Liam got them from a New Orleans antique store. The wood of the mantle over the fireplace had the maker's chisel marks and was once part of a hundred-year-old barn. Put them together, and Treddy's felt comfortably lived in, welcoming and warm.

"Hey, Sonny. You're on early today." Jackie, one of the servers, came by to pick up drinks for her table. Her Jersey accent stood out in the crowd of Richmonders, as did her Bettie Page black bob and bright red lipstick. She had always gone out of her way to make Sonny feel welcome and was one of the few people he counted as a friend.

"Been working a lot of nights. Needed to change it up a bit," Sonny answered as he poured refills for the crowd at the bar.

"Tips are better at night," Jackie replied with a shrug. She was a VCU student and one of the staffers who'd take any shift that came open to help pay for tuition.

"Nice to see some new faces. Keeps it fresh." He didn't want to get into what he'd told Liam, that he'd seen someone who looked like Mike, his stalker, and freaked out. *It wasn't Mike*, he told himself. Mike belonged back in Oklahoma. But that hadn't stopped him from showing up in Missouri and Ohio, popping up like a bad rash every time Sonny moved.

He rubbed his left forearm, over the spot where Mike had broken it. The injury didn't leave a visible scar, but Sonny swore it ached on rainy days. Worse, it hurt like a motherfucker in his dreams. *Three years later, and it's still not over in my head. Maybe it never will be.*

The police had taken his complaints, given him forms to fill out, and he filed a restraining order. Sonny had changed addresses, phone numbers, and jobs, deleted everything from social media, begged any sites with his photo on it to take down the information, started using a nickname at work.

Lately, he'd gotten up the courage to go on a few dates. Nothing serious, just some fun times and casual sex, which felt like an enormous step after leaving Mike's crazy jealousy and unpredictable rages behind.

And then, that guy showed up. *Not Mike*, Sonny told himself, hating the way just thinking about it made his hands shake. He'd come up with an excuse to get close enough to see for himself that the guy wasn't Mike. Yeah, there was a resemblance from a distance, but too many details were wrong to be Mike, even with a couple more years under his belt. Still, Sonny hated how it brought up old memories, dented his newly minted self-confidence. And the worst part was, stalker-Mike still wasn't as bad as his first boyfriend, Trey, whose tearful repentance over being gay betrayed Sonny's trust and got him kicked out of his house, his church, and their tight-knit small town. So he'd finally come back to Richmond, the city his parents had left when he was a kid, and hoped for a fresh start.

"Hey, over here!" A patron hailed him, and Sonny pulled himself out of his thoughts, hurrying to refresh the guy's martini before his hair caught on fire.

Jackie was right about nights being better for tips, but Sonny had enough put by that he could do without, for a few shifts at least. Give him time to clear his head, get some sleep. Treddy's did pretty well for a day crowd. Started at brunch and went on to the wee hours of the morning. The lunch crowd was split between corporate types and the "ladies who lunch" in their twinsets and pearls. Dinner picked up more mid-level executives plus the young professionals who liked the martini list and the atmosphere. Late night, the action shifted to the second floor, where the DJ made Treddy's a good place for a hot hook-up, while the first floor took care of those looking for a tasty meal, fine whiskey, and a nice place to take a date.

Sonny lost himself in the rhythm of the work, swaying to the music from the sound system, watching for signals from the barflies for another round, hauling ass on orders, so the servers got credit for quick response. Although he'd never been much for the "shoulder to cry on" bartender stereotype, he knew his regulars and noticed when they were off their game.

"You doin' okay, Pete?" He asked, leaving it up for interpretation whether that meant in life or needing another drink.

"Just a shitty day at work," Pete replied. He had loosened his tie and turned up his shirtsleeves. "What else is new?"

"Sucks, man," Sonny empathized. "But it beats a pink slip."

Pete knocked back his scotch. "Not always sure about that. Maybe."

Sonny gave him a commiserating smile. "Hey, you want to get something to eat with that?"

"Sure," Pete said. "Fries and wings. The usual."

Sonny put in the order, picked up food from the kitchen for the customers who were waiting, and scanned for who needed another drink. A glance out over the dining area told him they'd reached wait-list capacity, not bad considering it wasn't six yet. The early crowd drew a mix, young and older, professional and hipster. Treddy's had even found a new fan in a tired-looking off-duty cop who'd shown up a couple of times in the past few weeks. Something about the place just put folks in a good mood.

"What'll you have?" He said without looking up as he saw a newcomer pull up a seat.

"Jack and Coke, please."

The "please" made Sonny look up. Most people, even the polite ones, just put in their order, mumbling "thanks" if they weren't too deep in conversation or their own thoughts. "Please" stood out. On second thought, so did the newcomer.

*Well, well. That's a fresh face. Um-hmm.* Sonny took in the new guy without being too obvious. Tall—maybe a few inches over his own six-foot-one frame, a nice height to fit together. Broad shoulders, and the way the button-down clung in all the right places, Sonny bet on a toned chest underneath. Dishwater blond hair short on the sides and a little longer on top, fashionable without being trendy. Broad hands and long fingers. *Bet he's proportional.*

"Coming right up," Sonny said with a smile, meeting the blond's eyes with a hint of a wink, surprised to find them brown instead of blue. He came back with the drink and slid it toward the newcomer. "Taste it and see if it's what you like," he said, with a smile suggesting ideas of other things worth tasting.

If he'd had any doubts about whether the guy played for his team, the look that lasted a bit too long and the slight flush that came to the man's cheeks answered the question. Sonny watched as the newcomer sipped, then licked his lips.

"Just right," he said with a hint of a smile in return.

*Shit. He's cute. And alone.* Sonny knew the two patrons on either side of the blond had been there before he came, and it didn't appear the man intended to retrieve a drink and retreat to a table.

"First time at Treddy's?" Sonny asked as the regulars on both sides of the man continued their conversations.

"Heard it was good." He looked around. "Looks like it's got some history. That's…nice."

"It's the kind of place people keep coming back to," Sonny said with a shrug. "Makes people feel at home."

"Hey, Sonny—need you down here!" Izzy, a petite server with a pink pixie cut, looked ready to chew nails.

"What can I do for you, darlin'?"

"Don't darlin' me," Izzy said. "Table five is giving me an ulcer, but if you mix their drinks strong, maybe they'll ease up."

"You got it," Sonny said with a grin. Izzy had a temper, but for all her epic bitching, he'd seen her out back feeding scraps to the stray cats.

By the time he got back down the bar, he was afraid the blond would have moved on, but instead, the man nursed his drink as if he were in no hurry. "You want some food to go with that?" Sonny asked.

The man shrugged, and Sonny thought he seemed a bit uncomfortable in the press and hustle. "What's good here?"

"Everything on the menu, and a few things that aren't," Sonny replied, with a flirtatious tone. *Seriously? When's the last time I flirted with a customer? Shit, I must really need to get laid.*

"Any recommendations?" This time, there was no mistaking the way the blond held Sonny's gaze, shifting a little closer to the bar. Sonny felt a tingle go straight to his groin.

"I've got a couple of favorites," Sonny said, leaning in. "By the way, I'm Sonny."

"Seth."

"Nice to meet you, Seth. New in town?"

"Just visiting. I like what I've seen so far."

*That absolutely wasn't in my imagination,* Sonny thought. The new guy was definitely interested, but not overly slick. Either Seth was a master pick-up artist or his edge of self-consciousness was genuine—and very sexy.

"So here's what I order," Sonny said, bending closer to share the menu with Seth, just brushing his fingers for a second. He pointed to two or three choices, sure to please because everything was good. "What sounds good? And is that for here or to go?"

"For here," Seth replied, pointing to his choice. "Maybe I'll be up for some to-go later."

*Oooookay. Definitely on the same wavelength. This could be interesting.* "Let me know, and I'll go over the options with you," Sonny replied, making direct eye contact. Seth didn't blink or turn away, confirming that Sonny hadn't lost his touch with reading signals.

"Be back in a few," he promised, going to type the order into the system. Jackie came up to pick up more drinks.

"Since when are you in the game?" She asked just loudly enough for him to hear. "I've never seen you hit on a customer."

"Technically, he's hitting on me," Sonny replied. "I'm just responding. It's polite."

"Sure it is."

Sonny mixed her drinks and fiddled a few seconds longer down at the end of the bar. What was he doing? Not that Liam would care if he took a customer home with him. Wouldn't be the first time one of the wait staff—or Liam himself—had hooked up with someone. But that wasn't usually Sonny's thing. Then again, he'd been gun shy since Mike, practically a monk—if you didn't count the hurried hand jobs, porn, and jacking off in the shower. Pretty sure monks at least jacked off.

Maybe it was time to get out of his shell. Take the guy home, have a nice roll in the hay, and shake off the ghosts of the past. No strings, no complications. After all, Seth was just visiting, so no worries about him wanting more than Sonny was ready to give.

He set Seth's order down in front of him. "Watch out; it's hot."

Seth smiled. "I like it hot."

Sonny swallowed. Somehow, that didn't sound totally cheesy coming from Seth.

"If you'd like, I could show you around when I get off at seven," Sonny said. "Since you're new and all."

"That would be great," Seth replied, and a bit of pink colored his cheeks.

*Damn. Maybe it's been a while for him, too. This could be a great evening.* Sonny whistled as the next hour flew by. Even Izzy's gripes about cheap tippers didn't get him down. He had a date with a cute stranger. Okay, maybe a hook-up more than a date, but still, more company than he'd had in a while. This was just what he needed.

Seth took his time with dinner, nursing his drink and ordering fries and a Coke to give him an excuse to dawdle. That earned him points in Sonny's book. By the time Sonny was ready to clock out most of the customers in the dining room had turned over from the early dinner crowd. Even the cop had moved on.

"I need to cash out my drawer and hand off to Eddie, and then we can go," Sonny said, slipping Seth's bill to him. Seth reached for his wallet and paid in cash. Sonny held his breath, wondering how the tip would go. Too little was an insult. Too much felt like paying for his company, given their plans. To his relief, Seth came in at twenty percent, appropriate for good service, not trying to buy favors.

"Tell us all about it tomorrow, you sly dog," Jackie murmured as he passed her on the way to get his coat.

"I want pictures," Izzy added with a rare smirk.

"In your dreams," Sonny replied and found himself grinning. Fuck, what had gotten into him? This was hardly his first rodeo, and that thought led to wondering who might be riding whom. *It might not even get that far,* he warned himself, then tried to remember how well he was stocked for lube and condoms. *More than enough for one night. Even if he's...energetic.*

He met Seth at the door, and they headed out. The October wind was cold for Richmond, but Seth didn't seem to mind. "Not sure what you're used to or where you're from, but Richmond isn't exactly New York when it comes to nightlife," Sonny said. "Don't get me wrong; it's a great city. Plenty of history, close to the beach. And there are some good clubs. But it's not a big party kind of place."

"That's fine," Seth replied. "I'm not much for clubs."

That made two of them, although Sonny had tried hard to fake it to keep up with Mike before everything went to shit between them.

"How about I give you the five-cent tour, and then see what you want to do next."

"Sounds good to me."

Sonny pointed out a few landmarks like the Iron-front building and the park by the Capitol, as well as rattling off some local trivia he'd picked up from the last time he'd helped out on game night. Seth seemed comfortable, but a little guarded, and Sonny found himself wondering what the sexy blond's story was. Not that it mattered; they'd have a nice night together, and that would be the end of it. But still, something about Seth intrigued Sonny. Not to mention the fact that he had a great ass.

Sonny thought about what highlights to share from his newly adopted town. Richmond was a city torn between its past and its future. Glittering new office towers lined the waterfront, growing universities sprawled through the downtown, and well-groomed parks provided a great view of the James River. The Virginia Museum of Fine Art hosted world-class traveling exhibits, the State Capitol building and its fountain were photogenic, and tourists and locals flocked to the beautiful grounds at Maymont and the Louis Ginter Botanical Gardens. Downtown boasted a growing number of trendy shops, bars, and restaurants.

And yet, Richmond had a darker side, in the whispers suggesting that no matter how many years passed, the Civil War would never be over. At the Museum of the Confederacy and the Confederate White House, docents told a tale of the "martyrs of the Lost Cause" that could have come right out of *Gone With The Wind*. Monument Avenue's statues were popular with history buffs, but the men they memorialized had long ago ceased to be defensible, except to those who even now refused to surrender. Richmond, like Charleston, New Orleans, and Savannah, was a beautiful city built on rivers of blood, and that past might never completely release its grip.

"Richmond has plenty of interesting stuff, depending on what you're into," Sonny said. "Museums galore, concerts, and NASCAR. Plenty of ghost tours. It seems like everything's haunted—restaurants, hotels, churches, even an old collapsed train tunnel. Something for everyone."

As a bartender, Sonny had plenty of chances to watch people, and he counted himself pretty observant. One of his favorite ways to amuse himself on slow nights was to make up a whole history for a stranger at the bar, and then see if he could tease out enough conversation to validate his guesses. He was right—or close enough—more often than not, at least on the parts he could customers to 'fess up to.

*Hmm. He's alert, even when he's trying to be relaxed. Cop? Maybe ex-military?* He considered the haircut and figured on the latter. *So who's he visiting?* "Family" didn't feel like the right answer, and he'd shown up solo and willing to take Sonny up on his offer, so not here to meet up with a boyfriend. Somehow, Seth didn't strike him as the tourist type. *Maybe business, but not something he wants to discuss? Could be.*

They bumped shoulders as they walked, too close to be just friends. Sonny was pretty sure he'd seen Seth sneak a look at his ass. He liked Seth's long-limbed stride, and how confidently he moved, despite his height. Not graceful like a dancer, more the kind of smooth, seamless motion Sonny had learned in Tae Kwon Do before switching over to mixed martial arts. That would figure for ex-military.

Sonny had been gone from the heartland for a long time, but he thought he recognized a bit of Midwestern twang in Seth's voice as they chatted, and a little small town vibe around the edges. He wondered if Seth had left his family and home for the same kind of reasons that had forced him out. Although he hoped not, it was more common than anyone liked to admit.

*Quit overthinking. Take what's been offered and don't make too much of it. It's just one night. Not like it's gonna change anything.*

# EXCERPT | BADLANDS

## SIMON

At this hour of the morning, the boardwalk ghosts were silent. Simon Kincaide stared down the nearly empty, broad beachside walkway and breathed in the ocean air. Flags flapped in the breeze, waves pounded the shore on the other side of the dunes, and seagulls swooped. The tourists hadn't yet woken.

Simon looked, out of habit, to the places the spirits favored. The old man with his bicycle and his dog wouldn't appear until late afternoon, cycling down the boardwalk. Kevin, a dreadlocked man in his twenties, liked the stairs that led to the beach, perhaps near the spot where he drowned. Two children in Victorian clothing, spirits so faded that they could not even remember their names, would skip past near sunset. Other ghosts came and went, but Simon could set his watch by those appearances. Not everyone could see the ghosts—most of the people milling along the boardwalk could not and never would —but Simon did.

Sebastian Simon Kincaide had known he wasn't like other kids when he realized nobody else could see and hear the spirits he considered regular playmates. Discovering he got glimpses into the future from time to time made him even less like his friends at school. Figuring out that he was gay was just the icing on the cake. That all happened long ago, but the sense of being an outsider never really went away, Simon thought, not even now at age thirty-five, with a prosperous business and a few bestselling books to his credit.

He worked the key in the front door. Grand Strand Ghost Tours, a small shop on the Myrtle Beach boardwalk, shared a building with a beachwear shop but had a coveted location between the legendary Gay Dolphin Gift Cove and the popular Myrtle Beach SkyWheel mega-Ferris wheel. Simon paused in the doorway, letting himself enjoy a moment of pride and satisfaction in the business it had taken three damn years to build.

Simon collected the mail, pocketed his keys, and locked the door behind him since the shop wouldn't open for another two hours. He switched on the lights and music, then went to the back to start a pot of coffee.

His phone buzzed, and he answered. "Hey, Seth. What's up?"

Seth Tanner chuckled. "You haven't had your coffee yet, have you?"

"I'm working on it." Simon held the phone between his shoulder and ear as he readied the coffee maker. "What do you need?"

Seth sighed. "I'm looking into a vengeful ghost problem near Breezewood, up in Pennsylvania. Salt and iron aren't doing the trick, but I'm sure it's ghosts, not demons, so exorcism won't work, either. Got any ideas?"

"Find the anchor object the spirit is tethered to," Simon recommended, measuring out the coffee. "Might not be near where the appearances are happening. Have an officiant from the deceased's faith tradition say a blessing and urge the ghost to move on. If nothing else works, there's a banishment ritual, but it's brutal on the spirits. And no matter what you've seen on TV, don't get yourself arrested trying to dig up the grave to salt and burn the bones."

Seth chuckled. "I knew you'd have the answers. You're a rare medium, Simon. Well done."

"Ha, ha. As if I haven't heard that one before," Simon groaned, rolling his eyes. He pressed the button, and the coffee maker chugged to life.

"Seriously, thanks," Seth replied. "Send me the bill."

"When I have to do some research, I'll charge for the time. This, I can give you off the top of my head. Next time you're in the area, stop in and we'll do dinner. Your treat."

"You're on," Seth replied and ended the call.

Simon headed out to the main room and started to get the shop ready for business. Shelves in the front held books about ghost stories from all over South Carolina and the Lowcountry, but especially those with tales of spirits, pirates, or old scandals of the Grand Strand. Prominently displayed were the three books on local folklore and ghosts that bore his name as author. The glass case by the register held gemstones and silver jewelry for healing and protection, colored candles, and sealed bags of the most common dried plants and flours used in rituals and aromatherapy. Shelves behind the cabinet held an assortment of candles in tall glass holders with pictures of saints on the front. In the back, a table and two comfortable chairs supplied a homey place to do appointment-only psychic readings, and the table could expand to hold six people for a full séance.

A rack on top of the counter held brochures about the Grand Strand Ghost Tours that Simon led four nights a week, as well as the "Pirates and Scoundrels" special tours and the "Lowcountry Legends and Lore" talk he gave twice a month at Brookgreen Gardens. The large sign on the wall behind the counter advertised ticket prices for the tours and special events, with a prominent reminder to "ask about rates for private spirit readings and séances."

Display racks offered t-shirts with the Grand Strand Ghost Tours logo, while others bore catchy phrases like "Ghosts Gone Wild," "Grand Strand Spook-a-palooza," and his favorite, a cartoon of a ghost holding a beach drink that read "Chillin' Out." The nearby shelves that held cups, stickers, and shot glasses with the same designs were a concession to tourist tastes.

Simon straightened some of the merchandise when his phone rang again. "Mark! You're up early."

Mark Wojcik grumbled something in response, and Simon grinned. Mark hated mornings even more than he did. "No, I'm up late and still haven't gone to bed," Mark muttered. "And I'm bruised from head to toe after I got my ass kicked by a were-cougar before we brought it down, so forgive me if I'm not Mr. Sunshine."

Like Seth, Mark was a real-life hunter of things that went bump in the night; part of a loosely allied group of people who by talent or personal tragedy found themselves initiated into a shadow world most people could live happily never suspecting. Simon's gifts as a medium and clairvoyant—and his training as a folklorist—made him a part of that hidden network, and his research skills provided a second stream of income.

"I finished the research on the kelpies you asked for," Simon replied. "Sent the files to the secure share drive."

"Okay," Mark said. "That's what I was calling about. I'll shoot the payment back atcha. Thanks."

Simon ended the call and ran a hand back through his shoulder-length brown hair. Four years ago, if someone had told him that he'd be making a living taking beachgoers on ghost tours, giving readings, and selling tchotchkes, he'd have laughed. But how he'd ended up on the Grand Strand was not funny at all.

Three and a half years ago, Dr. Sebastian Kincaide held a professorship at the University of South Carolina in the Humanities Department, teaching folklore and mythology classes and writing scholarly articles on legends and lore. He kept his abilities as a medium and clairvoyant hidden, although his long-time relationship with another professor on staff had been openly acknowledged, especially after he and Jacen had announced their engagement.

Even now, the memory brought a sour twist to Simon's stomach. Emerson Baucom Tallmudge, the father of one of his students, turned out to be not only a donor and a board member for the university, but a hard-core fundamentalist as well, of the "thou shalt not suffer a witch to live" variety. Apparently, after he'd gotten a glimpse of his son's textbooks for the class, Tallmudge got his dander up and lobbied the board to be rid of such an "evil influence." Simon thought he had successfully placated the board, citing the importance of classical mythology in a well-rounded education, but then Tallmudge found evidence online that Simon admitted to being able to talk with spirits, and everything came crashing down.

The board dismissed Simon with a severance package that told him they also thought Tallmudge's complaints were bullshit, but in the end, the prospect of an endowment beat out standing up for one of their faculty. Then Jacen broke off their engagement, too afraid that Simon's dismissal would compromise his bid for tenure, and Simon's world went up in flames.

Alone, unemployed, and unable to find another teaching job, Simon drifted down to Myrtle Beach, intending to stay for a week or so to regroup and lick his wounds. When his aunt offered to sell him the cottage in Myrtle Beach where he was staying, Simon took it as a sign to rebuild his life from the ground up. He put his folklore background to use writing a book on local ghosts and used the self-published book to leverage himself into jobs as a tour guide, haunted attractions actor, museum docent, and speaker while he put his plan together. Grand Strand Ghost Tours wasn't just a shop; it was Simon's howl of defiance at a universe that had fucked him over.

And which was still doing so, since the coffee maker had not only failed to produce a cup of java-rich goodness, but had sent a gush of murky water and wet grounds all over the floor.

"Shit." Simon grabbed a handful of paper towels and began mopping. The smell of burned electronics told him without needing to use his psychic gifts that the coffee maker was dead. He dropped the machine into the trash on top of the sodden towels, ordered a new one on Amazon with expedited shipping, and then contemplated the prospect of a morning without coffee.

"Screw that," he said, glancing at the clock. He locked up, turned out lights, and headed for Mizzenmast Coffee.

Before he'd made it half a block, his phone buzzed once more. This time he smiled at the number that came up. "Hi, Cassidy. Everything okay?" His cousin, Cassidy Kincaide, ran an antique store in Charleston, just two hours south of Myrtle Beach. They hadn't been close growing up, but now that Cassidy had discovered her own ability to read the history of objects by touching them, they had bonded.

"Fine. Just busy. Mostly regular stuff, but some of the other too, if you know what I mean." Cassidy's shop proved to be the perfect opportunity to get cursed and haunted objects out of the wrong hands. Simon and Cassidy often talked over whatever weird or supernatural situation they were currently navigating. Not to mention Cassidy had a gorgeous gay Weaver witch best friend as a partner in her supernatural escapades. It was another sign of the universe's contempt for Simon that Teag was already taken. "Is the store open yet? Can you talk?"

"I'm heading for coffee," Simon replied. "What's up?"

"I've got a carved mahogany trinket box with the name *Jeremiah Holzer*' engraved on the bottom," Cassidy said. "There's a pretty nasty curse on it. I think Jeremiah was from the Myrtle Beach area, but Teag and I can't find anything about him online, and I thought maybe you could check some local archive stuff for me."

"Sure," Simon agreed. "How urgent?"

"We've got the box quarantined, so it's not doing any new damage, but two people were injured from the curse, and I have a feeling there's missing information that we need to break the bad juju. So, the sooner, the better."

"I'll work on it tonight, after the tour," Simon promised. "Say 'hi' to everyone for me."

"When are you going to come to Charleston? You know we've got the best restaurants on the Southeast coast," Cassidy replied. "Plus, Teag and Anthony have a couple of cute guys in mind they think you might hit it off with."

Simon cringed, glad Cassidy couldn't see his expression. Even after three years, he wasn't sure he was ready for a new romance. Perhaps he never would be. "It's the busy season," he begged off. "But maybe this winter. Or come visit me. Roads go both ways, you know."

"It's tourist season here, too," she reminded him. "But we'll get together soon, one way or another. And thanks for the research."

"You got that haunted painting off my hands," Simon replied. "I owe you." He hung up, but couldn't shake the melancholy that had settled in. A couple walked past, hands clasped, talking quietly, and an ache he didn't want to acknowledge flared in his chest. As much as he feared being hurt again, Simon couldn't deny the fact that he missed being in a relationship, having someone to wake up with every day and fall asleep with at night. For a while, he'd buried himself in his work, and that had dulled the loneliness. Now that he was no longer in survival mode, the evenings were not completely filled with busyness, and the nights stretched long.

Simon chuckled at his fears. *Here I am, backing up people who hunt real monsters, and I'm too chickenshit to go on a date. I need to man up and...man up.*